THE EMPR
A Novel of

E. BARRINGTON

This is probably the strangest true story in the world. Dumas made it the background for a novel where the principal characters are fictional and the part played by the Queen imaginary and unjust to her generous and noble character. I tell it, as far as I am able, as the facts were, compressing the time and giving it as a drama in which the true actors live and speak.

PART I

Chapter I

THE most famous necklace of history. Rippling diamond splendours, it lay on its bed of cool pearly satin which enhanced the fierce glitter of the magnificent stones. Such a necklace had never been seen before in the story of the world's great jewels — could not have been; for the means of procuring it did not exist. Not before the middle of the eighteenth century could men so have angled and netted the markets of the world to catch those radiant slippery fish of jewels. India aided from her Golconda, and Brazil searched dull earth for the cold hidden fire whose fame rang trumpet-tongued, and ancient caskets of high nobles were counted over in the hope that their owners might be induced by princely prices to sell. And sell they did and more than they would have told, for the ends of the earth were coming upon France, and there was the mutter of the far-off lion-roar which presaged the French Revolution and the downrush of things as men knew them into chaos. Many indeed of the more cautious sort of the *noblesse* were already realizing property here and there without attracting attention and buying little retreats in England, Holland and Italy which might be useful one day and, if not, were always a good investment. And what so easy to realize as diamonds — diamonds which that very accommodating Jew, Boehmer, could imitate in the cleverest possible paste so that great ladies might still sparkle at Versailles and the Tuileries, possibly themselves unconscious that their lords had taken thought for the morrow in this quite novel fashion.

Be that as it may, Boehmer the King's Jeweller (proud title with such a queen as the lovely Marie Antoinette to decorate!) sat in his private room with his chubby little partner Bassauger at his elbow, gazing at their completed triumph as it dazzled their eyes with flying arrow-points of colour unnameable as the outer arches of the rainbow. The spring sunshine played hide and seek with it, acknowledging a rival, earthy indeed but with all the fire of sun and star concentrated in its radiance of living light. Let it be described and visualized, for these stones were to make history and make and unmake — what? As this story shall tell. Here is the portrait by grave historians.

First, about the throat went a chain of seventeen diamonds of purest water, the size of filberts. It had taken years to match the seventeen and when collected only picked workmen of Amsterdam were permitted to give them the finish art lends to nature: cut, angled and faceted so that from every surface entangled rays flashed lucent.

From these were looped in three festoons another chain of splendour bearing pendants of massed diamonds, star and pear-shaped; and as if this were not dazzlement enough, from the back were brought forward two broad, threefold rows of diamonds only lesser than the throat circlet, diamonds of a queen's magnificence in hundreds, and from these two supple ribbons of diamonds knotting on the bosom fell lower, ending in tasselled diamonds, while at the back of the neck two similar ribbons, but in a sixfold row, fell scattering auroral lights from themselves and their tassels, and thus was the royalest jewel of the world complete in a blinding panoply of light to adorn only the royalest and most beautiful bosom in all the earth.

That certainly was its destination as far as Boehmer and Bassauger were concerned, but the expression with which they regarded their triumph was not triumphant — far from it.

"It was the curse of curses that Louis the Fifteenth died before it was complete," said Boehmer moodily. "A man will give his mistress what he won't give his wife, and Madame du Barry had lost her heart to the model in clay. The money was as good as in our pockets. He could refuse the slut nothing."

Bassauger curled a sarcastic lip and sniffed audibly: "Except constancy. If he had kept away from the girls of the *Parc aux Cerfs* he would have escaped the smallpox and death, and du Barry would have had her necklace. Hard luck for us!"

Boehmer lifted a glittering tassel with a meditative air; his Hebrew descent was very visible in his blond Germanic face, and obtruded itself also in the dull brooding look of his people when the hand of the Gentile is heavy on them — a man of the anxious nervous temperament which is bound to suffer in this best of all possible worlds.

"And yet — laugh at me, my friend, if you will — it would have been a bitter pill to me to see this about the du Barry's plebeian neck. It asks —

it demands — all that there is of most patrician and imperial to do it justice. You see it?"

He held the splendour dangling from his hand. Bassauger answered drily.

"No neck is plebeian with diamonds like this about it, and money doesn't smell whatever hands it comes through. In business is no sentiment. *Mon dieu*, I wish it were about the du Barry's neck this moment. She is a very pretty woman, though as coarse as a fish-fag. But that style suited his late Majesty very well. He was not particular in his tastes."

Boehmer's large full face bore a slight expression of contempt for his partner's grossness of expression. His own manners and tastes were nothing if not courtly. His position admitted him to the Queen's boudoir when she wished to consult him in matters of importance, and it was the rule that ornaments for repair or re-setting were always handed to him in her presence. He had acquired a strong liking for royalty and its magnificences in these surroundings and for dealing with a queen who was grace itself in the charm and kindliness of her manner to the Court Jeweller as to every one else. Romantic feeling combined with commercial in his sense that she and she only was worthy of the peerless jewels which he of all men had collected from the ends of the earth. Certainly business was business with him. No one was better aware of the qualities it demanded, but he could combine it with delicacies of sentiment quite unknown to Bassauger, whose hard commercialism reckoned everything in hard cash only. While the du Barry ruled France through her old voluptuary of a king, Boehmer had contrived to see a little romance even in her position and to think his diamonds not unsuitable to the First Sultana of the Most Christian King. Now that the King was dust and the lady of no consequence he thought mention of these doings a little unbecoming in connection with the necklace.

"That episode should be forgotten," he said stiffly. "Our present beloved monarch does not indulge himself in such distractions, and you should know that an ornament destined for a du Barry cannot be pleasing to a queen of France. Her mother, the Empress of Austria, brought her up with the strictest notions in the world."

"Which the bride of fourteen shook off as a dog shakes its ears when she cut her apron-strings. And besides, diamonds smell no more than money," retorted Bassauger with a pinch of snuff. "But let it be forgotten if you will. The main point is that her Majesty must see the necklace — and soon. The matter is frightfully serious for us who have terrible expenses to pay for it. The times are not too promising for a toy of this cost, and you should —"

"Toy? Good God!" cried Boehmer. To him the necklace was the one splendid salient fact of the universe. He had given years of his life to it, had toiled, plotted and intrigued to get those jewels, and now — that that coarse Bassauger should call it a toy! Anger choked him.

"After all, one can eat and sleep without diamonds," crowed the chubby Bassauger. "Better sometimes than one can with them, for that matter. But time is precious. Get permission this very day to see the King at the first chance. Since he fell in love with her eight years after the marriage he refuses her as little as Louis the Fifteenth the du Barry. So some say. But you who move in Court circles should know better than I."

"His Majesty is a good husband. He will realize that this ornament should be an appanage of the Queen of France and no other. Well — I will arrange it. By the way, has the Cardinal de Rohan made any purchases for any of his little favourites whilst I was at Meudon? He spoke of something."

"A pair of earrings set with diamonds and turquoises for little Madame Quesnel, and — yes — a ring to match. Nothing more. For a man of his wealth he has spent little of late."

"His loss of Court favour depresses his Eminence, no doubt. That jest he made about the Queen's mother was one of the unluckiest that ever left the mouth of man. It ruined him at Court —"

"But it was perfectly true," said Bassauger with his inveterate disrespect. "The Empress Maria Theresa was the hardest, most gripping old harpy that ever sat upon a throne. That's probably why our Queen runs to the opposite extreme and is a spendthrift, even for a queen and a beauty."

Boehmer was profoundly irritated: "For the love of God be guarded! Why criticize royalty? You may see by the downfall of the Cardinal, a prince of the blood royal, rich, handsome, gay, what comes to those who disparage their superiors. He has not been admitted to Court for years — except to say Mass."

Boehmer's raised eyebrows and hands might have illustrated the loss of heaven, so feelingly did he speak.

"But I," retorted Bassauger, "am not a cardinal and my heaven is with Madame Bassauger in our little cosy retreat at Passy with a good dish of *blanquette de veau*, before me, and a glass of Chambertin beside it, and my chimney corner after with a good book. Courts are not for me. But you, my friend — Well, let us put this dazzler away and you be off and make your appointment."

With all the care and ceremony that befitted its importance the treasure was locked and barred into safety. Bassauger had never said a truer word than that those who possess diamonds sleep ill.

It had become a nightmare to Boehmer. Fire — thieves — Heaven knows what, flitted nightly in procession about his bed and the mere thought of carrying the thing to the Tuileries brought out beads of sweat on his forehead. One must do it alone to avoid observation, but if there were a street scuffle, if his carriage were run down and himself carried unconscious to his house, they would strip him, they would find the treasure. O that it were in the keeping of the guardian of the royal jewels! He hated and worshipped the thing.

But he pulled himself together. He assumed his fine *tricorne* hat, his coat and breeches, his silk stockings, irreproachable as befitted the King's Jeweller, and with his gold-topped cane he stepped out daintily into the street, his large face as apparently untroubled as if he had not had the most gorgeous diamonds in the world upon his conscience. Verily upon his conscience, for Bassauger, honest man, had disclaimed the adventure of collecting them. "It is beyond us," he had said. "Just suppose the du Barry were to die!" — with a hundred more unpalatable supposes, and Boehmer, irritated, would have his way in spite of Bassauger and now, ruin, or success splendid as the diamonds, lay before them. "The game is worth the gamble," he said to Bassauger, but in his heart he knew he scarcely thought so now.

As he went down the street a coach drawn by four fine horses came lumbering noisily along the cobblestones, swaying from side to side on high leather straps, with gold-encrusted hammercloth, magnificent coats of arms on either door, everything imaginable suited to the coach the fairy godmother would have bestowed on Cinderella if she could have afforded anything so gorgeously unpractical. Four splendid lacqueys adorned the shelf behind, clinging on precariously by gilded straps. There were outriders. There was a coachman stout and imposing in a gold-laced hat. There was all that rank and riches could bestow. People stood respectfully aside and murmured that it was the Cardinal. What cardinal, asked the country bumpkins, tremendously impressed. Why, Prince Louis de Rohan, his Majesty's cousin, a prince of the blood — returning from a visit to the Archbishop of Paris. Men uncovered and women made reverences. The street was hushed and watchful.

A florid handsome face appeared at the window with a gracious salute for all and sundry. The glance, accustomed to homage, swept the little crowd and alighted on Boehmer, standing gravely back and saluting with deep respect. The face was immediately withdrawn, and an order evidently given, for the coach stopped and a footman sprang down from the back and hat in hand approached Boehmer, while the crowd turned like one man to see the happy being whom the great man delighted to honour.

"Monsieur, I have the honour to inform you that his Eminence desires a word with you at your convenience. Move on, good people, move on! Make way for Monseigneur!"

They moved on obediently, and Boehmer with profound bows approached the coach door and stood respectfully bareheaded beside it. Prince Louis de Rohan's extremely unecclesiastical face appeared at the window once more, full, jovial, self-indulgent, a prince of the Church indeed but much more unquestionably a prince of the World, the Flesh and ahem! That certainly was the thought which flashed through Boehmer's mind as he made his bow. Yet, after all, what could one expect from a man trained in the wicked school of the Court of Louis the Fifteenth, where it was much more profitable to propitiate Madame du Barry than the Queen of Heaven or the Queen of France, and the King had no use for any one who could not share his amusements? Generous allowance must also be made for rank and good looks, and such a prince would never lack for the profoundest respect and obedience.

"Eh, Boehmer! It's a long time since we met," said the deep condescending voice. "And how is my old friend and how is the world using him? You look a little thinner than you should. Take my recipe of a light refreshment of a few oysters and a glass of white wine before *déjeuner* daily. It acts like a charm in restoring vitality."

The high nobility of France could allow themselves familiarity with Boehmer because the demarcations of his position were so clear in his mind that he could be trusted never to overstep them. His bow was even deeper on this gracious recommendation.

"Permit me the honour of observing that your Eminence looks the very picture of health and younger instead of older," he answered. "I sincerely rejoice to see it."

Perhaps not the less because the Prince had been one of the best customers of his firm. Even Bassauger respected rank when it indulged in such lavish expenditure as that of Louis de Rohan. Could either of them forget the boxes crammed with costly trinkets which the Cardinal had taken with him as ambassador to Vienna after Madame de Pompadour (the du Barry's predecessor) had graciously promoted the marriage of the King's grandson, the Dauphin, heir of France, with the loveliest of that bouquet of rosebuds, the daughters of the widowed Empress of Austria, the famous Maria Theresa? Heavens! how Boehmer had rushed to and from the Hotel de Rohan — the town house of his Eminence — laden with pearl pendants and rings, delicately engraved *étuis* set with a discreet sparkle of diamonds, vinaigrettes and snuff-boxes of exquisite enamel, and all to conciliate the ladies and gentlemen of the Viennese Court who could be trusted to breathe pretty fables of his devotion to her Imperial Majesty into the Imperial ear! There was also a chicken-skin fan painted by Vanloo with Loves flying like bees to cluster round a girl attended by the three Graces, weaving a garland of roses under bluest summer skies by the silver spray of a fountain. The sticks of mother-of-pearl and gold, the diamond monogram M. A. surmounted by the crown of France — a masterpiece indeed and worthy of the young Archduchess Marie Antoinette whose fair features the girl bore. That was a gift worthy of the future Queen of France. Boehmer almost licked his lips in thinking of the price he had asked and the Prince paid ungrudgingly for that and the whole cargo of lovely frivolities. Was it for him to censure if some had been given to ladies dear to the Cardinal himself as well as to the Empress of Austria? No indeed, for those tendernesses had resulted in further orders for avalanches of rings on his leaving Vienna later — rings the ingenious settings of which (if you touched a cunningly contrived spring) disclosed the hidden face, a little flattered, of that most unecclesiastical of cardinals. Also there were many miniatures of the same attractive subject delicately rimmed with pearls. The Empress Maria Theresa was so shocked as to declare that she never would have believed in that epidemic of rings and miniatures if she had not seen it with her own eyes. There was indeed much to shock so pious a lady in the escapades of the Cardinal. Certainly the parting guest had been urgently speeded on his way to France. Boehmer was inclined to think that the rings explained, it. But that did not concern him. Summoned to the coach his one thought was, Could so excellent a customer be interested in the Necklace in case of — what of course could not happen — the Queen's refusing it? At all events his good word could do no harm, for the more pretty ladies flocked to see it the better its chances. And such a connoisseur in jewels! The very man to help an anxious King's Jeweller from a very terrible burden.

"And you truly enjoy the health, Monseigneur, which your very humble servant always desires for you?" he repeated.

"Why, yes, Boehmer, my good friend. But what I want to ask is, Have you any pearls of respectable lustre — but by no means a king's ransom — suitable for a ring? There is a little lady who has set her little heart on black pearls — the whims of women! — to enhance her white hand. Three, to be set with an illustration of diamonds. I wish it to resemble the famous ring which my father gave Madame de Boufflers when she first appeared at Court. You know the song:

When Boufflers was first seen at Court,
Venus' self shone less beauteous than she did.
To please her each eagerly sought,
And too well in his turn each succeeded.

Well, that ring — your predecessor made it — was one of the baits. I want the same thing but at half the cost."

"Certainly I know it, Monseigneur, and I have the pearls, moreover, fresh from Ceylon. But half the cost! Your Eminence did not use to bargain. Ah, these are hard times for my trade!"

"And would not bargain now if times favoured me. But the lady, though charming, is not worth more than half what my father has told me of Madame de Boufflers. Now, for *some* women one would give all the world were it all condensed into a single pearl like that of Cleopatra's."

"I have a jewel for such a lady!" cried Boehmer eagerly. "A supreme, a royally magnificent jewel for a queen of beauty or empress of the world.

There is no woman who could refuse anything to the man who gave her such a magnificence."

"There is only one woman who is queen of beauty and royal also," said the Cardinal with lowered eyes. "And she has diamonds too many to care for more."

Boehmer smiled discreetly: "Has a woman ever enough, Monseigneur? You know better than I. But have you heard of my diamond necklace?"

His Eminence yawned indolently: "I believe I heard a rumour of some such thing. But, Boehmer, the pearls?"

"I will bring them for your approval, your Eminence. At present I am on my way to present my duty and ask an interview later with her Majesty that she may see my necklace."

Life sprang into the Cardinal's dull eyes, colour flushed his cheek. That name always touched something in him apart from all other amours. There was somewhere hidden under the mud and murk of his life a stray sparkle of imagination, of romance, dimmed, befouled, but still surviving. And the exquisite Queen touched it. The thought of her alternately shamed and stimulated him. The lovely creature, proud, airy, the very embodiment of race and high sentiment and a girl's romance playing at hide and seek with a great queen's dignity! He had known her when as little more than a child she had believed in his devotion to her mother's interests and to hers and had given him a very loyal and innocent confidence which he had grossly misused. He had seen her arrival in France, a girl scarcely fifteen, fair and hopeful as the dawn, luminous with youth and life and beauty — a glittering jewel for a king's wearing. He had watched her before he lost Court favour, a virgin wife, as all knew, failing to charm or even to interest her dull young unripe husband though the very safety of France demanded an heir. He had seen that rose unplucked high on the topmost bough, wasting its sweetness on the desert air, while the man who might have worn it in his bosom never looked at her nor answered her half-pathetic, half-humorous little attempts to please him. And men, knowing this, climbed as far as they dared to reach the Unapproachable. There was the handsome Duke of Dorset, gay and beautiful as the long ago Duke of Buckingham who had won the heart of a queen of France. Had he — had they? No, the Cardinal would not believe it. He trampled on the thought. Marie Antoinette had coquetted innocently, she had spread out her charms in the sunlight as a peacock spreads his net of gold and jewelled moons. But more — no.

And then after eight years of marriage suddenly the Dauphin, now king, awaked as from a drugged sleep to the worth of his treasure that all the world envied, and his wife was his wife indeed and mother of the little Dauphin and Madame Royale of France.

Yet, knowing all this, the Cardinal longed still for the beautiful angry woman who let her eyes glide over him as coldly as a December frost when he must cross her path at the celebration of the religious ceremonies which as Grand Almoner of France he and none other could perform. It was his only approach to Court now — otherwise it was forbidden, and through her influence. And yet in his own way he loved her in spite of it all. Not a high love — desire backed by self-interest and stayed on thwarted pride — but still the best in him. And this fellow, this Jew Boehmer, a mere tradesman, might enter her cabinet and display his wares and hear her voice rise and fall, see her pleasure as she examined the treasures laid before her. And he, Louis de Rohan, whom the King must call "my cousin" might sooner hope to enter Paradise (in itself improbable) than that sacred sealed cabinet which held the one thing his soul coveted with the only passion left in his life. What was the use of his descent from Anne of Brittany and the blood royal of France? What the use of the proud motto of his House: *Roi ne veux, Prince ne daigne. Rohan suis*, if the only woman he valued never cast a glance his way? Hopeless!

"She will not buy your necklace," he said coldly to Boehmer. "Public affairs are too disturbed and the people are beginning to thrust their pigs' snouts into financial matters and others too high for them. The King would not hear of it."

"Monseigneur, the King is so madly in love with her Majesty now, making up for lost time, as all say, that if he once sees it about her neck —"

Had Boehmer fully persuaded himself or was it the desperate hope of getting rid of his glittering nightmare? He spoke with conviction and the Cardinal flushed at his words, a dull, jealous red. He made a sign to his men to drive on and Boehmer was left in the street, bowing and protesting that the black pearls should be at his service and at a price the most reasonable, and so forth until the great man was out of hearing. Then he pursued his way, tremulous with anxiety.

Chapter II

REACHING the Hotel de Rohan and dismounting from his coach in the imposing courtyard the Prince betook himself to the small and very luxurious room which none but himself and his intimates ever entered. There hung over the fireplace a portrait splendidly framed and surmounted with the united arms of France and Austria which Louis the Fifteenth had presented to him after the marriage of his grandson the Dauphin to the Archduchess Marie Antoinette. When the old King was dead and he himself had sailed to the North Pole of royal disfavour he had feared that that precious gift might be recalled. But, no — the young girl who was now Queen of France still smiled down upon him as cordially and trustfully as in days his heart remembered but too well. Sometimes it was almost too painful a reminder of the living smile which was once his and her cold averted eyes when last they met. Should he banish it and forget? But he could not. She was so sweet in her gorgeous dress of white satin embroidered in silver *fleur-de-lis*, the row of pearls about her stately little throat and the blue eyes above it. So, still she kept him company and the very light ladies who sometimes favoured that room with their perfumed presence would look up half in awe at the young royal beauty and dare no comment.

For once one of them, perched on the arm of the Prince's chair, had ventured a criticism on the curling Austrian lip — a jealous one. Her host, rising instantly, bowed her politely and in dead silence to the door which she never re-entered. That hint was sufficient for a companion who was present. There were no more criticisms even if the pretty ladies wondered secretly why a great crystal vase of the choicest flowers stood winter and summer before the picture as before a shrine.

Prince Louis de Rohan sat now with long silk-stockinged legs thrust out before him staring up at her and brooding over memories which Boehmer's words had awakened. They were not cheerful. He had held a brilliant hand in a great game and played it ill. Does Fate ever deal such cards twice over? Never.

His handsome eyes grew sullen with anger. Time, the merciless antagonist, was playing against him now. If he could have kept his gay youth — that youth for which he would have given any fortune but his own — there might be hope. But now! — He saw himself reflected in a long mirror, a figure still dignified but heavy and ageing. Invading flesh blurred the clear outline of his features, his flaccid hand trembled a little as he poured the priceless Tokay, the Austrian Empress's gift, into a Venetian glass where golden threads twined themselves in crystal. Age! and he a man who could hope for no more of the things he loved better than life — the dazzle and intrigue of Court life, high office — and above all, the favour of the queen to whom the king could refuse nothing.

That story of his jest against her mother was good enough for the world to believe, but it was not the truth. The truth was one which none of the very few concerned would be willing to pour into the world's greedy ear, and naturally it was his policy to encourage the common belief.

"Royal ladies!" he would say half-smiling, half-sighing, when sympathizers commented on the vindictive anger of the Queen, "they must never be blamed and her Majesty is the most dutiful of daughters. After all I should have known better!" — with a slight touch of regret.

And since the Austrian Queen was none too popular in Paris sympathizers agreed among themselves it was just like the Austrian venom to keep up a trifling grudge so long.

Oh, the cards he had held when she came to Paris with not a friend to steer her among the pitfalls and dangers! The Pompadour, proud of her power, had made the marriage to please the Empress Maria Theresa and was amply rewarded by delightful letters full of consideration and beginning, "My dear Cousin," from the greatest and most pious Lady on earth. The presents of jewels which came with them were pleasant but not for a moment to be compared with the letters. It was something for the King's harlot to be able to show them about the Court and to know that Europe had heard of the intimacy and envied her. Such a personal tribute to her position! Perhaps she would have valued it less, thought de Rohan, if she had known that to set a daughter on the French throne was so necessary to the Empress's policy that to attain her end she would have kissed the devil's black cloven hoof with as much zest as that with which she had written those enchanting letters to a lady whom she regarded as the prize goat of his flock on earth.

Madame de Pompadour meant to pay the debt owing for so much condescension. She would have honestly befriended the young bride, as she had promised the Empress. She would have spread the shadow of her august protection over the Austrian lamb. Not a dog would have barked where the Pompadour commanded! But she died, and when Marie Antoinette arrived in France the du Barry, pretty, coarse-minded, and furiously jealous, had stepped into the Pompadour's painted high-heeled shoes, and very serious dangers awaited the Austrian Dauphine.

Even the Empress could not condescend to court *that* omnipotent slut! She who knew everything which passed at the French Court through her ambassador the Count de Mercy and his spies, knew as well as the du Barry herself the disreputable old King's taste for green fruit. She knew also that the du Barry would therefore not only do all in her power to keep the bride in the shade but would actively plot and lie to injure her in the old King's eyes, lest she should gain not only his liking but more. What was the Empress to do to protect her lamb from a wolf so sharp of tooth?

De Rohan was then ambassador in Vienna and visiting at the palace of Schönbrunn. He occurred to her at once as a man too obtuse and absorbed in pleasure to be anything but a useful tool in her hands and those of her ambassador in Paris and yet, in virtue of his great position and ample means of collecting information, a most valuable friend and adviser for her daughter. The advice would of course be her own but it would be more likely to be well received by Marie Antoinette from the mouth of a man whom no one could afford to despise. His ambitions and hers might be made to coincide for, though she was but the Dauphine now, any day might make her Queen of France with endless gifts and possibilities in her hand if only she could be safely steered through the present dangers. So the Empress sent for him and received him with cordiality so winning and sunny that it obliterated all memories of escapades among the Court ladies which he also was very anxious to forget.

As he sat now he recalled that conversation, and the Empress, stately and smiling, little guessing that she was dealing to a very ambitious man exactly the cards he needed.

"You will understand my position, Eminence," she said, leaning forward in a confidential attitude from her great gilt *fauteuil*. "I really counted on Madame de Pompadour's influence with your illustrious Master for my daughter. She was in some respects a worthy woman and had a proper sense of responsibility to him and to the nation. You agree with me?"

Louis de Rohan could remember no worthiness in the Pompadour though a super-abundance of charm. Responsibility to the nation indeed! Who cared for the nation? Certainly not the lady who plundered it until she was gorged with gold and jewels. But he smiled as gravely as he bowed.

"And I know," pursued the Empress, gently waving her fan, "that Madame du Barry, though beautiful and no doubt deserving her high position, for none can doubt his Majesty's wisdom, is perhaps naturally so eager to preserve his esteem for herself that —"

The Empress was feeling her way. Who knew with a woman like the du Barry that she had not been — was not now — a *chère amie* of de Rohan's? He relieved her mind instantly.

"Madame, it pains me to speak so plainly to your Majesty, but the woman is a slut! A fury of jealousy! She is capable of spreading the most atrocious lies about your royal daughter, not only to his Majesty but throughout the Court — throughout France! It will need the utmost skill to pilot her through the dangers of that woman's tongue and deadly animosity."

"Animosity? But why?" hesitated the Empress, even yet uncertain how far she could trust him.

"Because, Madame, your Majesty knows how my Sovereign adores beauty, especially youthful beauty, and she will dread the influence of the Dauphine more than any other in the world. There are possibilities — "

He hesitated. Maria Theresa laid her fan down and looked him straight in the face with inscrutable grey eyes. "Your Eminence, can I trust you?" she asked.

"To the death, Madame." Cardinal though he was he dropped on one knee and kissed her hand, his heart beating like a lover's, but for very different reasons. The way — the way — was opening before him! She yielded her hand graciously, then motioned him to rise.

"I never trust by halves. You are worthy of knowing my whole mind. There is nothing — no anxiety I feel so deeply as the need of securing the support of France. I cannot hope to recover my lost province of Silesia, to move with any certainty in Europe, unless your august

21

Sovereign supports me. My dearest hope is that my daughter may acquire the strongest influence with him, if only she can use it wisely. Had Madame de Pompadour lived — Alas! hers was a heavy loss for Europe!"

"All must lament it," said de Rohan, with exactly the proper accent of regret. For all such niceties he could rely upon himself, but in deeper matters — No! He knew that the Empress's plotting brain was worth a round dozen of his. Lord, steer him straight through the shoals to harbour! He knew that she cared no more what happened to her daughters except as pawns in her game than he for a last year's love. Heavens, what a woman!

"She is so young, so inexperienced!" said the Empress mournfully. "What I desire is some friend, a man for choice, who will advise her kindly but firmly, not by any means sparing her home truths and who will confer with her tutor, the Abbé Vermond. I want a man who will in short act the part of a —"

She was about to say "father" but the look on the vain handsome face before her was a warning. She changed the word neatly to "friend" and went on smoothly: "— a friend whom she can trust. He must be a man whose birth and position ensure respect and whose grace of manner will attract her confidence. For choice, owing to my profound respect for the Church, I would say a great churchman. Need I say, your Eminence, that I speak of you?"

Again (strictly as a prince of this world, not of the Church) he fell on his knee and kissed the imperial hand. He was profoundly flattered. The tribute was one he could scarcely have expected after the episodes of the rings and miniatures and it was the more gratifying. She listened with a benignant smile to the torrent of thanks and vows and then motioned him to rise.

"And now that we understand each other perfectly," she said, "I will tell you, my dear Cardinal, that my poor child is making the most deplorable mistakes about Madame du Barry. One may think what one likes of that lady but what one *says*, what one *does*, is a very different matter, and unfortunately some officious fool has prejudiced her against Madame in the most shocking way. Imagine! I hear from Vermond that not long since your great Sovereign gave a supper-party for my daughter at which Madame du Barry was present. Three ladies who were there at once rose and left the table, considering it an affront to the Dauphine — Did you ever hear such folly? — and the poor misguided child in consequence wrote me a frantic letter to the effect that his Majesty had insulted her by Madame du Barry's presence and that she entreated I would interfere with a personal request to her royal grandfather that such a thing should never happen again! Need I say the letter was opened and read and naturally gave terrible offence in august quarters?"

"And what did your Majesty reply?" de Rohan asked, deeply interested.

"Ten simple words — no more. 'Where the Sovereign himself presides no guest can be objectionable.'"

"Most true!" said de Rohan with deep conviction. "And the result?"

"The result was unluckily too great a rebound in the other direction. My last report says that, being told Madame du Barry was the happy person who is most successful in amusing the Sovereign, my silly little girl said, innocently enough, of course! — 'Then I declare myself her rival, for I shall just try in the future which of us can best amuse my grandpapa. And we shall see who succeeds!' You can imagine Madame du Barry's feelings! I hear my Antoinette plays off all sorts of childish tricks now which delight his Majesty and drive Madame du Barry frantic. Is it wonderful, Cardinal, that I beg you to advise the unfortunate child?"

"What exactly does your Majesty wish the Dauphine to do?" asked de Rohan cautiously.

"To conciliate Madame du Barry's feelings in every way, while quietly consolidating her own influence with the King. To preserve her own dignity. I am told she even discards her hoops sometimes. Hoops! When she knows they are a matter of strict etiquette and, not only so, but most invaluable to ladies in delicate situations whether married or unmarried. Female reputation is really guarded by hoops and one may realize the animosity it provokes when she sets such a dangerous fashion. I sometimes think I have given birth to a fool!"

Not a sign of his inward mirth appeared on the Cardinal's face. He sat, gravely absorbing information which had of course reached him from his own spies at the Court long before, then slowly shook his head.

"I fear her Royal Highness's position is delicate in the extreme and the more so because her husband —" He hesitated and the Empress took him up smartly.

"— is not her husband in the true sense of the word and apparently takes no more notice of her than as if she were a perfect stranger! The unlucky child writes to me that he escorts her to her bedchamber door, takes off his hat with a bow and there leaves her!"

"Bless me!" ejaculated the Cardinal, who knew as much of the facts as the Empress, and indeed considerably more.

"But you knew that?" she questioned. The ignorance was a little overdone.

"Certainly I knew it, Madame, but I hoped, as all loyal subjects must hope, that such transcendent charms —"

"Oh, Antoinette is well-looking enough!" answered the Empress coolly. "But what is to come of it if she cannot win her husband's heart? What about an heir for France? I ask you!"

"Madame, I can only quote to your Majesty a reply of my Sovereign's to one of his daughters who asked the same question when in the same case. He replied, 'A prudent princess will never want for heirs.' It was apposite, I think!"

There was such humour in his face and twinkling blue eyes that for a moment the Empress softened into laughter, and they drifted more comfortably into gossip about the celebrities, men and women, of the French Court — a very highly spiced dish of gossip indeed, but valuable in another way also to the great Lady to whom it was of the utmost importance to know the character of every person in Marie Antoinette's *entourage*. Several of them indeed were already in her pay. Others would very shortly be. The Cardinal had never before been so graciously dismissed. He could remember now the charm of the smile with which the Empress bid him to return next day as she expected important despatches from the Abbé Vermond on which she must have his opinion.

He had scarcely reached his own room before he sent for his secretary, the Abbé Georgel, and told him the whole amazing story, delighted to observe the changes of hope, doubt and gladness on that keen vulpine face with close-drawn black brows and narrow lips. He was the Cardinal's faithful confidant and adviser in all but his lighter amusements. Those were kept strictly apart from business and the secretary attached no more importance to them than to the choice of his master's very rich and fastidious wardrobe. Princes did these things and the ladies came and went and he scarcely knew their names and cared less. That was a department altogether distinct from his.

But the Empress — the Empress!

"Of course," said the secretary, "she would do anything to conciliate the King. It is vital to her policy. But, for the love of God, remember, your Highness, how the Empress and the Austrian marriage are loathed in France. France has never loved Austrian marriages and will never forgive the Empress for her cruel conduct to us after the battle of Prague. So far even the youth and beauty of the Dauphine have not conquered the prejudice. Indeed you are shouldering a most anxious responsibility."

"I see no cause for alarm, and much for ambition. One has only to please all parties alike and —"

But the Abbé was too deep in thought to listen. He went on earnestly: "If his Majesty really falls in love with the Dauphine the marriage with the Dauphin may easily be annulled as it has never been consummated, and in that case his Majesty might marry her himself. Would that please the Empress?"

"I should say that even the Empress might have scruples there," said the Prince with affected coolness. "But who can tell?"

"I doubt any scruples!" replied the Abbé eagerly. "Does your Eminence know what happened when she designed her daughter the Archduchess Josepha for the King of Naples? The marriage by proxy had actually taken place, when just before she left for Naples the Empress happened to ask her if she would second her mother's plans in everything at the Court of Naples and — "

"Don't tell me the girl refused!" said the Prince. "Every one of them has been brought up to think their mother a pope in petticoats."

"The new Queen answered demurely: 'Scripture says, your Majesty, that when a woman is married she belongs to her husband's country.'"

"The little prig!" cried the Cardinal.

"'But what about State affairs?' asked the Empress in consternation. 'Are they above religion?' answered the young Queen solemnly. The Empress reflected for a moment in silence. 'My daughter, you are right and wrong!' she said. 'It is a case where we must implore Divine guidance! Go tomorrow to the tombs of our family and in the sacred vaults of your ancestors pray to Heaven to illumine you.' As a matter of fact the unfortunate young Queen was sent to pray by the tomb of the princess who had just died of the smallpox (her name I regret to say has escaped me), but the young Queen of Naples caught the disease and was dead in a few days."

"Bless me! What a woman!" repeated the Cardinal. "And then she sent Marie Caroline, the next daughter, instead!"

"Certainly, and when she arrived in Naples that young lady discovered that it was not etiquette for the Queen to dine at the same table with the King. The old lady immediately sent a despatch to the Neapolitan Prime Minister to say an Austrian army would fetch her daughter home if she were treated as inferior to her husband. But before this reached Naples the young Queen had already dismissed the ministry, upset the Cabinet and forbidden her bedchamber to the King. it is a very singular family indeed, and for that reason I entreat your Eminence to go warily not only with the Empress but the young Dauphine. It is not because a head is lovely that there may not be deep plotting instincts hidden within it."

"My friend Georgel," replied the Cardinal with a superior smile, "you are a very wise man and sometimes a very great fool. If a man of my age and experience cannot fathom the mind of a girl in her teens I give you leave to write me down an ass!"

The Abbé bowed submissively and remonstrated no more.

"She is as innocent as a lily, as fresh and guileless as a lamb!" cried the Cardinal. "She and her sisters have been brought up like nuns. Whole pages alluding to even the most refined love-affairs were chopped out of their books before they were allowed to read them and —"

"*That* I should think might arouse a very unwholesome curiosity," replied the Abbé grimly, "but I own I am unacquainted with the minds of young women."

"Pooh, my friend! What can girls imagine who know nothing? They were not even permitted anything but female dogs and birds as pets. Only women attended them. Excepting their confessor, who was all but a dotard, they never beheld men except on State occasions. I am told the Dauphine has no understanding whatever of her husband's neglect. All she complains of is his negligent manner. What can surpass such innocence?"

"I question it — I should indeed, your Eminence. Your Highness's information may be correct, and yet — Since you have done me the honour to ask my advice I would say: Go most warily. Remember the two queens of Naples. The Archduchess Josepha had the courage to defy her terrible mother; the present Queen of Naples had the kingdom by the ears before she had been in Naples a month. Possibly the Dauphine —"

"Bah! she is the sweetest little innocent alive!" said de Rohan laughing.

"She will not always be and who can say when the age of enlightenment begins," replied the secretary seriously. "However, one may safely say that few men have such a magnificent position thrust upon them and I congratulate your Eminence with all my heart."

Would the congratulations have been so heartfelt if he had guessed that for the first time in his life de Rohan would fall in love, and desperately, with the girl he was set to watch and influence? Had such a possibility occurred to him he would on his knees have besought his master to leave the danger-zone for others who had more taste for ruin. Ruin would certainly come of the smallest slip on the ice of such altitudes. Georgel who cared for his master's interests because they were his own would have gone half-mad with terror if he had guessed what was in that master's mind but, thinking as he did with the austerity of a churchman, passion was a force outside his estimate. The love affairs had never interested him and never would.

The rest can be briefly told.

Trusting in his own skill, keeping secret from his one adviser his true motive, de Rohan attempted to play a double game and to make his royal marionettes dance on his strings. He kept the Empress in a constant state of terror as to her daughter's indiscretions and follies that she might feel his advice and protection indispensable. He fed her upon lies and exaggerations and at last she could endure her anxiety no longer and sent a man whom she could trust to report upon the girl's conduct. Discovering the utter falsity of de Rohan the Empress forbade him her presence and he left Vienna in haste and secrecy for Versailles. There he set himself to the task of winning Marie Antoinette by embittering her against her mother.

Sitting in his own room and staring at her portrait while he recalled these things he remembered her trusting confidence and amazement when he seriously warned her against the Empress.

"It is painful but true that her Majesty feels you have failed, Madame, in carrying out her plans for Austria. Keep the secret I am about to tell you if you value your future. It is her intention that your grandfather the

King should marry your younger sister the Archduchess Elizabeth and —
"

He could never forget the look of dismay on Marie Antoinette's young face.

"What? And I am to be nothing, and my sister is to be set over me, and if she has a son my husband will be nothing!"

She broke down sobbing. She had tried so hard — what had she left undone?

She sobbed on and de Rohan resisted the longing to throw his arms about her and comfort her as a man may. She had nowhere else to turn and no position could be lonelier or more dangerous.

"But, Madame, hear reason. The Empress has confided this negotiation to *me*. Do you not know that in my hands it is safe? Can you believe I will let it go a step further? Not if it costs my life. I am returning to Vienna now to put a stop to such a hideous imagining."

She believed him. How otherwise? And he, speeding, got himself back to Vienna and straightway assured the Empress when he could gain an audience that he had set on foot a negotiation with the old King for his marriage with her daughter the Archduchess Elizabeth.

"For we shall never make any impression on the Dauphine, Madame. She is engrossed in her amusements and perfectly careless of the Austrian interests. Austria will make no progress in France while the august Dauphine represents her."

It is useless to open out the web of intrigue in which he snared the mother and daughter, intercepting their letters, playing a desperate game desperately. And in the midst of it the old King died and Marie Antoinette was Queen of France! Had he lived longer her marriage would have been annulled and she sent back to Vienna, so fatal had been the plottings of de Rohan and others to her hopes and future.

So the house of cards built upon deceit fell to the ground and the truth became known both to the Empress of Austria and the Queen of France. The Empress declared he should never enter her dominions again. Marie Antoinette, who dared not reveal all to her husband lest it should cause an open rupture with her mother and with Austria, could only use her influence to have the man forbidden the Court. That was in itself a sentence of death to all his hopes and in the glories of the new reign he faded into the background, a thwarted man, bitter with disappointed love and ambition, weak and dangerous alike to himself and others, waiting listlessly for some chance he might turn to better account.

Recalling all these things as he sat there he felt the past to be irreparable. She would never — could never forgive him. It was only the old King's death that had saved her. No, life would go on in this dull succession and he would see other men rise to power and favour. He had had to bear as best he could the knowledge that her husband had become her lover and to see her mother of the Dauphin of France. He had lost all. She could be generous to her other foes. Even the du Barry was allowed her pension and retired fat with ill-gotten gains. The Queen's influence was always for peace and a better understanding. For him only she had no pity. Could she have suspected that the traps he had set were to drive her into his arms for safety? Was that the explanation? He sat still staring at the picture, his mind wandering through the mad past and hopeless present.

She had her dangers yet in spite of her queenship. Not all her beauty and charm could soften the French hatred of Austria which he himself had helped to strengthen by his intrigues. To the French people she was always "The Austrian," she still walked in the midst of pitfalls where even her gaiety and grace were her enemies. But queens are safe enough, thought de Rohan. It is only those who trust them who pay their debts.

He rose at last sullen and wearied and blew a note on a gold whistle.

"Send to Madame de Lamotte and say I should like to see her this evening!" he said curtly to the lacquey who appeared. He could bear his own company no longer.

Chapter III

THE two most charming women in France sat in the Queen's cabinet a few days later, Marie Antoinette and the Superintendent of her Household, her close friend, the young widowed Princesse de Lamballe. They shone sweet as flowers against the rose satin hangings, but by no means the simple flowers which make sweet constellation in April meadows. Each was the product of centuries of race and training inherited from dominant ancestors surrounded by submissive slaves. The power of kings and pride of warriors asserted itself in every line of delicate nose and lip together with the imperial coquetry of long dead women who had swayed courts and camps as the moon swings the tides to her cold changes. If breed tells in the kennels it tells far more surely in the more sensitive human stuff of brain and flesh.

Each was "the last word of a thousand years, fine flower of Europe's slow civility," and therefore no garden flowers for the pleasures of lesser men but exotics fenced with glass, fostered in artificial warmth, worshipped at a distance but never made for daily love and household uses.

Yet both were perfectly at ease with their kind and each other, dressed at the moment more carelessly than the wife of many a rich *bourgeois* in Paris, full of gaiety and simplicity of manner also where they knew themselves on their own ground, yet capable of stiffening in a second into fair frost-pieces of majesty if any hint of familiarity should come between the wind and their nobility. "It would be interesting," thought a man who waited in the antechamber within sound of their voices though not of their words, "to speculate how either or both would act in a moment of dismay or danger." Ridiculous thought! he ended with a smile. Such could never confront these darlings of fate. God himself would think twice before damning princesses of their quality whatever their sins. His smile took a tinge of bitterness remembering certain stories which had reached him. But no. Impossible!

A man passed him, preceded by one of the Queen's ladies, on his way to the cabinet. Lucky dog! Count de Fersen thought, with a movement of surprise, looking up quickly.

After all it was only Boehmer, the King's Jeweller, and he, of course, was a necessity of majesty. What shining toy tempted the Loveliest now, he wondered. Of all earthly wishes would that he might be the one to offer it and see those proud eyes soften for a moment over the beauty of a stone cold as her own royal heart. He watched Boehmer's discreet entry with a smile half-melancholy, half-bitter, and returned to his idle talk with the officer on duty outside, for the door was now closed.

As for Boehmer, he was at the moment inaccessible to sentiment. He knew, none better, what was due to majesty, but the necklace filled his universe and on entry, after the necessary obeisances, he saw only two lovely young women who, being what they were, would certainly succumb to the glittering temptation. He congratulated himself on the Princess's presence, for her amazement and delight would carry the Queen off her feet, if that were needed. Every one knew the influence possessed by the young Mistress of the household and how in matters of taste Marie Antoinette would take her opinion before her own. And who could find a flaw in his necklace where the whole was as super-perfect as every jewel in it? His heart bounded in his breast with certainty and pleasure. The scene was striking. The room had an effect of dim richness and splendour very impressive. There were magnificent commodes, the doors gleaming with the richness of red lacquer and ormolu, and behind the Queen a glorious cabinet with Sevres medallions of the loves of goddesses and nymphs, roseate, azure, smiling as only loves in porcelain are likely to be. The carpet was in powder-blue and rose from the looms of Aubusson and the gilded chairs glimmered in white brocaded satin, the patterns delicately illuminated in hand-work of flowers and garlands. If one counted the treasures of that room together with the pictures they would outweigh the value of the necklace itself. But these were treasures of the Crown of France, the other, the property of Messieurs Boehmer and Bassauger.

A lady-in-waiting was present in stiff hoops and powdered eminence of hair; she stood erect behind the chair of the young woman in white with straightly falling India muslin with a crossed fichu over her bosom who represented the majesty of France. Thérèse de Lamballe sat beside her on a low seat without arms, but rose on his entry. There must be no familiarity with the Queen of France on a stranger's arrival. She was on duty at once. Both returned Boehmer's greeting with friendly grace. He was so far below their sphere as to render any precaution of manner unnecessary.

"Madame, I thank your Majesty with deep humility and gratitude for the favour accorded me of presenting a very wonderful work of art to your gracious notice."

"But what is it, monsieur? I must beg you not to tempt me, for, as you know, I am still in debt for the diamond earrings. It is true I meant to be economical, but what would you have?"

"Madame, it would not be for the happiness of their people that great queens should be economical. It is known to your Majesty that the people love to see the splendour of courts and realize that money is circulated."

He addressed her always in the third person so impossible to represent in English. She laughed like a girl.

"True, but yet — Where is it? Have you left it in the antechamber?"

"Madame," protested Boehmer, "one does not leave jewels worth the City of Paris in the antechamber even of kings. Nor does one carry them visibly. I drove through the streets with terror today."

"Come nearer, Thérèse, and prepare to be astonished. I will wager it is the diamond bracelets the Grand Turk had made for the chief sultana. I had heard they were to be sold in Paris."

Not a word said Boehmer. With the solemnity of an archbishop officiating at High Mass he put his hand in the deep breast pocket of his soberly handsome brocaded undercoat and drew out a slender case especially made for such conveyance of the treasure. It was not its state receptacle, so to speak, but an incognito though elegant enough for a queen's handling, and with the intention of suggestion he had had a crown-royal stamped in gold on the purple leather.

Before her Majesty was a small table enamelled in miniatures of shepherds and fashionable shepherdesses in the gardens of the Trianon. On this he laid the case and kneeling on one knee opened it, then rose and drew back.

Heavens! how the light imprisoned sprang to light released. Bright sparkles danced on the very ceiling as it laughed at its lover the sun. The Queen, laughing also, put her hand over dazzled eyes as bright. The Princess opened hers in amazement. The one had known the Austrian crown jewels from her cradle until the happy day when those of France

32

were lavished to illuminate her beauty, and for the other the jewels of the great House of Penthievre were a fitting setting. But this was a world's wonder. Such a thing had never been seen before — might never be seen again.

"But, monsieur, impossible! Can they be real?" cried the Queen at last. "Naturally I have seen a few larger, but such an assemblage, never. Thérèse, what do you say?"

"Magnificent!" The Princess was hovering over them like a bee above roses. She showed unashamed, unconscious, the primitive longing of the woman for adornment and glitter. "Can a bride forget her jewels?" asks the Scripture and if not a bride certainly not a queen and her mistress of the household.

They lifted them, fingered them, commented, gloated, and Boehmer stood back delighted, sure at last that his day of happy release was come. Foolish Bassauger who had croaked like a raven of loss and ruin! What news he would carry back to shatter the gloom into triumph.

"Put them on, Thérèse, that I may see the effect!" cried the Queen, alive with curiosity and interest.

"Oh, Madame, your Majesty first. Permit me!" and in a moment her fair fingers loaded with emeralds had clasped the happy jewels about the beautiful throat made, it would seem, for such decoration. In the combination of simplicity and splendour was the most bewitching contrast in the world. Such diamonds with such beauty clad in white muslin were a dish for playful Graces. Thérèse de Lamballe clapped her hands, laughing aloud with gentle pleasure.

"You should make it the fashion, Madame. A white ball at Versailles, with avalanches of diamonds. A winter fête — I have it! White, white everywhere like snow, every head powdered, swan's-down, white fur, and the glitter of diamonds for frost crystals and your Majesty in these!"

The Queen flew to the wonderful Louis Quatorze mirror in gilt claws which reflected the room, sumptuous casket for the jewel it held. Her figure, startlingly white and slender with rivers of light on shoulders and bosom confronted her. She turned, flushed and lovely to her friend. "Oh, if only I need never wear those abominable hoops again. I look like a woman in these draperies and in the hoops like a painted Queen of Diamonds — no better than the rest of the pack. What figure need a woman have in hoops? One might be knock-kneed and not a soul the wiser."

She halted, remembering Boehmer's presence and the Princess released her from the splendid harness, laying it on the table while together they counted the stones and admired the pendants.

"Really there is no choice!" Thérèse de Lamballe said at last. "To permit any one else to wear it would be to acknowledge oneself vanquished. It could not be. It is too magnificent for any one but a queen."

"I feel that too," the Queen said seriously, "but then — the cost! And times are so bad. Bad harvests, trouble with the English, discontents everywhere. What *is* the cost, monsieur?"

"The cost, your Majesty, is infinitesimal for such a jewel. You will laugh when you hear it. Roughly, four hundred thousand pounds. And that —" as he saw the quick look of alarm — "not by any means to be paid at once. Only in instalments and perfectly at his Majesty's ease. Madame la Princesse is right. For the honour of the royalty of France there is none other who should wear it. So convinced was I of this that I had the crown stamped on the case."

The Queen sat staring with great blue eyes at the necklace. It had been a bitter winter, delightful for sleighing at Versailles in gilt sleighs, shaped like swans and the last word in luxury. She had leaned back buried in a warm snow of furs, delicate feet slipped into costly muffs heated to protect them, only the sparkle of bright eyes and frost-rosed cheeks emerging from the warmth to meet the gay inspiriting cold. How her children had loved the sight of long white wastes of snow blotting out all the familiar lawns and landmarks, how they had clapped their little hands at sight of the snow statues of the Queen reared in her honour by a loyalty as short-lived as its memorial. Yes, a heavenly winter. She could not remember that she had ever enjoyed one more! But then — the people. Terrible reports came in from the provinces of starvation and death in the biting cold. Versailles itself was in the grip of poverty. As the sleighs glided over the sparkling surface one saw women huddled in rags leading gaunt children, the very ghosts of famine. The snow was not so amusing for them.

Naturally one stopped, one caused the equerry to ray golden louis into hands unused to gold. One received thanks and blessings and glided on conscious of queenly grace in the action. It would be reported far and wide. But a louis here and there did not go far. The King had spent much money on cart-loads of wood to warm wretched homes and one reason why she was delayed in her payments to Boehmer for the diamond earrings was that she had joined him in that gift to poverty.

And still the people died. Ill-fed, ill-clothed, what chance had they? But who could deal with such wide-spread misery? Who was responsible? Not she — not the King. These things simply happened and were most unfortunate. The way was to forget them if one could and continue sleighing.

That was possible and she had done it. But these diamonds? No doubt it was a moderate price but for what immoderate luxury! Quickly sensitive the tears gathered in her eyes as she sat looking silently at the necklace. That a queen of France whose right to splendour was unquestioned must doubt and hesitate before the purchase of a mere necklace seemed at the moment the cruelest injustice of fate. Her mind wavered to and fro like a flag in a gale, while Thérèse watched her half-smiling, as one watches a pretty child hesitating between its toys, and Boehmer looked on in satisfaction. At that moment he was as sure of his money as man could be.

At last the Queen roused herself from her reverie: "The King must see it. He has expressed the wish. I know the price is moderate enough for such jewels, but you are aware, monsieur, that there are many poor — poor moreover who do not realize that it is fate and not the King's Government which stints them. If it were to get abroad that I had made such a purchase there would be pasquinades, satires. In short, it would be misrepresented in every possible way. You could not have chosen a worse time."

Boehmer bowed and protested without a tinge of fear for the result. The Princess's first look of doubt reflected her own. Yes, the times were bad, even dangerous, if one considered such things! Boehmer urged that no time could be ill which placed such stones, the collection of patient years, at the foot of the throne. He would be profoundly honoured if his Majesty would condescend to inspect them. The Queen, sighing, despatched a messenger.

"And, I think, Thérèse, that when the King comes we had better see them alone. I want his frank opinion. The necklace is magnificent, but you see well that I must not be rash."

With gravely lowered eyes and her charming *reverence* the Princess glided out of a concealed door leading to the inner apartment and at the same moment the King was announced and the royal couple were alone with the happy Boehmer. His Majesty nodded to the jeweller and threw himself into a chair.

Very far from the model of an accomplished gentleman was Louis the Sixteenth, King of France and inheritor of much unfulfilled renown and a descent that most other European kings must envy. Yet let none judge by appearances. No man can increase the stock of intellect with which he is launched in life and there the patron saints of the House of Bourbon had not been lavish. Knowledge a man may acquire if he have the chance and will. Louis had had neither and a deplorable education distracted by Court intrigues for tutorships had left him as ignorant a young man as any in his dominions except for such morsels of statecraft as he could not avoid in the life he was compelled to lead. By way of accomplishments he might be called a fair shot and horseman. By way of tastes a clever mechanic. As an artisan he might have made a decent living and earned his keep honestly. He was a really clever locksmith and if the workmen were busy with repairs about the palace it was his delight, not to look on with a condescending word of encouragement, but to pull and haul paving-stones, toss a plank over his big shoulders and so forth, much to their dismay and contempt. Horrible indeed for delicate-handed courtiers to witness; horrible for a royal bride to endure who expected sugared flatteries, a plumed hat swept to the feet or pressed to the heart in bows and had none of this from her strange uncouth husband. She had curled her lip often to watch him loafing in the courtyard, dully, idly, sometimes lending a hand if he got the slightest encouragement rather than lounging in her perfumed salon.

But the wife was wiser than the bride as wives are likely to be. That had been her first impression. She knew now that under that hulking exterior lay one of the kindest hearts in the world, a heart oppressed with a sense of destiny too great for its powers and therefore condemned to a most misleading reserve. There had come a day when she knew her charms and graces had not blown away like thistledown on a wind as she had supposed but that the rough boy had watched, had learnt that graces as well as conscience are necessary upon a throne and that though he could not shine himself and would never develop more than a dull reserved civility with which to meet his people he could yet delight to see her shine beside him while he toiled with false or inadequate ministers to retrieve the burden of an irretrievable past.

At first she pitied him, as one may pity a spirit prisoned in the rough bark of a cleft tree, and if such pity is not love, it is at least its kin and may one day develop the psyche wings folded in its chrysalis. Difficult and clumsy the elegant courtiers beheld their Dauphin and King and smiled in safe places, but the bright blue eyes of his Austrian wife were clearer — she knew there was a something inarticulate but fine, if one could reach it. Something that spoke of conscience in a conscienceless world ruled by his shameful grandfather and his shameless du Barry. And so it came about that to the shy young man's consternation one day she rushed into his room and clasped tender arms about him, crying with tears: "I care for you more every day, my dear, dear husband. Your frank honest character delights me, and the more I compare you with others the more I trust you."

Was it any wonder that though he could never speak of that moment even to her he was henceforth the lover of the one woman who understood him.

"Everything she does is lovely," was all he said to a great lady who hoped to catch his attention. His eyes were fixed on his wife. "We must own that she is perfectly charming."

She was that and more in his eyes, something spiritual, exquisite, from a higher world than his own, a wonder clasped miraculously in his very earthy arms. And what could he deny her? Better if he had done it sometimes and affected an austerity he could never feel. She desired the Trianon, that charming country house by Versailles, the only place where she could be less than the Queen of France — a great lady playing at rusticity — and she had it and the cruel embittered comments of the journalists and pamphleteers who now began to rule France, comments on the frivolities and senseless extravagance of the Austrian. And now she wanted a new jewel — Well, it would be hard if the Empress of Hearts could not be the Queen of Diamonds also. It would be a difficult matter to manage just now, this awful winter; but if she wanted it — That was the mood in which the King entered the room that held his treasure, heavy and clumsy of gait, but a true lover in his heart's heart.

"Show me the rubbish!" he said with would-be levity and held out the big flat-fingered hand of an artisan from the ruffled lace of his velvet sleeve. The Queen lifted it in almond-white rose-tipped fingers delicately as befitted its worth and laid it in his — those hands of hers were celebrated throughout Europe for their high-bred beauty and the very touch of them sent a light thrill through the coarser hand they brushed in passing.

"Most beautiful!" said the King, and did not mean the necklace.

Chapter IV

HE sat a moment, turning it over curiously, causing the light to play upon it from different angles. To him it was extraordinary that any one should care for such things. What did they mean? Nothing. A bit of honest handicraft such as a well-wrought lock was worth it all. But yet beauty and rank claim their adornments and that also was a bewildering part of the odd necessities life forced on one, for to him she was more lovely in the muslin gown she wore at the moment than in all the hooped and glittering splendours that held him at a distance and made a goddess of her. But how natural — how natural she should desire this wonder! Think of the ugly Charlotte of England sparkling in the diamonds an Indian Prince had laid at her flat feet! She had laughed over that news the other day. His eye fell on the arched and high-heeled shoe pressing the gilded footstool beside him. Watteau and Lancret might have taken it as an inspiration and lovers kissed its print upon the velvet. Where else could such beauty be found — and, more than beauty, charm crowning it with an indescribable attraction that drew all hearts. Rank, yes, but she could have laid that aside and yet been a world's wonder.

He sat so long musing, his slow mind taking its own devious track to the goal, that Boehmer began to quake in his shoes. Did his Majesty disapprove? Had he forgotten? The Queen observing it put a light finger on her lip and remained looking steadily at the King.

"Of course you must have it, Madame," he said. "I would not speak of it until you saw it, but Boehmer submitted it to me the other day and my mind was made up then that if you approved it could be no one else's. It is suitable to you and you only."

Bright red flushed up into Boehmer's sallow cheeks. Praise be to God! The relief was painful. He drew a long breath like one released from bodily torment, but not a word did he utter. He watched while the Queen let the jewels fall through her fingers like water, her head bowed over them, her eyes invisible. And it seemed that much time went by.

Suddenly she looked up and made a sign to the jeweller which waived him away to a distant window. He went, stationing himself half behind the heavy curtain. The two were virtually alone.

At last with downcast eyes she said in a low voice: "Will it be difficult?"

"Not to you, Madame."

"But difficult?"

"It can be done. That is all the Queen needs to know."

His heavy mouth relaxed into a very kindly smile — as when the little Dauphin snatching at the magnificent order of the Holy Ghost dragged it off his father's breast. The child could not gauge its value. He wanted it. That was enough, and it was enough now also. But she was speaking: "I am more than the Queen. I am your wife. Again I ask, will it be difficult? What will Calonne say when he hears?"

Calonne was the Comptroller General and his very name in those days that were coming upon them seemed to her a word of sinister omen. He was a man whom her every instinct distrusted and whom the King had called to the Ministry much against her will. De Calonne knew this very well and her fine perception felt an enemy. The thought of him took life and colour from the heap upon her lap.

"He has found money before. He can find it again."

"But the means?"

"That I cannot tell. It is his business. Put it on that I may see it."

"But it is believed that with Thérèse and the Polignacs I fill my hands from the Treasury whenever I please. It has done infinite harm."

"That is a lie. What matters what liars say? You should know better than to listen!"

She hesitated, then lifted it mechanically and clasped it about her throat. Even the King's dull eyes lighted at the rainbow lights it flung about her and the new meaning with which it irradiated her beauty. That beauty was of a type as unusual as the woman herself. She could wear a hoop with the stateliest dignity but in a hoop all figures are pretty much alike. Who but the Queen could wear that white drapery clinging about her and melt from one perfect pose of grace into another as unconsciously and naturally as a flower swaying on the stem?

None. His heart knew it.

Others also might have that blended beauty of lily and rose and the great blue eyes, but never their witchery of gaiety and melancholy. Another woman of Marie Antoinette's colouring would have crowned it with golden hair and become banal and obvious with what is in itself a beauty. There too nature had been lavish to her. Her hair was the last touch of refinement and distinction — *blonde cendrée* — masses of almost ashen blonde hair making the most exquisitely softening background for colouring too brilliant had the frame been golden. That was exquisite — no one had hair like the Queen's. It was as though it had been etherialized by a delicate veil of powder, and there were those who predicted that when it became grey it would still further stress the unapproachable distinction that all her Court envied. But how the diamonds lit it up! She glittered star-like from the darkening depths of the mirror, then turned to meet him, smiling doubtfully: "You like it, Sire?"

"I like it, Madame."

She stood, her hands dropped beside her, while Boehmer trembled in the distance anticipating the recall and decision, then lifting her arms she unclasped and laid it on the enamelled table.

"I will not have it, Sire."

Dead silence, the King staring at her mutely.

"I will not have it," she repeated slowly, as if to strengthen herself.

Something in his acquiescence must have struck a vibrating chord of pity in her heart. Yes, it would be difficult, difficult indeed! True, Calonne must carry it through, but the King would suffer in deep anxiety, and for the King — not that squalid form of suffering if she could help it! For the voice of France was going up in cries and groans, the people wailing for bread. Taxation was frightful and yet did not bring in enough to pay the daily way of the country. There were sounds of rebellion, muffled and sinister stealing on the ear, not to be traced to this source or that but all-pervading, terrifying. And the world knew well that the dead King with his appalling vices, his appalling lavishness to the women who shared them, had left a debt which the people must exact with interest one dreadful day. Also, across the Channel English ships were watching, biding their time, fiercely resentful of French participation through Lafayette in the breaking away of the American colonies from the dominion of George the Third. They too had their score to settle. These thoughts and many more passed like grey phantoms of fear through her brain as she replaced the diamonds, slowly and delicate-fingered, in their purple case. Her husband's voice roused her.

"You shall have them, Madame. I say it."

She raised her own, soft but clear as a bell of crystal, and addressed not the King but Boehmer.

"Monsieur, have the goodness to return. The decision is made."

From the velvet curtains which half-draped him Boehmer advanced elate, bowing deeply at every second step. Never a doubt now clouded his face or thoughts. The nightmare was lifted and prosperity rose like a dawning sun. Aha! what would Bassauger have to say when he returned empty-handed but full-hearted? He could see him rubbing his fat little hands and rallying "the man of affairs," as he called the senior partner.

"Madame!"

She held the case towards him with a gesture of finality. "Monsieur, France needs ships of war. The Queen cannot buy a diamond necklace."

There was dead silence, the King staring mutely at her, his face indecipherable; Boehmer with dropped jaw. He had not heard a word they uttered, had taken all for granted from the King's acquiescence, for who could doubt the Queen's? Something seemed to snap in his brain. He did not intend it, did not even know what he was doing, but acting on the irresistible impulse of the moment fell on his knees before her making as if to clutch the folds of her white dress.

"Madame, Madame!" was all he could stutter. The blood charged to his brain and the sparkle of the diamonds seemed to fill it with fire that dazzled his eyes.

"Madame!" he gasped again and awed by her look, half-angry, half-startled like a surprised goddess, got himself clumsily on his feet again and faced her, while she stood with one hand laid on the table. The King watched both with his heavy gaze, veiling so much more feeling than he had power to express.

"Madame!" he stammered, his breath catching in every word. "Have pity on your old and faithful servant! This is a matter of life and death to me — of more, of much more: honour! For, will your Majesty's goodness realize that not only have these jewels been a dreadful cost, but I have payments to make —" His voice failing for the moment trailed into nothingness, but he rallied it again, speaking with a violent effort that flushed his face purple.

"Madame, it shall be on any terms his Majesty imposes; spread out over what years he will. There is nothing I will not accept to facilitate your possession of these jewels that become you as they can no other in the world. I swear I had this honour before me all the time I was combing the earth for them. Oh, Madame, have pity!"

The Queen gathered herself together, the King dead silent beside her.

"I have listened, monsieur, and with sympathy, for I understand your emotion in view of the immense cost of the jewels, but you compel me to remind you now that you are a Frenchman and a loyal one. Consider the state of the country, known to you as to all. Is it a time when you would wish to see your sovereigns lavishing treasure on a thing so useless, however beautiful? Suppose it were not yours. What would you feel if you heard of such a purchase at such a crisis! No, you must sell it in happier countries. There is no time or place for it here."

One does not argue with the Queen, but Boehmer's misery thrust him beyond the pale of custom. He was sobbing, dry breathless sobs, while his hands clutching each other expressed the rigid tension of failing self-control.

"Madame! No one need know! Keep it for happier days and make only such payments as you approve. Sire, I beseech you! I am a ruined man! You were favourable. Oh, plead with her Majesty for me —"

The King moved a step forward.

"You are resolved, Madame?"

"Absolutely. With what face could I wear it? And as to hiding it —" Her look of disdain said the rest.

The King advanced on the man in his disconcerting short-sighted way which had the effect of seeming to drive people back against the wall. Boehmer shrank before him.

"Her Majesty has expressed her will, and I, the King, say she is right. There is no more to be said. No, I am not angry, but take your diamonds and go!"

Even to Boehmer's anguish it was clear that the fiat of doom had gone forth and there was no more hope. He could not comprehend what had changed his world into hell. What had they said to one another? But what matter? All was lost. Trembling like an old man, his face a sickly white now, he gathered up the rejected treasure and secured it in his breast pocket, then bowed pitiably, piteously, and crept towards the door.

The Queen stood still as an image until it closed, then turned to her husband, her eyes brimming with tears that spilt down her cheeks.

"The poor man! But what could I do? I was right. You know I was right."

He caught her clumsily in his arms and held her close, kissing her hair and brows.

"You are always right, my dear heart. I was wrong to say a word, but I thought you wished for it and if you had — But to me it looks more like the du Barry than — my Queen." His tone was love's homage alike to wife and queen. He could say little but there were moments when his look said much. It spoke then.

"You are too good to me!" she said sadly, disengaging herself. "If I had wished for it I should have been a wretch! Wear it perhaps four times a year, and see the veiled glances when I did! No, you are right. It is for women like the du Barry, for whom they made it. Forget it, Sire, and let us talk of happier things. But that poor Boehmer's face! It haunts me."

"Let him sell it elsewhere!" the King said stolidly. "We have heard the end of it now, and he will never dare to trouble us with it again."

But a cold premonitory shudder shook the Queen, as when someone walks over a grave as yet undug. She clung against the King's shoulder like one in fear, and knew there was no strength in it to save her from the poison-wind of calumny which had begun to breathe through the palaces of the kings of France.

"I wish with all my heart and soul that I had never seen it," she said.

As to Boehmer, not knowing what he did, walking stiffly lest control should slip from him altogether, he passed almost unnoticed through the antechamber. The Count de Fersen, Colonel of the Regiment of Royal Swedes looked up from the game of cards he was playing in a recess with an officer of the Garde du Corps.

"The favoured Boehmer does not look particularly happy!" he said.

"I suppose he has not got rid of as much as he hoped!" answered the other carelessly. "But it is madness of the Majesties to buy so much as a diamond snuff-box now. The talk of the Queen's expenses is frightfully dangerous and grows daily. Curse these cards! You have all the luck,

Comte! It seems to me that a foreigner has always more wit or good fortune!"

"And yet she is probably one of the least expensive queens that ever sat upon the throne!" said de Fersen, ignoring the cards. "It's the left-handed queens that cost the money. The Pompadour and du Barry spent as much in a month as the Queen in a year. And the King's life is simplicity itself in so far as he can control it."

"True! but, oh, curse it, Comte, you can't talk and play. At least I can't. And the poor devil is gone with his hangdog face. Do forget him and play."

De Fersen picked up his cards but without interest and his look was absent. The poor devil had made his way out by a long corridor leading past the apartments of the Queen's waiting women. As he stumbled along, half-stupid with shock, a door opened and a pretty woman came out tripping coquettishly on ridiculous heels, the latest note of fashion; exceedingly well-dressed too. She turned to the friend inside.

"Good-bye then, *chèrie*. Tomorrow you shall have the almond-water for the skin. It has an infusion of tree-bark in it from the Orient that acts like magic in effacing wrinkles. Try it and see. Yes — two louis. But what's a louis for beauty renewed? Not that yours wants renewing — it's a case of prevention with *you!*" She looked at Boehmer and halted. "Who's the gentleman with the long face?" she asked in a tone of languid interest.

"That's Boehmer, the King's Jeweller, Madame Lamotte. I thought to hear you talk you knew all the people about Court. I daresay he's been selling something to make your mouth water. He's coming from the Queen."

"Mighty fine, I've no doubt," said the other edging up. A pretty woman with brown black hair and bright dark eyes, a heart-shaped face and slight tip-tilted nose. But, to a knowledgeable eye, distinctly lacking in refinement. She cast a sidelong glance after Boehmer and added: "I wager her Majesty doesn't stint herself these hard times."

The Queen's woman was condescending.

"Those who are about queens, madame, know that they must be fine. It is a part of their business."

"A business that's getting a bit out of date, I imagine. I wonder what she bought."

"Perhaps the diamond necklace!" the other said yawning. "Well, I must dress for my attendance."

Lamotte pricked up her pretty ears for more.

"The diamond necklace? Which? What?"

"Why, the one Boehmer made for the du Barry. One of us overheard the Queen and the Princess de Lamballe talking about it. There never was anything like it in the world. As big as a big crystal lustre! You ask the Cardinal to give it to you!"

This was a roguish side-dart that brought a becoming little flush to the Lamotte's face.

"How you talk! You pretty women are always suspecting others of the same tricks as your own! Well, I too must be off. I have an appointment in the apartments of Madame de Provence. She's most awfully good to me. You'd be jealous if you knew. Adieu!"

With a parting giggle she minced off on her little high-heeled shoes, her hoop billowing about her. The other turned to her friend inside.

"She knows as much of Madame de Provence's apartments as I do of the King's. The King's sister-in-law indeed and a wench like the Lamotte! Not likely, I should say. Still, she knows a lot about face and hair washes. Don't you think I look a different creature since she took me in hand?"

They closed the door on the corridor. Lamotte, with her little contemptuous smile, was well out of sight following on Boehmer's track. To her quick observation he had not the air of a man who has sold a diamond necklace or anything else. He looked stunned, dazed, almost unconscious.

She watched him with interest until he disappeared, for in her trade all was fish that came to her net, and Heaven only knew what might turn up. Finally she went slowly along the corridor which led to the apartments of the King's sister-in-law, calculating the exact point at which she could turn and give herself the appearance of having just left them in case anyone should be coming along that way. Then she would read their interest in a quickened curiosity. They would be thinking: "That woman must be somebody. She has been with her Royal Highness. Who can she be?" The thought pleased her.

Chapter V

OF the scum flung up by the revolutionary waters fermenting before the storm Jeanne Lamotte was one of the strangest elements and in view of later events one of the most unforeseen. It appears incredible now that a woman of her insignificance could have achieved the colossal mischiefs for which she was responsible. She was ill-born, ill-bred, ignorant and greedy as a monkey. Yet a woman who fights the world with her handicaps and only a piquant dark prettiness for her weapon must be owned to have quick wits if nothing more. Quick wits she certainly possessed and a conviction in spite of repeated disappointments that much might be made of fishing in troubled waters if the rod were in the right hand. Her own. She had unshaken confidence in herself. That was a weapon too.

Though she kept it hidden as close as a guilty secret there were one or two who knew that her father was a mere peasant of Auteuil. But here was a very odd contradiction. A peasant, but of all names in the world he called himself Valois, stuck to it doggedly however much people laughed! And they did laugh, consumedly. Valois! the ancient knightly royal name of France. It was exactly as if some guttersnipe of an Englishman should announce himself as Plantagenet. There were days, now almost forgotten, when the Valois name would have run like a trumpet call from the Pyrenees to Normandy, but they were long over, and in the reign of Louis the Thirteenth the last known Valois had occupied a poor little property called Gros Bois and occupied himself with the somewhat adventurous business of coining. He died and the family was finished. Then who was the peasant of Auteuil who bore a name so much too stately for his hovel and muddied *sabots*?

Some years before Boehmer presented his diamond necklace at Court a great lady, Madame de Boulanvilliers, walking inside the wreathed and decorated iron gates of her estate at Auteuil and looking down the road happened to see two picturesque little peasant girls toiling along in clattering wooden *sabots*, each bowed double under a load of wood. They were pretty enough to rouse some idle curiosity and the *curé* of the village who accompanied madame in her stroll looked through the gate with her and laughed with amusement.

"Those children, madame — It is the oddest thing in the world! If you guessed for a year, you would never guess what their name is."

"Something extremely common, poor little angels, I have no doubt," said madame, yawning behind jewelled fingers.

"Something extremely uncommon!" her companion retorted with a pinch of snuff. "Those children have some curious papers relating to their descent, and their name is — Valois!"

"Good God!" cried madame, halting so suddenly as to startle the lap-dog she led by a ribbon. "But no, it's impossible! How should that be?"

"Why, only in one way, madame, and that common enough. Those children are descended from the illegitimate son of one of the Valois princes. It will probably be Henri the Second. There is a great deal of good blood scattered about the country in that way, if people did but know their good fortune!"

Madame dropped the conversation. As a woman of rank it displeased her to think that any privilege of hers was shared even illegitimately by the child of a peasant. Still, the thing stuck in her head. Madame de Boulanvilliers, herself of high birth, might not have pitied the ordinary child but it pinched her pride of race to think of a Valois however illegitimate drudging in the filth and poverty of a village. She decided to make an experiment, to take the eldest into her house and bring her up as some sort of attendant. Surely one could count on instincts of refinement in the Valois blood which would make it pleasant for a great lady to have the girl about her!

It may be imagined the wild bewildered hope that such a change would waken. To Jeanne Valois, for her neighbours never conceded the aristocratic "de" to the family, her life had always been a problem with deliverance waiting round the corner. One could not be a Valois for nothing! Every scrap of knowledge she could gain about the past had always convinced her of that and now already the illustrious name was bearing fruit. It should bear more, she resolved once and for all.

But meanwhile she had much to endure, from her point of view. The house was dull as ditch-water and madame, far from being a pretty painted coquette of the Court such as Jeanne could have admired and imitated, was religious, dogmatic and stern. But though she could cheat her mistress behind her back and mimic her with such skill as would have delighted the company of the Comédie Française if it could have sat as audience she was quite clever enough to realize that here was a school for learning to speak like Madame de Boulanvilliers and her friends, and pick up their very burdensome manners for use when necessary. She was a sedulous ape, always watching and practising and every day the skin of the peasant sloughed and disclosed a highly varnished surface beneath. Her mistress saw and admired, congratulating herself on a well-applied charity and Jeanne was satisfied that it was worth all the boredom a hundred times over even if she had not tempered it with epigrams and coquetries as she did; for much went on which Madame de Boulanvilliers never guessed as, growing older, Jeanne spread her little lures so poorly aided and abetted, fighting for her own hand as audaciously as any Valois of history. She was indeed to make history herself though after a somewhat different fashion.

She was certain that something must come of her life. Was one pretty, a Valois, quick as a weasel and sharp as a needle, simply that one might comb a dull old woman's lap-dog? No indeed! Marriage — marriage was the open gate! There, she would make her fortune.

Meanwhile her patroness, foreseeing that the girl must soon strike out for herself, procured her through her own Court interest a microscopic pension of fifteen hundred francs a year as a fallen Valois. It was worth little enough, but Jeanne was quick to see that it altered her standing and confirmed her pretensions. Her mistress, now extremely anxious to be rid of her for various reasons, remarked that she was quite above her work and strutted like a peacock. The need for marriage grew urgent on both sides.

Alas, she was obliged to realize as she grew older that there were plenty of chances for love-making but very few for marriage. It seemed as far off as heaven and much less hopeful. Men grew shyer every day, it seemed, of pretty adroit young women with sparkling eyes and coquettish tricks who held off for a wedding ring. At last however, virtue, or what passed for it, met with its reward, though far from the reward it deserved in its own opinion. She married a private named Lamotte in the Bodyguard of the King's brother, the Count de Provence and was promoted from Auteuil to a poor enough little furnished house at

Versailles which went by the name of Belle Image. And then her patroness died and hope with her, unless they could live by their wits.

Now, if any one thought that the lady of Belle Image would settle down into domestic life and mend her private's hose and cook his stews that person was grossly deceived. She could not tell where her star would lead her but somewhere else it must, and with progress in view she took her measures. Monsieur Lamotte was perfectly willing to slip into the background at any time to further his wife's little plans. A most good-humoured husband: first, the name. It had served her already; it should serve her again. Her husband was quite good-looking enough to carry a title and a title he should have. She set her quick lips resolutely and had cards printed giving her name as Madame la Comtesse de Lamotte-Valois. Why not? Had not her pension acknowledged her as a Valois? In that land of many titles it would pass excellently well and neither she nor her husband would be the worse for a high-sounding one. At first it frightened him a little — the arrow was aimed so high, but he knew his social wits and knowledge were no match for hers, though he had his own department in the firm for all that! Therefore he agreed and became the Comte de Lamotte-Valois by grace of his busy little wife.

One could not live on it however, nor on fifteen hundred francs, and Madame la Comtesse was obliged to consider what she could do next with her good looks and her title. It flashed upon her. A *clientele* of ladies interested in preserving their good looks who would buy washes and lotions for the skin and duly appreciate their provider, who would open not only their boudoirs but their hearts, in whose company she would hear all the Court gossip and the secrets of the wealthy idle women — that was the career for such wits as hers! Her own clear pale skin and brilliant eyes would bear out her knowledge of cosmetics and her glib tongue would do the rest. Her husband fully agreed. She would be the heaven-born beauty-priestess with her armoury of attractive little pots and bottles. She fixed her mind upon it steadily and began to haunt the back-stairs of Versailles where once the great doors had been thrown open before her royal ancestors, if indeed they had ever been her ancestors at all.

It was not really difficult to live upon people's foibles and upon what else could a woman with her hard luck hope to live? Especially with a little help from flirtations quite in the manner of the gay world. Monsieur de Lamotte-Valois was no Puritan fortunately, and had besides his own little interests and engagements in that way. It all looked very promising as clients and flirtations increased and the gossip which came her way enabled her to extend her business.

A veil drawn with discretion over this stage is perhaps desirable. It is enough to say that as her purse filled her ambition increased and that it was a very grateful client who upon a very glad day mentioned her attractive title and person to no less a grandee than the Cardinal, Prince Louis de Rohan, a personage certainly not too high for a Valois but high enough to please even a lady of that august family. A very pleasant and lucrative little friendship was the result.

Indeed on the very evening after Boehmer's agony she was seated in the comfortable apartment of an intimate friend, the blear-eyed wife of the Superintendent of the Cardinal's household, waiting the arrival of his Eminence in pursuance of an appointment made some days since.

There was no jealousy on the part of Madame the Superintendent, for Jeanne occupied a position she could never hope to fill and she had made herself extremely pleasant to all the household. No one had more grace in offering a smile and pleasant little compliment instead of a louis, and her hints as to the management of madame's troublesome complexion were invaluable. With the Cardinal himself she not only avoided all foolish jealousies but made herself generally useful in any little affairs which interested him at the moment, and there were many in which a lady with the *entrée* to such charming boudoirs could show her gratitude.

In the Hotel de Rohan her position was really very strong.

"And here is the lotion for your eyes, madame," she said to her friend as they sipped their coffee. "Not that yours need it as far as brilliance goes, but it strengthens the lashes wonderfully. I am planning the most amazing lotion — But how is his Eminence?"

"Very well, madame, and in good spirits, so says my husband, but, oh, how I wish — how all his friends wish — to see him restored to Court favour. I know none who would use his influence more nobly for them!"

"None, none!" Jeanne echoed with unfeigned fervour. There were few things she herself wished more sincerely and believed to be more hopeless. "Ah, I am never at Versailles but I think of it and long to see his coach rolling up to the grand entry."

"And you, madame, with your influence with so many great ladies, is there nothing you could do? The ladies rule everything at Versailles, they tell me."

Jeanne winced. She had never got as far as the door of any great lady's boudoir whatever her little under-world might think, but that it should be believed she had did nearly as well at the moment in her hand-to-mouth existence.

"I must watch my time, madame," she said gravely. "But the mouse may help the lion some day. Who knows! And I can never fail in gratitude to his Eminence. Like yourself I grieve that his influence is not equal to his generosity. But let us hope, hope always!"

The elder woman threw up her eyes and hands to heaven.

"Ah, madame, the angel who could achieve that for him! Curse the Austrian with her pride and angers! It was a bad day for France when she came over the frontier. Austria never was lucky for France and the feeling against her is frightful. God knows her own virtue is not so high that she need object to a little gallantry in a fine gentleman like his Eminence, who after all is not a priest though a Cardinal. The stories —"

Jeanne put up her fan as if to hide her blushes and laughed merrily.

"Ah, we must only whisper when we talk of the Austrian, madame. But our day may come —"

"Well, all I can say is that it's a frightful thing that a de Rohan should be left out in the cold while the mushrooms of yesterday are warmed in the sun of royal favour. And for what is his Eminence cold-shouldered? For a well-deserved jest and a little gaiety perfectly natural in his position! But are things likely to better, madame? What do you hear at Versailles?"

For the Comtesse Jeanne whose intimacies consisted in extracting all possible information from her intimates and giving little in return had possessed Madame the Superintendent like all the rest of the world with the belief that she was in the confidence of persons of the highest influence in the royal *entourage,* far too great in fact to be mentioned by name while even their utterances must be guarded like grains of pearl. And so artfully was all this insinuated and substantiated that never a soul doubted the Arabian Nights stories with which she regaled them. It had no definite aim but to increase her own consequence but it served for that.

"Why, as to that, madame," she said with her own mysterious air which yet conveyed so much, "I have heard things both at Versailles and Marly which lead me to suppose that the tide may be turning and that if his Eminence has the courage to take advantage of it —"

A shrewd nod completed the sentence as the rattle of the Cardinal's wheels were heard in the courtyard outside. She was on her feet in a moment.

"I have a most interesting bit of information about that, for you and you only!" she whispered, kissing her finger-tips as she whisked out of the door to catch the Cardinal's valet and make her way by the back stairs to the room where his Eminence laid aside the purple and took his ease. The room of the portrait of the Dauphine.

Chapter VI

BEHOLD the pair in conference half an hour later! Prince Louis de Rohan, large, fleshy, imposing, in his great chair, his legs stretched out to their full luxurious length, and the Comtesse de Lamotte-Valois (whose title caused him some contemptuous amusement) perched on the velvet settee before him. She had always the effect of perching, of alighting for a moment like a bright quick bird to pick up her worm or crumb and flashing off again into the unknown.

"No, no, it is hopeless!" he said with the moody downturn of the lips which that subject always brought with it.

"But again, no, Highness." She always called him Highness and he preferred it. "I assure you the tide is changing, is changed, and the Queen regrets the coldness of the past years. It is no news to you that she has an eye for a handsome man, and who can wonder when they look at the King! Whitworth, Dorset, de Fersen —" She began ticking off the names on her finger until some dregs of manhood left in Louis de Rohan stopped her sharply.

"Silence. I forbid you to speak of her Majesty in that way. Pass on to what else you wished to say."

She stared at him in sheer amazement, stammered, regained self-command with the quick assurance of the adventuress and went on.

"I know, Highness, on the very highest and best authority that the time is ripe for you to regain the Queen's favour, and it follows that if once you let it slip it will never return. Strike now — and success is yours!"

"Yes, but how, how? I care nothing for these glittering generalities. You have said this before and nothing came of it. Be precise, my friend. Condescend to details, and tell me how, and you will never find me wanting. But first of all a detail on my side. I who hear of you flitting about the boudoirs of Versailles find it a little difficult to believe you have any access to those who can tell you the thoughts of the Queen."

She leaned forward with a silvery peal of laughter and touched his cheek playfully with her finger.

"Foolish Highness! Are all men as innocent as that? Don't you know that in the boudoirs far more of truth can be learnt than in the King's

Council chamber, and especially of the Queen's mind. She does not spread it out before statesmen or his Majesty but she shares it with her Princesse de Lamballe and her Duchesse de Polignac and — and (she smiled like a tantalizing fairy) — your humble servant holds the key!"

He stared at her incredulous. And yet who could decipher the ways of women? He knew that those she had mentioned would certainly know the mind of the Queen, if any. And every one would admit that if a little adventuress could gain access to the boudoirs of these very great ladies and to their confidence she might also gain access to the Queen's thoughts. But still he stared at her incredulous. If it were so, if it were conceivable, he must certainly revise the carelessness with which he was accustomed to treat the Comtesse de Lamotte-Valois! Not that he had any hope, not a vestige. It was only that anything concerning the Queen moved him while it hurt him.

She looked at him with gentle dignity.

"How well I comprehend your doubt! The misfortunes of my life have been so crushing that any friend of mine may be pardoned the doubt whether I can ever rise again. And yet for me, poor trampled forgotten me, the tide has turned at last, and I have felt the first rays of the Queen's favour. She has heard of me as possessing the pension of a Valois through the ladies I have mentioned and was pleased to pity the blood of Valois fallen to such misery. Oh, she is much slandered. She has a generous heart. I shall not seek the boudoirs of others, Highness. It is they who will seek mine!"

She threw up her head gallantly and for the moment was a Valois indeed. She had given him vague hints before but never spoken so plainly. The Cardinal stared at her stupefied. Her proud look softened and she shot a bright glance at him under long lashes.

"But so well can I understand the uncertainty of my friend that I am content to submit my truthfulness to a stern test. Go to Count Cagliostro, that most marvellous seer and prophet. You believe in him as passionately and profoundly as I. Ask him to look within his wonderful crystal and see what my occupations have been and will be. By that I am content to stand or fall. Do you accept my offer?"

There was no question as to what the Cardinal's answer would be.

Cagliostro had come to Paris on his invitation and the French nobility had run wild after his signs and wonders. His predictions, horoscopes, prophecies, flew from lip to lip and it would have been a bold man or woman who would have ventured to cast a doubt upon the reality of his inspirations. It was freely rumoured that the Queen herself would have consulted him if she had dared and that her two sisters-in-law had already done so and had been enormously impressed and awed by his revelations. As for the Cardinal, he was Cagliostro's slave. There was much talk between them of alchemy, of retrieving the clipped fortunes of the House of Rohan by the transmutation of the baser metals into gold and such singular results had already been achieved that the Prince of the Church was ready to take the word of the Prince of the World-Magical for the rest.

The conversation had suddenly become of the deepest interest for him. He sat up gravely in his chair and regarded her with new respect.

"My friend, it is casting no doubt on your veracity, which I never have had reason to doubt, if I say that the opinion of Count Cagliostro would be of the utmost value to me at this crisis, for it will amaze you to hear that he has already predicted that this year, this very month, a great and startling change occurs in my fortunes owing to the aspects of the ruling planets. I did not pay the heed to this that I ought, for I could see no betterment in the affair that most concerns me and never expect to. But if you are right —"

She clapped her little hands and laughed until the room rang again.

"Joy, joy! Judge if I am proud to be the servant of the mysteries of the prophet! For it is my doing, mine! that he foresaw. Let us go to him tomorrow and he shall look in the crystal for us and it may be an assistance to me to see exactly how I should train my batteries. I pray you to do this. Then we shall walk in clear certainty instead of in doubt. That man *cannot* err! He is the most wonderful creature that ever walked on earth. We know it, don't we?"

The Cardinal agreed eagerly. That was his opinion in common with the opinion of all Paris. Cagliostro had caught the public by its love of the marvellous; had dazed, bewitched, bedazzled it, until every word that fell from his lips was gospel where the old gospel no longer compelled belief; and as gospel the Cardinal received it.

She could not have made a proposal better calculated to win him — a fact which Madame Jeanne could grasp as capably as another.

He summoned his confidential valet and despatched a message to Cagliostro fixing the following evening. The man lingered a second on the threshold.

"Monseigneur, there is a gentleman who entreats an audience of you. He will not delay you more than ten minutes if you will have the goodness to accord it. It is Monsieur Boehmer, the King's Jeweller."

The negative was cut short on de Rohan's lips by the name, and the look of sharp interest that sparkled in the face of the Lamotte.

"Why, I saw him at Versailles yesterday!" she said under her breath. "He had been with the Queen about the diamond necklace. Permit him to come up, Highness. It may be of the utmost consequence to us."

"But how did you know what his business was with the Queen? Yes, show him up." The Cardinal too was tense with excitement.

"Ah, Monseigneur, that is my secret — a part of the secret we were just discussing. You will yet believe I have friends who are in the know! And I say this to you very seriously — even if he has come on quite other business lead him to that — find out what happened and let me know. It may be of inestimable value to your interests. See — I will hide in here. Perhaps I had better listen. You agree?"

He agreed with a nod, pleased at her candour.

She opened a door she knew very well and with one of her bird-like movements flashed through it and was gone.

A vague scent of lilac and a little ruffle in the air was all that testified to the late presence of a woman in the room when Boehmer was shown in and he was not likely to notice a trifle like that for his grief-stricken aspect pierced through even the Cardinal's selfishness.

"You are ill, Boehmer. Have you had bad news? Be seated."

"Monseigneur, let me not trouble you with my affairs. I have come about the black pearls you had the goodness to order and to take your commands about the setting. Here they are."

From a little box he extracted three exquisitely matched black pearls and laid them on the table, but with an expression as absent as if the thing meant nothing to him. The Cardinal with his idle good nature looked at the man instead of the pearls.

"No doubt they are beautiful, and if we agree about the price — But you were never extortionate. Be candid with me. Has anything gone wrong? Is there anything in which I can serve you? *What* is on your mind? I fear you are ill."

The man made a poor attempt at a smile which almost ended in a sob.

"The black pearls, Eminence. I was about to say you shall have them set in small diamonds and all complete at the same price as the ring of white pearls you ordered last month. And if that meets your approval I will withdraw."

"It suits me very well. But it does not suit me that an old and faithful servant should withhold his confidence in a matter in which I might possibly aid him."

The look and words were kindly. They were the first words of sympathy which had met the miserable Boehmer, for Bassauger on receiving his news had unleashed himself in a passion of anger and terror of which the less said the better. Breaking down utterly he hid his face on crossed arms on the table and wept, a cruel nerve-storm of long pent-up and violently released misery.

The Cardinal rose with his heavy gait — more than a hint of gout in it — and opened the wing-doors of a richly carved cabinet. He extracted a bottle and two twisted Venetian glasses of purple frosted with gold, brimmed them with Imperial Tokay, no less!, and raising the glass with relish to his own lips commanded Boehmer to do the same.

"I wait on you myself for I will not permit another to see your distress. Drink, calm yourself, and give me your confidence."

The natural result followed. The rich wine ran like hope and life through the poor man's veins and the condescending kindness warmed them. He poured out the whole story, giving every word, every gesture to the life but, naturally, as seen through his own hopes and prepossessions.

"Her Majesty longed for the diamonds, Monseigneur — longed for them with all her heart and soul. What woman could do otherwise? What passed between herself and the King I cannot tell, but I am convinced that it was only her high sense of duty that stood in the way, and that if any way could be found — Oh, if it could but be found!"

"You think she would take them?" the Cardinal asked in a muse. Every word Boehmer uttered bore the stamp of truth upon it. It gave him much to consider.

"I think, Monseigneur? I *know*. I have revolved every expedient. As I suggested to the Queen, let her take the necklace and pay by any instalments that please her. She need not wear the jewels immediately. They can be laid by, of course. She seemed to resent that suggestion, but why? I cannot see. Possibly she feared to displease his Majesty. But as for me I am in such desperate straits that anything which would relieve me of the diamonds would be salvation. If I had her Majesty's signed agreement. But why do I talk? It is hopeless. I must go, but with the undying memory of your condescension."

It was not long before he went. There was much to say and hear in the details of the royal interview and the time did not seem long to the greedy listener in the next room to whom it opened vistas of delightful intrigue that never had dawned as yet upon her horizon. She must think deeply, must consult her husband. Not a word, not a word as yet.

She crept in noiselessly when the door was safely shut upon Boehmer and knelt before the Cardinal, looking up, her dark intelligent face subdued into a seriousness he had never before seen upon it.

"I heard all he said, Highness. I knew you wished me to. And now I will tell you what I heard at Versailles today — what I *know*. I dared not before. It was this. He is right. The Queen longs with all her heart and soul and strength for the jewels. She will give anything to the man who will procure them for her. Nothing will be withheld. I have her ear, Highness. For God's sake don't tell any one else, but it's true! Didn't I tell you before Boehmer came? Catch Fortune as she flies! Be that happy man and the world and more, much more is yours."

She drew herself up by the arm of the chair writhing upward like a snake until her mouth touched his ear, and whispered, drawing a little back now and then to note the look of joy and hope and confidence which passed across his face while he listened.

Finally he flung his arms about her and kissed her cheek, then stood up, stretching them above his head with a gesture of enormous relief. Not a word had he uttered but she knew he had listened with his soul in his ears.

"Tomorrow we will go to Cagliostro!" he said.

PART II

Chapter VII

COUNT CAGLIOSTRO, the Grand Cophta (which being interpreted means the Founder or Restorer of the lost Egyptian Freemasonry) claimed for himself the most extraordinary powers in virtue of his office and, appearing from nowhere in particular, had succeeded in getting them acknowledged by a larger number of true believers than the King of France could at that moment command, belief in powers and authorities being at a pretty low ebb so far as any influence upon life and conduct goes. Paris raved about him. All the pretty ladies and many of the most accomplished beaux repeated his revelations and prophecies, exaggerated his marvels, fanned one another's belief and made a half-divine hero of him. His notice was honour. His presence at any gathering conferred distinction which the Court itself could scarcely command. But the surest proof of his influence was the handsome sums of money which fashionable people, headed by the Cardinal, were willing to lavish for every word that fell from his lips. Whatever else they distrusted they certainly believed in their cash most truly and devoutly, and that like all else was flung at his feet. If it be objected that this was only in the hope of doubling it, the answer to that is that such faith is not found in Israel — perhaps least of all there! And if there still be those who disbelieve in the miracles of the Grand Cophta (which history has used rather cruelly on the whole) none can deny one miracle, surprising to stupefaction: that is, that he converted Prince Louis de Rohan to steadfast trust in something and someone outside his own indulgences, his Grand Cophtaship and himself, a feat hitherto impossible to the Holy Father and Sacred College. In Cagliostro the Cardinal did most devoutly and utterly believe. Thus Jeanne de Lamotte-Valois had appealed to the person in all the world most sacred to him and it was with a feeling of true awe and suspense that he presented himself next evening at the holy portal of the Grand Cophta, bearing her with him masked and hooded in the unobtrusive coach he used on such occasions. But the darkness and the hour made both precautions unnecessary even supposing the Cardinal or the lady had had any reputation to lose.

"It will be the stronger test because you have given our Great Friend no idea of our errand, Highness!" said the Countess in soft flute tones a little tremulous with feeling. "I almost wish you could have been masked as I am. I could have said — not that it matters much however, for if you were masked a hundred times I would engage to detect you anywhere by your stately and noble way of entering a room. That is where race can never be denied. The Valois, the Rohan blood, stamps its own through life and death."

His Eminence agreed with the utmost politeness. Only two days ago that consummate reference to the Valois blood would have sent him into shrieks of delighted laughter, for nothing in this world amused him more than to see Madame Jeanne on her high horse and caracoling with the best of them. But today all was changed; could she be less than a Valois whose happy fortune it was to build up the fortunes of the Rohans in their latest and worthiest representatives? She who was distinguished by the proudest of queens and Austrian archduchesses? He could have kissed the pretty hand that lay like a snowflake on the black satin domino — kissed it with heartfelt devotion. As a matter of fact he did.

They descended carefully on the steps let down by the senior footman and Jeanne heaved a long soft sigh as she unmasked. That, that — indeed — was the life she relished, the life that claimed her as its own. She saw herself riding always in luxurious coaches with obsequious peers beside her — cold as marble to others not of their world but warm and fruitful of good as summer rain to her interests. What a Pompadour she would have made had God been good to her! Dream-diamonds sparkled in her powdered hair, dream-toilettes by the Queen's own milliner Mademoiselle Bertin graced her elegant little person. Whether Madame de Lamotte-Valois reverenced the Grand Cophta in her inmost soul was known only to herself, but her reverence for Mademoiselle Bertin he who ran might read with never a fear of error.

She tripped as lightly up the stairs now as if Grand Cophtas were matters of everyday experience, his Eminence following, somewhat tremulous about the knees under his deep sense of the unspeakable importance of the oracle he was about to consult.

"Madame, I beg you won't hurry and flurry me after this fashion. You are surely aware we are enjoined to approach the Grand Cophta with minds and persons in a state of complete tranquillity. Where is the sense of racing upstairs at this break-neck helter-skelter?"

"True, most true," murmured the devotee, gently slackening her pace. "The truth is, Highness, I am so eager for the glorious news which I dare swear awaits us that I feel as if wings sprouted at my ankles. Forgive me, but I *know* what has happened. You only receive it on my poor hearsay! Until you have my certainty we cannot feel alike."

It was a nice distinction, cleverly drawn, and it calmed the princely indignation. With measured steps they completed the next flight of stairs and stood at length before the veiled and solemn portal which concealed the mysteries.

It was a singular fact that though the Cardinal had often met Cagliostro in private life (where he unbent to some purpose), he was as deeply impressed as ever when the Grand Cophta pontificated in his robes and mysteries. At this very instant his heart danced like an autumn leaf in a wind.

Soft strains of distant music welled from within; faint and delicious odours of a strangely scented incense wafted through unseen crevices. To the highest in the land it was forbidden to knock. So there was nothing to be done but wait. The acolyte stood without until the Grand Cophta became mysteriously conscious of his or her presence and then —

The door touched by unseen ministrants opened noiselessly on darkness — darkness illuminated only by two trembling stars at what seemed an immeasurable height and distance above them. Nothing else was perceptible but the dim sighing of music and the heavy pungent scent of the unknown incense — extremely unlike what the Cardinal was necessarily familiar with and imported, as was known, from the Fan Lung Mountains in the northern extremity of China probably by obedient spirits. It had at all events this much of mystery about it that its fumes mounted to the brain like alcohol. Before he had gone far the Cardinal experienced an effect as of many glasses of the Empress's Tokay and clutched the cool firm hand of his companion with a feeling that the ground was heaving under him like cloudland.

"We cannot stop here. It would be dangerous," she said in a hurrying whisper. "You know the rules. This is the Entry of Probation. Let me lead you. You are anxious, and no wonder, but advance fearlessly. It is only the evil-minded who have cause to fear!"

They went on with reverent steps, in so far as the Cardinal's vertigo permitted reverence, and passed through another portal as could be told only by the parting curtains. There they were suddenly arrested. A cold clear breath blew on their brows and a voice from a seemingly immense distance, low yet distinct in every letter, pronounced these words.

"I give you this breath to cause to germinate and become alive in your heart the Truth which we possess: to fortify in you the means whereby you may receive our immortal and mysterious knowledge. In the sacred names of Helios, Mene, Tetragrammaton."

As the last words were pronounced the two distant stars appeared to fade and recede in the faint dawn of a rosy light, stealing from unknown heights and suffusing the air by slow degrees. As it strengthened and grew a very singular sight was revealed.

They stood in a spacious hall octagonally shaped and of startling height — the roof lost in darkness, the walls and floor covered with black cloth painted with flames and menacing serpents. And in the midst of this sea of midnight black stood a small couch startlingly white in the midst of its surroundings and on it a girl asleep or dead in motionless quiet. This was the Columb, the innocent means of approach to the Invisible. The Grand Cophta buried in profound meditation, his hand laid on a great open volume, sat at a small table beside her. He was robed in purest white and at his elbow was a small ebony stand supporting a crystal ball at the angle of the earth in its revolution about the sun. The two figures, the one lying like death, the other buried in thought, stood out as if by their own light against the gloom. The visitors stood silently awaiting his pleasure as he turned a leaf and yet another, then placing a marker in the page, shut the great clasps of the book and raised his head.

"Seekers after truth!" he began, his really beautiful voice pealing organ-noted along the hall. "You are welcome. What is so dear to Truth as her own element in faithful hearts? Here lies the dumb oracle that shall answer all your doubts. Her spirit wanders at this moment in the formless world of luminous verity. Standing in veneration of that immortal Presence ask what you will!"

At that moment the Cardinal was so flurried that all presence of mind deserted him and not a question could he recall or articulate. The oracle lay still as marble, black lashes sealed on a cheek pallid as death. There was no smile upon her lips, nothing but a solemn stillness which forbade those thoughts of human beauty to which he was peculiarly accessible.

"You first!" he whispered hurriedly to his companion, slightly urging her forward.

With a deep reverence to the Grand Cophta she knelt, covering her eyes with her hands at the foot of the couch, and spoke in trembling accents.

"Sacred Lord of the Dawn-Star, since I dare not address myself to the Purity before me, I beseech you to be the intermediary. Let her declare to me through your great self whether the cloud of misfortune which has shadowed my life is about to break in sunshine at last?"

A moment's silence and the Grand Cophta drew the ebony stand with the crystal towards him and gazed steadily into its lucent depths. The girl on the couch lay motionless. Her lips were rigid, but from his broke suddenly a girl's voice clear, high, confident, as a linnet in the morning. The effect was really terrifying in its strangeness.

"It will break. It will break! I see in the crystal which represents the rolling world a woman honoured as she deserves by the greatest. Secretly that favour has been showered upon her. The day is at hand when openly, before all eyes, she shall be known as the friend of kings."

The silence that followed vibrated with triumph. For a moment the Lamotte did not speak. She knelt still with bowed head in an attitude of the utmost reverence. At last, scarcely stronger than a whisper, she uttered her next question: "And how, by what means, shall this miracle happen to one who has only faith and humility to offer?"

Again the musical answer.

"In the crystal that cannot err I see an act of self-devotion involving much danger, cruel misunderstanding. I behold the gratitude of a great person. More it is not lawful to reveal."

Silence again. The Grand Cophta sat absorbed in profound thought, gazing steadfastly into the crystal. At last without raising his eyes he made a commanding gesture to Louis de Rohan who fell immediately on his knees beside the Countess.

"Ask!" cried a sonorous voice, pealing through the hall like a trumpet.

Stuttering, stammering, de Rohan put his question. "For me also is the cloud lifting? What is my future?"

The linnet voice of a girl took up the story.

"Success, honour, glory. A deed of courage and self-sacrifice. High favour rightly earned. And — love."

The blood beat in his temples — his throat and eyes were charged with it. It hammered in his pulses and almost choked his utterance.

"Highest, enlighten me. What am I to do? How shall I know the way?"

"Accept the guide so strangely sent, and go forward in confidence. Fear nothing. A glorious success is within reach. Take it and be glad!"

There was a profound and terrifying silence, and the minutes glided by.

The Cardinal would have asked another question but, the pressure on his brain prevented it. The fumes of incense grew sickening, overwhelming. He swayed sideways on his knees and lurched to the ground unconscious.

In a moment Cagliostro had pushed the crystal aside and was beside him, the girl on the couch sat up in terrified astonishment, and horror distorted the face of the Lamotte. If a prince of the Church were found dead there, and in their company — Heavens, what an appalling *contretemps*!

The Grand Cophta seized a carafe of water and discharged it over his face while Jeanne held a vinaigrette to his nostrils and the Columb, an extremely handsome girl, chafed his hands. But the face of the Lamotte! No life in the world could be so precious to her at that moment as de Rohan's. She was the only one of the party who kept her wits about her and to some purpose. She turned on Cagliostro as furiously as a tigress.

"It's that horrible incense. There's too much of the narcotic in it tonight for a man with a thick neck like this. I was sure there would be an accident sooner or later. I told you so before. Marie, get back. He may open his eyes at any moment and if he does we're done!"

His eyelids twitched at last as she fanned him. Swift and silent the girl glided back to the couch, the Grand Cophta composed himself by the crystal. The scene was set. Madame de Lamotte-Valois knelt, the picture of gentle anxiety by her patient.

"What has happened?" he muttered thickly. "Did I faint? What was it?"

"A wonderful thing!" she assured him. "As the Columb warned you to accept the guide so strangely sent —"

"Yes, I heard that. Go on!"

"You cried out that you saw a glorious light, a crown, a woman, and appeared to swoon with excess of joy. Tell me — if you can — But not here! We must not disturb this holy atmosphere. It is profane. We should go now."

He raised himself gradually to his feet, and gradually his full senses returned and the sacred stillness restored him. The fumes of incense were dissipated by a cool air blowing from unseen heights.

The girl still lay quiet as death. The Grand Cophta rose with majesty and approached them.

"Monseigneur!" he said gravely. "I have seen that it is by direction of the High Powers that a glorious destiny is reserved for you. I have nothing to add to what the pure tones of the Columb speaking through me have revealed. Go on with confidence. Fear nothing. And when you stand in full sunshine I ask but one reward. Come then and assure me that my teachings were a lamp to your footsteps."

De Rohan bowed with as much veneration as he would have offered to the King, and even while he did so the rosy light began to fade and surrounding objects grew indistinct. Jeanne took his arm and as they groped toward the door the two trembling stars reappeared in utter darkness and a cold breath like the dawn was about them.

They were in the Cardinal's coach before either spoke again, and by that time the Cardinal had completely recovered.

"I regard it as providential that Boehmer paid me that visit yesterday. Not that the way is clear as yet, but the mist is gradually lifting. The next step must be for yourself and me to see the diamond necklace and then through you I must have clear and definite assurance of her Majesty's pleasure in the matter. Without that I dare not move. Even now I can't see a step ahead and every step is dangerous. I can't even imagine —"

"Nor I, Highness. If not you — how much less the poor de Lamotte-Valois? No, if she wishes faithful service her Majesty must be explicit. It is she who must declare her wishes and then — devotion to the death!"

"Devotion to the death! All must come from her," repeated the Cardinal solemnly. "But I should see the necklace and should ascertain Boehmer's exact views with regard to price, payments, deductions and so forth. I will arrange that you should see it later. And remember I state no intentions. I regard this merely as a survey of possibilities which pledges me to nothing. I have yours and Boehmer's assurance that the Queen longs for the necklace, but I know nothing more."

"Nothing. Nor do I. All I can promise is full information and complete devotion. And every step must be taken with the profoundest caution. If the Queen were compromised by so much as a hairbreadth —! Frightful! Indeed, in spite of the august encouragement we have just had, my courage fails so far that I think myself unworthy to proceed!"

"No, no!" said the Cardinal, pressing her hand. "That must not be. But being, in spite of all your talent, a woman, let me impress upon you the awful secrecy needed in this affair. Not a word, not a breath to a living human being! Can you be trusted to the death? Speak freely."

The Countess's "I can" was so simply and gravely said that it reassured him more than many protestations. Besides, as he reflected, the Queen's confidante would never dare to break secrecy and destroy all her own hopes. More — the penalty might be dreadful — There was still the Bastille for those who offended the ruling powers. He dropped a hint to that effect which she received with a melancholy smile, apologizing instantly when she replied.

"I did not need that reminder, Monseigneur. If you can trust me on no other grounds than fear, do not trust me at all, I beg of you. But before we part on this wonderful night let me recur to one thing I mentioned yesterday. I would not mention it now but that I think it may lead up to matters more important. When last I saw her, the Queen lamented to me in the most touching way that she had no money to relieve a case of wretchedness brought before her by the Princess de Lamballe. She cannot bring herself to touch the public funds for such things, and you know how small her private income is for what she must do. Little more than twenty thousand pounds a year."

He did not know, but shook his head pathetically.

"Imagine such a position for the most generous of queens!" cried the eloquent Lamotte. "It brought the tears to my eyes. It is an officer's mother, with a large family, and she dares not see the poor woman because her hand is empty. Need I tell you my thought?"

"My good angel need tell me nothing. I can divine for myself. Her Majesty has but to write me a line and all I have is at her service in so sacred a cause. Here, my friend, is an earnest. Carry it yourself to the poor mother, and tell the Queen that my heart bled for her. The rest may follow."

"Generous and noble heart!" she said as she dropped the rouleaux of gold into her bag. "She shall know, and, oh, the contrast it will form to the niggardly avarice of de Breteuil, the present Minister of the King's Household. That is the office I covet for you. That is where you would shine — where you would be in closest contact — for that position gives every opportunity for conferring favours which your noble heart could wish. The Queen said — but, no, no! I dare not tell even you yet all I have heard and know. I am indiscreet. Do not tempt me. I should never have said as much as this but for the miracles of tonight."

In vain he entreated. She laughed, all arch and pretty malice, teased him divinely, raised every hope and expectation to burning point, called herself his fairy godmother, then, as the clock struck twelve, vanished with her little curtsy. They parted the best of friends, the closest of confidants.

Yet there were matters of which the Lamotte kindly kept her friend in ignorance. Why mention to him, for instance, that the pure, chaste Columb was her own niece? That fact surely could not affect the sanctity of her message? Nor was it necessary that his Eminence should know that her day's work was by no means concluded when she stepped from his coach at the entrance of the little apartment she occupied in Paris. It might have surprised him for instance to learn that the owner of it was an old admirer, a very capable and stirring gentleman known by the name of Retaux de Villette, who had advised her in matters of importance before and would never have the heart to refuse assistance in any important undertaking.

After all, can a poor little woman be expected to imperil herself blindfolded to make the fortunes of a great gentleman like the Cardinal de Rohan? No — she needs backing and must have it.

A rainy dawn was breaking over Paris before Jeanne de Lamotte-Valois and Monsieur de Villette had finished their long and interesting conversation, and she had succeeded in convincing him that such an enterprise was not too dangerous for cool brains and strong hands.

Surely it must be owned that the vanished night had brought a prince of the Church and a Rohan into company sufficiently strange.

Chapter VIII

MEANWHILE Boehmer drew nearer and nearer to despair. If he had had a hope from the Cardinal's known lavishness that was soon dispersed as the days went by and he made no sign. Bassauger was absent from business. Anxiety had made him ill and he was not reticent as to the cause with Boehmer, whom he blamed violently and cruelly for the crushing blow that had befallen them. So Boehmer sat alone in the room behind the shop, biting his nails and brooding. There was very little trade of any kind. The distant mutterings of revolution had frightened the people who spent their money with him, and it seemed that days passed without a buyer crossing the threshold. It was not really as bad as that, but he saw black nowadays and had lost all belief in sunlight and everyday life became more unbearable. He could see no hope anywhere, but at moments it seemed that perhaps the least hopeless effort would be to see the Queen once more. She was all kindness and courtesy with those who served her, as he might consider he did, and surely when she realized his cruel plight she would not condemn him to despair. She could not realize his bitter need unless he forced it upon her careless royal notice. What could great queens understand of bankruptcy and ruin?

It was not difficult for him to obtain an audience, for some of her jewels were in his hands for repair and his office gave him certain rights of entry at Court. In a few days he was able to steady himself sufficiently to ask for an audience at Versailles. No difficulty stood in his way, for the Queen had almost forgotten the necklace and for her the unpleasant episode was a thing of the past.

Boehmer stood at the door of the royal cabinet. The lady who had announced him retired, thinking the Queen had heard his name, and Boehmer under the same impression stood at the door until the conversation should be ended and the lady in attendance summon him. She was Madame Campan, to be known later as a writer of Memoirs of this especial period. A bright-faced amiable-looking woman with soft brown hair and eyes, she stood laughing at some story which the Queen was telling with the utmost relish, laughing herself as she told it.

Boehmer could hear every word. The grave little princess, Madame Royale, sat beside her mother listening and stitching at a simple embroidery.

"You were not there this morning, Madame," she said, "when I tried on the wonderful new headdress Mademoiselle Bertin has invented for me. Crowns are completely outdistanced by its magnificence. When I went to have my hair dressed with all the ladies in attendance what was my amazement to see that Chabot my hair-dresser had brought a step-ladder with him. "Good God!" I said, "and what is this for?" He bowed with outspread hands. "Because, Madame, Mademoiselle Bertin has so enormously increased the height of the head-ornaments that my stature not being gigantic I cannot have the honour of placing it on your Majesty's head unless I have your permission." And with everybody choking laughter in their handkerchiefs and I myself in mine, he scrambled most decorously halfway up the step-ladder and fixed it on my head. Very nonsensical, isn't it? And yet I do think it is becoming."

"It is ravishing, Madame!" cried the lady, and indeed it was true. The Queen's figure permitted her to wear what few others could dare and the famous milliner had known very well what she was about in adding height to a presence which already dominated most other women; not seeing Boehmer she rose for a moment that Madame Campan might note the effect, and stood, a goddess confessed.

It was very late in the afternoon and she was already dressed for a public dinner and reception in the evening in a dress of gold tissue from India widely distended with hoops, the magnificent stuff displaying its glossy surface shading from milky gold to orange and dim shimmering splendours in the shadows. The bosom, cut low, was veiled with old Brussels point and diamonds, and on her powdered hair was the astonishing coiffure wreathed with small roses, plumes of ostrich feathers curling softly about it and loops of diamonds. So she still sits for us in more than one portrait which strives to reproduce, but cannot, that lost beauty and majesty.

But to Boehmer listening in his despair it seemed a frivolity too cruel to be endured. Why should queens smile and be glad while honest men were pushed downward into a pity of ruin? Why should she wear a smile while he suffered? He ventured a movement, a cough, and she turned and saw him and suddenly the smile vanished and her air of majesty was alarming until recognizing him she smiled again in acknowledgment of his bow as Madame Campan ushered him in.

"I am glad to see you in health, monsieur. Madame Campan had heard you were suffering and it caused the King and myself regret. We look upon you as a faithful servant. I suppose you have brought the emerald bracelet?"

"Madame, with your Majesty's permission, I have, and I hope the setting may now meet with your approval."

He laid it before her respectfully, and she examined it with care, calling Madame Campan's attention to the emeralds which now had a tiny miniature of her son, the little Dauphin. Her eyes softened as she looked at it and something in her expression gave courage to the unhappy man before her.

Suddenly — suddenly even to himself — he flung himself on his knees at her feet, his voice dry and hoarse with passion, the heartbeats almost audible in it, his features working as if he sobbed.

"Madame, once again I beseech your Majesty to hear me and to save a desperate man from desperation by purchasing my necklace. Since I saw you I have made enquiry from the agents of their Sicilian Majesties, for I had hopes that their well-known magnificence might claim the necklace. But no. I have offered it in several directions and again, no. My position is appalling. My partner has become an enemy, my creditors are sharpening their teeth, and there is no refuge for me in heaven and earth if you will not hear the prayer of my anguish. Oh, Madame —" His voice choked finally and he could say no more, but knelt before her speechless, with upraised hands.

Her first impulse was to reply indignantly that she declined to be annoyed with his affairs any further. But her natural kindness of heart checked her. She would try reason with him first.

"Rise, Boehmer. These rhapsodies give me pain and can do you no good. You should not inflict this upon me. Remember that these diamonds were collected for your own profit and without any reference to the King or me. They were intended for Madame du Barry. Why do you not ask her to buy them now? Her means are large, and I own I consider the necklace more suited to her than to me."

But Boehmer did not rise. The grave little princess suspended her needle and watched him with open-eyed interest and astonishment.

"Madame, I have tried, and she will not. At least she would if it were possible but she has not the means. There is none but the gracious Queen of France who can rescue the lowliest of her subjects from misery. O that she would hear me!"

"Monsieur, I command you to rise. Your emotion is in every way unbecoming, and thus continued it would move me only to anger. I neither can nor will buy your necklace. It would be absolutely impossible at the present time, and my jewel-cases are overflowing, not to speak of the unset diamonds in the *garde-meuble*. But to prove to you that I am not insensible to your anxiety I will say that I spoke to the King after I had seen you and suggested that if he thought the price favourable he might buy the necklace for the marriage of one of our children, and put it aside until then, for I will never wear it myself. But his Majesty replied that the Children of France are too young to justify such an expense, which would be greatly increased by the years during which the diamonds would be useless, and in short he has finally decided against them. There is now no more to be said."

The miserable man clasped his hand before his face and burst into tears.

"There is this to be said, Madame. Life is over for me. I cannot live ruined and disgraced. I will fling myself into the Seine and end my misfortune thus. You shall indeed be troubled no more. A word from your Majesty would save me, and that word you refuse to speak."

The little princess, thoroughly frightened, rose from her stool and drew near the Queen as if to shelter behind her — a pale shrinking little creature very unlike her beautiful mother, who also rose but with dignity, clasping the girl's hand. Madame Campan stood as like a graven image as etiquette demanded.

"Again, I tell you, monsieur, that these rhapsodies are offensive. Honest men need not fall on their knees to beg for mercy. If you destroy yourself as you threaten in this unmanly way I shall regard you as a madman, and shall not hold myself at all responsible. You knew well I proposed to add no more to my collection of diamonds and I was even ignorant that you had the necklace in view until I heard after the late King's death it had been collected for Madame du Barry. There is however another way which seems to have escaped you. Take your necklace to pieces and sell the diamonds separately. You will then have no difficulties. I am indignant with you for making this scene in the presence of a child. Go, and let me never see you behave again in this manner. *Sortez, monsieur!*"

She was angry at last and towered above him entirely unapproachable and remote, the Queen of France addressing an offensive tradesman.

There was no more to be said. He had played his last poor card and failed. Still kneeling, he implored the Queen's pardon, promised she should hear no more of the matter, and crept from her presence. That threat of the Seine had been uttered in a moment of madness — he could not do it, for he was only at the beginning of the bitter lesson that it is possible to exist without hope, and there is no realization so engrossing. It leaves room for no other thought in all the wide world. He could feel rather than see the Queen turn indignantly to Madame Campan as the door closed.

Two days later he was sitting in the room above his shop and was staring at the necklace lying on its satin bed. To him indeed it shot evil fires, and yet his soul acknowledged it supremely beautiful. How could he take it apart and destroy the chief work of his life? True, the diamonds would survive but the soul of the thing would be dead. In his mind's eye it had become part of the beauty of the Queen and the royalty of France. Centuries hence when some queen — perhaps even more beautiful than Marie Antoinette — shone in all her splendour at a new Versailles or Fontainebleau, men and women gazing in awe would say: "That necklace was made by a man named Boehmer, King's Jeweller to Louis the Sixteenth. Men do not make such things now. Was there ever such a story!"

For diamonds are immortal and these must carry his name with them so long as their light mocked the stars. But dispersed — a sparklet in the ring of a citizen's wife, a star in the pendant of any nameless woman — he himself would be lost. Well — no matter! There was no hope now. It must be endured and he must reckon what each stone should fetch in the falling diamond market. Falling indeed, for England had her own troubles of war and depression, and in France the nobility were selling eagerly instead of buying.

And as he sat thus, miserably noting prices, a young man in his employment knocked at the door.

"Monsieur, a lady wishes to see you on a matter of the first importance."

"Delay her two moments. Then attend her here."

The young man lingered a moment at the door.

"She came in an equipage of Monseigneur the Cardinal de Rohan's and is evidently a lady of distinction."

Boehmer looked round in astonishment, then hurriedly secured the necklace and papers, and cast a hasty glance through the window to assure himself that the Rohan arms graced the coach-door. They flamed in gold before his eyes.

There entered a young woman most elegantly dressed according to the Ten Commandments of the mode. Complexion, hair, eyes, dress, cloak, silk stockings, high-heeled shoes, gloves, fan and ornaments were all according to the spirit as well as the letter of the law. She might have served for a walking illustration of what should be worn in Court circles for an expedition on business to Paris so important as meeting one's jeweller.

There was perhaps one respect in which the newcomer did not conform to the mode — one only. Her face was keenly intelligent behind its prettiness and she entered with perfect self-possession based rather on consciousness of her own powers than on the arrogance of a woman of quality. That difference would have been perceptible in the quality of her entry if Boehmer had not been too wearied and sad for observation. Bowing, he offered a chair, and she slipped into it easily, then looked about her with close scrutiny.

"Monsieur, my business is peculiar, of the gravest character and for your ear only. Are we absolutely private? No possibility of listeners?"

Boehmer reassured her. A man could not have been a leading jeweller in Paris for as many years as he and escaped many delicate and difficult transactions with ladies of the world and the half-world, but he had no difficulty at the moment in deciding to which the lady present belonged. The half-world does not speak with that clear unaffected simplicity, devoid of any lure and addressing itself with an entire absence of self-consciousness to the matter in hand. Her manner from his point of view was perfection.

She motioned him gracefully to a chair beside her and began, and at the very first words the colour fell away from Boehmer's face and left him livid.

"Monsieur, I have heard from the Queen's lips of your despair with regard to the necklace, and I come as the messenger of hope."

He stared at her stupefied. Was it one of the Queen's ladies? If so, which? Some of their faces were familiar to him. He knew the names of several of the chief ladies, but naturally not of those in lesser positions, and except for such outstanding names as those of the Princesse de Lamballe and the Duchesse de Polignac, and the confidential attendant Madame Campan, could certainly not have passed an examination in the subject. But "from the Queen's lips"? Then this must be a lady in the Queen's immediate presence — in her confidence. And yet — in a carriage of the Cardinal's — the Cardinal who for years had been virtually forbidden their Majesties' presence! Here indeed was a mystery beyond him or any other man! He could only bow deeply, murmuring something indistinctly polite and await the lady's pleasure.

"I decipher your thoughts as if you spoke them, monsieur, and find them perfectly natural. I will explain, but it must be under seal of a secrecy that nothing earthly shall break. You yourself will be the first to recognize this necessity when the matter is before you."

Much bewildered he gave his pledge and the lady proceeded, speaking with soft precision.

"I am the Countess de Lamotte-Valois — and as my name speaks for itself to every French ear I need no further introduction. That family has met with historical misfortunes, and mine had the happiness to reach an ear that is never closed to distress — the Queen's. Do not think me arrogant if I say a friendship has sprung up between us. Our positions in the world are far apart, but there must always be much in common between a Hapsburg and a Valois, and she can perhaps exchange thoughts with me more freely than with others."

Boehmer was wildly rummaging his memory for the name. Valois — No Frenchman but must know that name! But Lamotte? He bowed deeply and waited for more.

"I need not tell you, monsieur, that the Queen was deeply distressed by your anxiety about the necklace. That goes without saying. But that in itself could not entice her to act in a manner inconsistent with her sense of honour — yourself would be the first to admit it. But — do I speak under the seal of certain secrecy?"

Renewed protestations from Boehmer. His eyes were fixed upon her with painful intensity, his tongue was dry in his mouth.

"Then I will be frank. Her Majesty desires passionately to possess the necklace. I have it from her own lips. She could not speak freely before Madame Campan, who is not in her confidence. But her wish is to know definitely from you what deferred terms of payment you would accept. She will not mention it to the King until a part of the payment is made, and until she gives consent in writing the matter is to be kept secret by you. You are to understand that this visit of mine is no promise to take it. It is merely to ascertain whether the price would be within her means. I understand she mentioned to you that she has large expenses at the moment!"

Silence. Boehmer, in breathless agitation, was considering how best to convey to the fair ambassador that he could not deal with a young unknown woman in a case of such magnitude. With her calm lucidity she discerned that thought also and met it clearly and sensibly.

"You are reflecting, monsieur, that it would be unusual and unwise to deal with a young woman in the circumstances, and doubtless you are desiring a personal interview with her Majesty. That cannot be. She parted from you in anger and she may withhold the annual cleaning of her jewels from you as a mark of her displeasure. Consider! You were not alone with her Majesty, and you spoke in a very unbecoming manner which she was compelled to rebuke. She cannot act inconsistently, but you will understand that her anger which was very real will avert suspicion from the arrangement she now proposes to make with you. Of that her Majesty is confident."

Nothing could be more reasonable than this brief firm statement, especially as the Countess added: "You must also be well aware that for the same reason the Queen could not use any of her official ladies to communicate with you and that is why a stranger like myself is here. But I have had the happiness to serve her in many little matters to which the same objection applied. The role is not new to me."

Boehmer was partly reassured.

"Your goodness, madame, overwhelms me, and if I seem to hesitate your intelligence, extraordinary in one so young and beautiful, will comprehend and make allowance. But shall I be favoured with no written instructions?"

"In a manner very carefully guarded certainly, monsieur. That is necessary. But you must understand — and this is of the first consequence — that to outward appearances you will still remain under the Queen's displeasure. This also is essential. She requires that if any enquiries are made about the necklace you will reply that you have had the good fortune to sell it to the Sultan of Turkey for his chief Sultana. That too is vital, for she wishes the necklace forgotten. On hearing your terms she will then decide. Her view is that payments should be made by her quarterly. I beg you would now take time to consider whether these proposals are agreeable to you, and whether you are prepared to submit terms through me."

"Not only prepared, madame, but joyful beyond words to express. Her Majesty's displeasure lay like lead upon me, apart from the disappointment, for I have served her long and faithfully and may truly say I have a most respectful love and admiration for my Sovereign. But may I beg a gracious reply on one point. Her Majesty declared she had not the means herself, and would not put the King to that expense. How can the difficulty be met?"

"Nor will she, monsieur, put the King to any cost. It will be otherwise arranged."

The lady smiled mysteriously and was silent. It was then that another doubt flashed into the jeweller's mind.

"Madame, a thousand pardons, but — am I mistaken? — did you not arrive in a carriage belonging to Monseigneur the Cardinal de Rohan?"

The smile disappeared in gravity.

"Monsieur, you are acute. I see your point at once and you shall be met with perfect candour, though here we touch upon a most delicate part of my commission. The Cardinal is an old friend of my family and has had the goodness to treat me with confidence. Would you have received me in a matter of such consequence if I had come in a carriage unknown to you and without *this*?"

She extended a delicately gloved hand with a missive sealed with the arms of the haughty House of the de Rohans.

Boehmer tore it open and beheld the Cardinal's writing which indeed was as familiar to him as his own.

"Monsieur Boehmer, I request you to deal with the Countess de Lamotte-Valois as though you were dealing with myself in the matter she lays before you."

There was no mistaking writing, signature, or seal. But still more perplexed he stared at the Countess.

"Madame, I understand and obey — But surely this command of his Eminence's can have no relation to the other subject of your visit?"

She met him still with the unembarrassed simplicity of her manner — candid as a young girl who cannot suppose herself doubted.

"Can you suppose, monsieur, that I who am the Queen's friend, though a humble one, would do anything so displeasing to her Majesty as to accept any service from one she regards with displeasure? My arriving in the Cardinal's carriage was, it is true, intended to inspire you with confidence — and I beg that when I have left, you will wait upon him at once if you need reassurance. But it also implies — and here I must remind you of your promise of secrecy, for this is a State secret of the deepest consequence — that the Cardinal stands high in the Queen's favour, though for obvious reasons that fact cannot yet appear to the world. Ask himself!"

To say that Boehmer was amazed, stupefied, is to state the case mildly. He could scarcely believe his ears. How — when — had the tide changed? The whole world had long believed it impossible that it should ever change. He did not know, but then the point was that neither he nor anyone else should know — and State secrets are well kept. For what seemed a considerable time he sat with his eyes fixed on the carpet instead of on the very attractive face before him, trying to piece together this flood of information, and trying in vain. Of course he would see the Cardinal. Of course — But on the whole he believed, partly because no one ever would have invented such a stupendous improbability.

The lady rose.

"It was never expected, monsieur, that you could reply on the spur of the moment in such circumstances. That would be impossible. You have much to consider first. I beg you will consult with Monseigneur as to my reliability and that you will communicate with me through him. Or if you address to me care of the Queen's Gentleman Attendant Monsieur Leclaux — that also will find me. At Versailles will be best. But bear in mind that Leclaux is not acquainted with any of the facts I have mentioned and your letter must be sealed. Possibly through Monseigneur is safest. If the matter is to go further you will see me again. If not, I beg you will forget the whole thing — that being the only possible alternative. You fully understand that the Queen can in no way appear in the matter and that you are in no case to approach her. She was dangerously indignant at your last visit and only her intense desire for the necklace conquered her anger."

She made a slight but gracious salutation and turned to go. Terrified lest he had been distrustful Boehmer bowed to his knees.

"You shall hear through his Eminence, Madame la Comtesse, and I implore you to accept my humblest, most grateful thanks for the trouble you have taken. Her Majesty is well served. Would it interest you to behold the famous necklace before you go? It has been thought worth inspection."

"Monsieur, I am exceedingly obliged. Yes, I should like to see it if it is convenient to you."

There was no undue eagerness in her tone. A mild, well-bred interest was all it expressed. Nor when the case was laid before her and its glories disclosed, was she moved to any vulgar excitement.

"A beautiful work of art, and I suppose of very great value. But I am no judge of diamonds nor am I much of a lover of any precious stones except pearls. Those I cannot resist. No doubt this is a gorgeous jewel, but there is too much display here for my taste."

"But not for a queen, madame. I hope that is your opinion?"

"Certainly, monsieur. And now I must depart. We shall hear from you soon. His Eminence will reassure you as to his knowledge of me, and I am far from blaming you for your necessary caution. On the contrary, it will be needed all through this matter."

"You shall hear immediately, madame. Immediately. Again I thank you for the favour of your visit and I implore you to assure her Majesty of my humblest devotion. The only time I need is to work out the terms."

"Perfectly, monsieur. I understand."

Leaving even the precious necklace unguarded, he escorted the Countess to the carriage and saw her drive off, attended with the utmost care by the footmen of the Cardinal.

Then he returned and secured the necklace, the first gleam of hope shining like a rain-washed sunbeam in his heart.

That done, he sent a written message begging an interview with the Cardinal.

His last thought was that some graceful ornament set in pearls would be a very suitable offering at the shrine of the charming messenger when the transaction should be carried through.

Chapter IX

To the Cardinal, sitting eagerly expectant, entered a few days later the Countess in the same charming garb which had dazzled the eyes of Boehmer, crowned with a large black hat swept above a pretty ear and garnished with swaying ostrich plumes — the whole a gift, as she explained, from the Queen and a masterpiece at the hands of Mademoiselle Bertin. She brought an air of gaiety and hope with her that sounded in the very rustle of her silks, the tapping of her Watteau shoes. Her eyes sparkled and danced with pleasure as she swept the archest little curtsey ever seen.

"Good news, Highness! Good news! But yours first. Did Boehmer visit you?"

"The very same day. Naturally I reassured him as to your standing with the Queen and myself and he went away full of raptures and invoking blessings on your head. He was in the seventh heaven and looked twenty years younger. His gratitude was a song of praise!"

"That really is more than I deserve! I am only a go-between. The Queen and yourself are the benefactors."

The word go-between pleased him. She saw the light in his eyes, heard the suppressed eagerness in his voice, and played on it most skilfully.

"Since you wrote that little confession of past mistakes and promises of amendment which I counselled, things have moved much more swiftly. When I put it in the Queen's hands I withdrew respectfully to a window, yet, for your sake, my friend, I will own I managed to peep through the curtain!" The Cardinal in breathless agitation seized her hand and caught it to his lips. "And I saw her rather haughty expression — you know it! — change and soften, her proud lips trembled, and finally — finally — I saw two tears drop upon the paper!"

"If I could believe it!" he cried in ecstasy. "If any words of mine could so move her. If —"

The Countess interrupted gently but with decision.

"Monseigneur, I said to her Majesty that care with regard to all writing must be our motto, and that I would beg her to return your letter to me when she had read it that I might destroy it. She hesitated. Why? I cannot tell. But at last, sighing, she put it in my hands. And I will burn it according to my promise. But first, Highness, look here!"

She displayed the paper before him and there, touching indeed, was the mark of tears, the round starred splash of grief — or love. De Rohan caught it from her passionately, covering the paper with kisses.

"Destroy it! Never. It shall be buried with me. Only my own words — So who can object? No one could decipher from that?"

"Highness, my promise!" said the Countess austerely. "Neither you nor anyone else shall compel me to break it. With me a promise is sacred. Remember I am a Valois and must keep faith. What else I have to say must wait until that matter is settled."

He surrendered it unwillingly and she lit a taper on his bureau, and watched it burn, then turned smiling to him.

"I have saddened you, but now for better things. Look here!" From a pocket concealed in her dress she drew a little stitched packet of pale rose-coloured silk brocade, and from an ivory case a tiny pair of scissors with mother-of-pearl handles. With careful precision she snipped the stitches along the top and took out a folded paper.

"Read, my friend, and do not die of joy."

He opened it with hands so shaking that the paper rattled. In long-ago glad days he had known that broad gilt-edged paper very well — had seen it at Vienna when the then Princess wrote to her mother the Empress, had seen it in the hands of happy people at Court, had known the writing intimately though never a line of it had come his way — a letter from the Queen! Brief, naturally — how could it be otherwise.

Jeanne added gravely: "She struggled with herself, saying, 'I must write. I must answer this touching letter.' And again, 'No, I dare not. He would misunderstand.' But I remained silent, Highness, knowing that nature is best left to herself. Not a word from me! And at last she snatched a pen and wrote. But the contents I do not know."

He read them greedily, but to himself, and then said in a smothered voice: "She pardons me. She gives me hope. It is very shy — timid like a girl, but yet a queenly note in it also. It is signed with her name. Oh, Jeanne, what would I not do for you who have done so much for me? You have brought hope and joy and all the angel visitants with you. You have only to command and be obeyed. Have you need of anything in which I can oblige myself in obliging you?"

She smiled a sweet, half-melancholy smile.

"Highness, I only acquit myself of a debt of gratitude. You helped me when I had no friends. When I had little hope you were loyal. It is my turn now. But to business. I am not so inhuman as to ask you to destroy *this* treasure. But put it in the most guarded safety. I know you will. Now as to terms? Has Boehmer stated them?"

"Certainly. Here they are." He put a paper in her hands and while she read it, devoured the letter with his eyes, reading it again and again.

"That seems reasonable — quarterly payments, and your guarantee for them. He exacted that?"

"Well, scarcely. I offered it. To tell you the truth, madame, I wish to have a share in the matter which will put her Majesty under some sort of real obligation to me. My heart cannot relinquish that pleasure. I believe Boehmer would have taken the simple guarantee from the Queen which you were empowered to offer. He is to hand over the necklace on receiving the Queen's signed agreement!"

"Your wish is very natural, and can be managed!" the Countess said reflecting. "It can be put to her as a matter of business. And have you seen the necklace? Did you think it worth the price?"

"Certainly. I thought it magnificent. And you?"

"To me it appeared a little heavy. Too much of it. I did not covet it. Were it mine I should have a diadem made of the flat rows. But then I am not a queen and the Valois were ever fastidious."

"You are a queen of women!" cried the enraptured Cardinal and kissed her hand in an ecstasy of homage. That reference to the Valois did not even appear humorous to him now. Why should not a lady in whom every grace met have her little whim? And she *might* be a Valois after all. The gentlemen of that family had never been reticent where women were concerned and some of the ladies had not walked entirely unspotted through a censorious world.

"Then you have settled it with Boehmer — that you will pay the first instalment on receiving the Queen's command, and that then and not till then the necklace shall be delivered —"

"To you."

The Countess threw up her hands in horror.

"Not to me. For the love of God, no! I would not handle such a treasure for the world. Am I a madman? To the Queen's own gentleman, here at your house and under your own eyes. There must be no loophole for doubt or carelessness. I insist on that, or I shall withdraw instantly from the whole business."

"You are as wise as you are charming. Of course you are right. You could not devise a better plan. Boehmer shall attend here with the necklace after I have made the first payment. But — alas, madame, have pity on a lover's impatience! I have one little condition to make. You who have managed so many marvels can achieve another. I must see the Queen and hear from her own lips that I am forgiven. No —" seeing her about to interrupt — "I wish no confirmation about the necklace. I would not soil such a meeting with business. But I must see her — I must."

The Countess looked him gravely in the face.

"Highness, you know what you ask? It is that she shall run the risk of infamy — no more, no less! Consider it yourself. That this meeting shall come in time she is resolved. She has said so. She desires it ardently. But to press it now — now when all the world believes she is at enmity with you! Is this chivalrous? Is it worthy of a de Rohan?"

"Madame, your words are gospel. But a little glimpse, a passing word, a flower dropped. No more. Consider it, I beg you. Put it to my sovereign lady. Be merciful in your strength."

There was more, much more to be said and pleaded, and he ran the whole gamut of emotion. He was in desperate earnest, the Lamotte opposing only a yielding resistance. She would think it over. She would lay it before the Queen. It was for her only to decide though the Countess would not even promise that she would not oppose it.

"For I think it rash in the extreme. It may cost us all our lives. No — I will promise nothing but that I will convey your wish to the Queen. Nothing else. Forget it for the present. Let us think only of business. Oh, by the way, I must tell you that her enchanting Majesty has offered me the dearest little house in Paris! I shall not be long in my poor little apartment. If it were not for my devotion to you and my beloved Queen, I have little to gain by embarking in this anxious affair, for I already have her full confidence and promise that she will advance me. My future is secure."

This was obvious and charmed the Cardinal into remembering only the good fortune which had given him such an ally. She asked him to describe his vision at Cagliostro's house. Was the crown the crown-royal of France and the woman wearing it the Queen? Wonderful! She suggested so cleverly that it convinced him he had seen a great deal more than he remembered. The story grew in his mind with every word she said.

He overwhelmed her with congratulations and she went off in the end with a flutter of smiles and graces leaving him a little subdued by her serious attitude towards his heart's desire. For it certainly seemed to the Cardinal that the large sums he was guaranteeing himself to pay demanded an unusual return, and though a week hence a letter would have seemed unattainable as heaven, each step now led to the one above, and he trembled to think of hanging between earth and heaven when a leap might set him in heaven itself.

The Countess's next appointment (upon leaving him) was of a very different order but quite as important. It was natural enough that she should visit the little apartment she used when in Paris, now that better times had come her way, and to that not even the Cardinal could have objected. What might have startled him was the fact that a gentleman was also in occupation who bore no resemblance to the Count de Lamotte-Valois. Yet a personable man after a gay dissipated fashion. In short, Monsieur de Villette, black-haired and narrow-eyed, full-lipped and jawed, a little tarnished as to the embroidery on his wide cuffs, a little brazen as to the showy buttons adorning it, but otherwise well enough.

He lay in one chair with his feet on another, extremely at home, and as the Lamotte entered did not stir except to raise his eyes from the pamphlet he held and kiss his hand gracefully.

"*La petite Jeanne*, and more charming than ever! — fresh from the homage of Monseigneur. And what happened, my friend?"

She disengaged her satin cloak and sat down beside him, with an anxious expression.

"Much — but all good — better than good! except one thing."

"What?" He sat up straight and eager as a terrier after rats, his very ears seemed to prick and listen, the whole man changed and alert. "Danger?"

"No — difficulty. That's all. But first, the letter went off excellently. He never doubted, not for one second, that it was her hand. You should have seen his rapture. And my idea of the tears on his letter was stupendous. I would have exploded, only I was so anxious."

Villette giggled — there is no other word for it.

"I told you so. The old fool is a mass of sentiment and folly. No wonder he has made a mess of his life. He will make a worse one of it yet before he has done. Is he really in love with her?"

"*Mon dieu*, how can I say, when the same words mean an utterly different thing with different people. In his own way — I suppose, yes! But what a way! Sentiment, self-interest, desire, vanity; stir them all up with a few more ridiculous ingredients and you get what the Cardinal calls love. It is not what I mean by it, if you ask me that!"

"But business, chèrie — business! Has Boehmer stated his terms as we expected?"

"Exactly, with the quarterly payments which Monseigneur will guarantee. If she delays one Monseigneur will pay and be repaid at her leisure. The necklace to be delivered after Boehmer has her signed agreement. It was to be given to me at the Cardinal's house. The fools people are! One cannot but think of that. Of course I refused and desired that it should be handed to the Queen's gentleman. He agreed."

"Yes — all that was correct. You are a good little woman of business, madame. The gentleman will be there!"

Jeanne de Lamotte smiled at his expression.

"He will certainly be there!" she said. "And now for the difficulty. He insisted on seeing her 'a glimpse, a word' — but he *must* see her. I foresee that that demand will become urgent. What in the name of God are we to do? I hadn't expected that. I thought he could live on letters getting warmer and warmer, until — well, until the affair was settled."

Villette looked down with frowning brows. One might almost see the swift working of his mind in that stern concentration. Not a word from the Lamotte. She knew when to be silent. It was a part of her trade. The ticking of a cheap gilt clock on the mantelpiece filled the gap of speech. At last he looked up.

"An interview is of course out of the question. That stands to reason. But I have an idea. No — not a word yet. I want to think it out in all its branches. Did you gather that he was not prepared to pay up without an interview?"

"He never said that — but yet — Yes, I almost think it was implied, though I don't think he would hold to it. It would certainly make everything easier if you could see your way. We shall not feel sure of the necklace being handed over unless you can. If he tells Boehmer he has had an interview — well, it's obvious. We are on velvet."

But again Villette was lost in thought — hard concentrated thought. She might not have been there for all the notice he took of her, and at last she rose rather impatiently to go. Then he emerged from his profundities.

"Yes, I'm a dull companion, I know, but I can tell you it wants a pretty active brain to see my way. I'll let you know presently however. Have an evening free to dine out with me next week, and keep the pot simmering meanwhile. Have you shown him the Queen's letter to you?"

"Yes, yes, excellent. He is as convinced that she and I are bosom friends as you that we are not! I answer for it that all is right there. And he is keeping Boehmer in play so that all's right there also. Then good-bye, *mon ami*. We can easily meet here at any time."

He looked at her with narrowing eyes.

"What would you say if I knew a handsome young woman with ashen blonde hair, full blue eyes, and an exquisite complexion, *ma petite Jeanne*?"

"I should say — another?"

He laughed with relish.

"What? — there have been so many? But we are not jealous, no, no, we are not jealous. We little clever women are far too sensible for that. We know we are indispensable and the others are not. And as a matter of fact this girl is better known to your husband than to me, and a sensible woman is never jealous of her husband. This might be a very useful young woman though I cannot say her morals would stand examination by a jury of matrons."

She stopped, suddenly arrested, and stared at him with wide bright eyes, dumb with astonishment. He laughed, pleased at the effect he had made, a touch of braggadocio in the laughter.

"For God's sake be careful!" she said at last, paling under her rouge. "You may lead us to the scaffold if there's a single false step. I can face most things but —"

"But leave it to me, my little Jeanne. We are playing for big stakes. I take the risks; am I likely to forget the dangers? Leave it to me."

She was turning silently to the door when he called her back.

"You are making the Queen commit herself too quickly to him. Tell him that on consideration she does not approve of his guaranteeing the payments. It does not become her position and her word is enough. Also that the first payment is to be made at a date fixed for some months after the necklace is delivered. You are making her too cheap with herself. Make her proud, high, capricious — what she is. They are honoured to serve her. You will know how to do it, and you can always bring her back again. Don't forget you dine with me next week."

It is certain that Madame de Lamotte-Valois may be called a dispenser of happiness. Retaux de Villette had welcomed her with joy. Boehmer at the same moment hummed a tune as he looked over his jewels. The Cardinal sat in his pompous library (where he never opened a book) in close converse with Cagliostro (the Grand Cophta) in the ordinary breeches and silk stockings of the period, and disclosing a pair of sturdy legs — the objects of adoration of half the ladies of Paris — and the Cardinal glowed with happiness. He looked ten years younger than his wont. Cagliostro beamed mild benignities at him and was evidently in the best of spirits. Again the good fairy, Jeanne de Lamotte-Valois!

"It was a wonderful revelation, Monseigneur!" said Cagliostro. "The like has been vouchsafed to few. And I own I expected you to greet me with the news that already some miracle of good fortune had befallen. But we must not fret the Powers with mortal impatience, and I read from your expression that you are not wholly dissatisfied with the promise of the future. Aha! the ineffable Powers do not deceive their faithful votaries and the whole world's treasure-house is open to them."

"My great friend, wonders *have* befallen!" cried the radiant Cardinal. "Yours is my gratitude when the supreme day arrives. And the beautiful Columb too! She shall not be forgotten. I suppose even that pure intelligence does not disdain a ring or some such pretty trifle?"

"My disciple, when the Columb is not inspired she is a girl like others — pure, immaculately pure, but full of an innocent gaiety. The same with myself. You are aware that I unbend."

The Cardinal was well aware of that fact and said so gratefully. The Grand Cophta unbent now over more than one glass of wine from his host's famous cellars. It warmed them both, but not a word could the magician extract of what really was the object of his visit — the game that Jeanne de Lamotte-Valois was playing. There a dead wall met him. He could only reiterate that the sacred knowledge had revealed to him that the Cardinal was on the eve of startling developments to which the most brilliant success was attached, and the Cardinal replied with glowing smiles. No more.

At last the questioner drew back gravely and with dignity.

"I never question, my beloved disciple. I never need to question, for the knowledge of the spirits is at my command. But where the greatest forms of good fortune are indicated it is well to have more than one consultation with the High, the Mysterious Attendants in the heaven where wisdom opens her book. It has appeared from there that royal personages and events are intimately connected with your destiny and that great skill is needed. Beware!"

"Has there been any further revelation?" asked the Cardinal, trembling. Who could hide anything from the all-seeing eye of the Grand Cophta? — and yet what could be more terrifying than to think that Marie Antoinette's confidence should be even remotely approached by men or spirits? He yearned for the bright intelligence of Jeanne at his elbow to prompt him with some swift and ready reply. He could only stare with much embarrassment at Cagliostro and mutter something about all developments being as yet in the future.

"Certainly, my disciple, certainly! we must not attempt to hurry the Eternal Wisdom, but where royalty is concerned —"

His shrewd eye could not miss the tremor of the nerves round the Cardinal's mouth, and like lightning he pieced things together. A woman — a crown — those were the words Jeanne de Lamotte-Valois had put into his mouth, and the commonest gossip of Paris was the hate of the Queen for the Cardinal. Could it be possible that there was some intrigue on foot for restoring him to her good graces? For if so and it succeeded there would be brilliant prospects indeed for himself with de Rohan in power. That would be a thing worth forwarding with all the wisdom of the Attendant Spirits of Wisdom and his own Grand Cophtaship thrown in. He would apply a careful test but with the utmost finesse.

"No, no further revelations which it would be proper I should communicate now beyond saying that I have seen a thick cloud dissipated and honours and love pouring on my cherished disciple. So be it! So it will be! Never doubt it. Singular revelations come my way however. I only yesterday heard of a rising star at Court and high in the Queen's favour, a certain Comte de Fersen — a Swede or some such thing. Do you know anything of him?"

"Only that he is in favour both with King and Queen," de Rohan answered, flushing purple, "but there is nothing in that, nothing whatever. It would not interfere —"

He pulled himself up, and the stop was enough for Cagliostro's sharp ear and eye. So that was it — so the Cardinal was hoping to be the favoured lover of the Queen. His bait had caught the fish and now he knew.

Heavens, what colossal folly! Like the rest of Paris the Grand Cophta had heard scandalous reports of the Queen's unchastity, mud flung in hopes that at least a grain or two might stick and play the game of her enemies. But he was much too shrewd a man to believe it. It would not pay her to be any man's light o' love. That one consideration settled the matter for him. But if there were an intrigue for regaining her favour and friendship that indeed might be possible. Endless is the caprice of women, royal or otherwise. He smiled smoothly and made a careless gesture as though he blew de Fersen away like thistledown. He would have to consider this carefully and alone.

"Certainly nothing in that," he said, "nothing whatever, and so far as I can see the stars foretell a bloody death for him somewhere in the north."

De Rohan smiled — the notion was not unpleasing.

"And too good for a presumptuous puppy!" he answered.

The Grand Cophta tried once more the delicate process of working out a secret delicately and failed again. Finally, warmed with wine he made another desperate attempt and failed.

"But I will know what that little woman is up to," said he within his soul as he left unsatisfied, "if I have to comb Paris with a fine-tooth comb to find her secret. Does she think a kiss and a few louis sufficient payment for the play I staged the other night? By no means!"

And at Versailles the Queen sat unconscious, and read the comedies of Beaumarchais, "The Marriage of Figaro" and the "Barber of Seville," with bitter foreboding, seeing the merciless attack upon the Court and aristocracy, and hearing the far-off derision of Paris kindled by the scorching wit and humour dared for the first time in public.

The plot was thickening indeed.

Chapter X

IT was the misfortune of the Queen that she had always despised the trammels of etiquette and fetters of ceremonial. Brought up in the more homely atmosphere of the German court in Vienna, where the relations between monarch and subjects were those of a father with his children, the stately laws of intercourse at Versailles had always filled her with weariness touched with contempt. When she arrived in France a girl of fifteen vivid with youth and high animal spirits, the little Archduchess found a guide appointed for her dancing footsteps, calculated to freeze the dance-measure in any heart however young and gay — the prim and starched Madame de Noailles.

This lady had every rule of the French Court at her fingertips, from the time of the Valois downward. She could not err, and the slavery she sought to impose on her victim was dreadful. Yet after her fashion she was not wholly wrong and when the young Queen objected that these usages were only ceremonies, might well have replied with the Spanish courtier, "Your Majesty herself is but a ceremony," which really goes to the root of the matter. But Madame de Noailles had not the wit to infuse reason into her precepts nor the Queen the experience to perceive for herself the French tendency to become too easy and familiar even with the institution of royalty and to guard against it. Not for nothing had the fence of etiquette been devised at Versailles in the long experience of centuries. But she was young, headstrong and unwise.

There was not a creature in her *entourage* to teach her the wisdom of gradual and carefully planned advance and she charged at the fence of etiquette and broke through but at her peril. Life speedily resolved itself into a battle between the old *regime* and the new, the last headed by Marie Antoinette, the first by Madame de Noailles and all the conservatives of the Court fighting with the spirit of the age for a lost cause.

The Queen nicknamed her "Madame Etiquette" and mocked her precepts unmercifully. They were many and foolish. There was even one which regulated the width of her skirts, that a royal lady might not be guilty of the indecorum of stepping with too wide a stride over any rivulet or muddy patch in the forest of Fontainebleau. She revenged herself by springing across light as a deer, while Madame Etiquette flung up shocked hands in mute appeal in the background. There was a masterpiece of etiquette in use every morning which drove her youthful Majesty into open revolt. It was necessary that her ladies should attend her toilette and the one highest in rank present her chemise and the rest of her linen in turn. Well and good. But if a princess of the blood were there that honour fell to her share, and in such a case the lady next highest in rank must present the chemise to the Princess, receiving it for that purpose from the bedchamber woman. These ceremonies culminated one wintry morning in an explosion which nearly wrecked the usage of ages. The Queen stood entirely undressed, waiting to receive her chemise, Madame Campan held it unfolded for presentation when the lady of honour entered, slipped off her gloves and of course took it. A scratching was heard at the door (knocking being forbidden by etiquette) and in came the Duchesse d'Orleans, cousin by marriage of the King; she removed her gloves and came forward to possess herself of the chemise. The lady of honour handed it to Madame Campan, who presented it to the Duchess. More scratching at the door — the King's sister-in-law, Madame la Comtesse de Provence, appeared and the Duchess handed her the chemise, the Queen, her arms crossed upon her breast chilly as a marble statue, shuddering with cold. In her sympathy Madame de Provence did not wait to take off her gloves (much to the horror of Madame Etiquette) and put on the chemise, knocking the Queen's cap off in her haste. Marie Antoinette forced a laugh to hide her annoyance and muttered under her breath, "How annoying! How tiresome!"

Small wonder that when she took to the harmless sport of donkey-riding with her ladies in the forest of Fontainebleau, and a ridiculously curvetting beast tossed her on to a bed of leaves the Queen sitting and rocking herself in helpless laughter cried out: "Run, somebody, as quickly as you can and ask Madame de Noailles what is the etiquette when the Queen of France falls off a donkey!"

Absurd — and yet — a queen is a queen and when she breaks through the hedge the brambles scratch her!

She made many mistakes kindly but lamentable. For instance, she permitted her own sacrosanct hairdresser to increase his income by attending ladies of the Court and of Paris, who were only too eager to employ such a fashionable personage and pick his brains as to the Queen's tastes and little personal anecdotes of what went on at the royal toilette. It followed that gossip on the intimate details of the royal Household multiplied, was grossly exaggerative and broke down the awful distance expected by the people as part of the royal dignity of their Queen. The man in the street could now chatter familiarly of the Queen's toilette, temper, and what he was pleased to call her spendthrift ways. All about her noted and were alarmed. She alone could not perceive the danger.

She drove herself about with only one lady in attendance in a neat little two-wheeled carriage known as a cabriolet, and again the people stood in horror that was not desirable to see a Queen of France acting as her own coachman and flying to God knows what rendezvous in the wilds of the great royal parks and domains. Hatred of Austria prompted gross and horrible suspicions and slanders as to every innocent freedom and they were taken for truth and discussed as matters of political importance.

But a worse and more dangerous mistake lay before her. Better tutelage to twenty Mesdames Etiquette than that error which seemed so natural and delightful at the moment. The King had permitted her to use the little theatres at Fontainebleau and Trianon, and there the courtiers, men and women, presented plays for her delight with all the excitement of rehearsing, dressing up, and what not — gay and brilliant children as they were! But what was the horror of Paris and the world at large when the Queen herself took to the boards and postured and mouthed (royally badly) behind the footlights. Nothing could have been madder.

Never since Nero acted in Rome was such a tempest of condemnation raised by that fact — the Queen, the QUEEN — exposing herself to plaudits or disapproval! Great heavens, was the sky about to fall! It was and in real earnest, but again the Queen did not perceive it. The King detested the performances, but was too much the slave of his love for her to interfere. And there was no one to plead for her that the Empress her mother had caused the famous Metastasio to write some of his finest work for the performance of her children and that Marie Antoinette passionately loved reciting them and had had them translated into French that her new people might enjoy them as she did herself. Though many knew this, the opinion of the people was not worth contradicting. What did the masses matter? What had they to do with the diversions of a queen of France? Fatal contempt and inaction hindered the opening of her eyes to the danger of signals. The very simplicity of her dress on other than State occasions gave the deepest offence, and in these ways Madame Etiquette was reduced to an impotence of dismay, and so she went at her own fatal pace along the road to ruin accompanied by many dangerously frivolous friends.

So by this and much more the way was paved for the horrors of the diamond necklace, which, had it blazed with the fires of hell, could not have been more terrible in its results while in the gaieties and anxieties of her queenly life she had forgotten its very existence.

She sat one morning, sipping her chocolate when the Princesse de Lamballe came in fresh as a June rose in one of the frilled white muslin dresses which the Duchesse de Polignac had made the rage in the inmost circles of Court favour. She wore a straw hat curved like a flower-basket and covered with roses and blue ribbons, conveying the notion of a fashionable shepherdess whose white hands laden with great jewels were entirely in keeping with the piquant contradictions of the whole effect. Perhaps her expression and serenely dignified beauty emphasized these contradictions more strongly than anything else. She could not speak or smile without betraying the great lady in every gesture — a contrast indeed to the Polignac Duchess whose one restless effort was to outdo her own eccentricities at every turn, a pretty smiling ape of fashion.

"But sit down, Thérèse, sit down, and do not literally stand upon ceremony. It is really too early in the day to begin my prison discipline. What have you to say?"

"Some things which I am at a loss how to begin, Madame, but your kindness pardons everything to good intention. It is on that very question of what you call prison discipline that I am here."

The Queen sighed impatiently.

"My dear, is not Madame Etiquette enough? Well, be it as you will. Go on."

"It is this, Madame. Some person, I do not know whom, in crossing the courtyard dropped a small packet which someone whom also I know nothing of placed in the hands of my head waiting-woman and she immediately brought to me, saying she thought I should see the contents. I have forced myself to read them. I say 'forced,' for they are the vilest collection of songs, pasquinades and libels upon your Majesty that ever the mind of man conceived. Nothing can be more horrible. I will not show them to you. No —" for the Queen, pale as death, mechanically put out her hand — "for I consider myself defiled even by looking at them. But they have started a train of thought which I think it my duty to reveal to you."

"The monsters! The wretches!" cried the Queen, in towering indignation. "They cannot understand a virtuous freedom. They mistake it for licence. Yet there is no single detail of all my life which they might not see if they were worth convincing. But they are not. They are only worth silent contempt."

The Princess sighed, her beautiful face calm and sad.

"True, Madame, who knows that better than I? And yet — I will confess my own misdeeds. I consider that I have been wrong in promoting and sharing the harmless gaieties which have drawn down this frightful retribution. I am ashamed when I remember the risks I have let you run."

"You think," said the Queen haughtily, "that Madame Etiquette was right and we were wrong? Then I can only say the Queen of France is the one slave in a land where slavery is forbidden."

"Madame, will your Majesty pardon me if I speak frankly? Surely the Queen embodies and represents the dignity of the nation — and if — but I see it is necessary that you should read at least some of these atrocious papers. Here are some of the less filthy."

Marie Antoinette took them with eyes sparkling with anger, determined to resist and repudiate every feeling but that of contempt while she read the coarsely printed sheets as though she disdained to handle them. But the woman in her overpowered the queen.

A burning blush covered her face. It tinged even her throat and bosom. It forced the scalding tears into her eyes. Her hands trembled pitiably.

"And these are circulating in the country?" she asked in a stifled voice.

"By thousands."

There was a painful silence, until a faint scratching was heard on the door, when the Princess at a gesture, glided to it and forbade entry, then resumed her former seat.

"Madame," she said earnestly, "I entreat you, on the knees of my heart I entreat you, to stop what we have called in our merriment the *descampativos* instantly. You see what is said. You know I have never joined in them and it is impossible to deny that they have lent colour to the dreadful song in your hand. That at a meeting in the royal gardens his Majesty's brother or any man should be placed at an altar of friendship with power to pair off the assemblage, man and woman alone for an hour with orders to return and disclose the secret of their intimate conversation — Oh, Madame, in that song you behold the miserable result! I mourn the day when your Majesty took part in it. It should never — never have been! His Majesty's sister, Madame Elizabeth, young as she is, has always deeply disapproved of these things."

"The King took part in it more than once and was himself paired," answered the Queen in an attempt at excuse, but with shaking hands. "And as for Madame Elizabeth, she has the spirit of a nun."

"Yes, Madame — but let us be honest — his Majesty joined only to give you pleasure. And see the vile use made of it! You are accused in these dreadful papers of having wished to engage his Majesty in other interests that you yourself might be free to pursue your own. I implore you to let the *descampativos* be stopped at once. Is it fit that men and women should hide together in your gardens at Trianon for an hour — and one of them the Queen? The very name is enough. It savours of the frolics of creatures I would not name in your presence!"

She had gone too far. The Queen sprang to her feet glaring at her like an image of Fury — a mask of Medusa to strike the beholder to stone. The Princess hid her face in her hands.

"Since I did it it is right — and can you suppose I should own myself conquered by the vilest scum of the earth like these? To end my amusements would be to own myself found out and penitent. We will have one this very afternoon at Trianon and I command you to join it. Where the Queen leads the Princesse de Lamballe may certainly follow."

Her nobler nature was entirely in abeyance for the moment. The spirit of tyrannous ancestors looked out of her bright blue eyes and lips cruelly tightened above the little line of teeth. The woman before her sat with bowed head like a mute grief. So they remained while the gold clock ticked solemnly on beside them.

At last the Princess raised her head and looked the Queen in the face, mildly but resolutely: "Madame, you crush me with shame. I own myself utterly in the wrong. I entreat your forgiveness for a false friend. I feared to speak — I feared to lose your friendship, to drive you into the arms of

Madame de Polignac, and in that base fear I have exposed you to dangers which I might have lessened. Now you have given me courage. I will relieve my conscience at last."

Her head drawn up to the full height of her stately throat, the Queen answered: "You shall not speak, madame, nor I listen. Go. You have my orders for this afternoon."

"Madame, I desire to ask your forgiveness. If I appeared to criticize your actions I humbly ask your pardon. But — I shall not be in the gardens this afternoon. I refuse obedience."

It was impossible that Marie Antoinette should grow paler. Words choked in her throat. There was a tense silence, each looking into the eyes of the other. Then the Princess curtseyed deeply and without the customary dismissal glided to the door and was gone.

The Queen stood alone, flashes of light seeming to burst in her brain, the vile papers on the table beside her, rage and disdain in her heart. Her very queendom was abased and shattered before her. That she should be rebuked, defied, vilified, burnt the tears dry in her eyes. But she did not relent. It hardened the Hapsburg obstinacy in her until her heart felt like marble. Not an inch, not a single inch would she give in. She was driven on a cold fury.

*

That afternoon the merry party assembled in the green glades of the gardens of Trianon — lovely as the Paradise of Mohammed with plashing fountains catching the sun in rainbows of silver mist. The peacocks strutted on the long perspectives of a velvet lawn displaying their trains shimmering with emeralds and sapphire, and all round the blossoming trees drowsy with heat dreamed in ardent sunshine. In a white marble pavilion supported on marble columns but open on all sides was a little altar sacred to the genius of Friendship, wreathed with roses both sculptured and living. Behind it, in a black robe powdered with stars, stood the Comte d'Artois; the gay young brother of the King in a pose of solemn authority, one hand raised to enforce obedience. Before him the laughing group of courtiers headed by the Queen — loveliest of all the women in her shepherdess hat and skirt hooped and looped with roses, bright feverish roses also burning in her cheeks. The Princesse de Lamballe was not present.

"Ladies and gentlemen of the Fellowship," cried the Prince, "you await the orders of the Grand Lama of Friendship — my honoured self. I command you to pair and disperse for an hour by the watch of every gentleman present, I myself choosing the partners. Madame my sister — " to the Queen — "I allot your tender mercies to the Comte de Fersen."

And so on through a list which he had compiled with the utmost love of mischief and provocation in the highest degree. It had not by any means escaped the eyes of his Royal Highness that the grave reserved gentleman from Sweden lingered long at the Court and evinced a special devotion to the service of her Majesty. And might one not at a haphazard guess suppose that Marie Antoinette in her turn might look with some little flutter of interest on the tall fair Norseman — for so they called him. His height, his bright hair and calm thoughtful manner picked him out among the quick dark Frenchmen all fire and *verve* and swift wit and repartee. D'Artois was inclined to think Axel Fersen slow in talk, possibly stupid, yet — a case of the hare and the tortoise! — he generally arrived even if after others, and with some remark that summed up the rest. Women liked him extraordinarily, but he did not seem especially attracted by their light lures and laughters. He answered, dropped meditative eyes upon them, smiled a little, and passed on. Now supposing his heart were touched — touched where he dared not declare it — what a triumph for a charming queen! And supposing *her* heart were touched — not seriously of course, for that would be impossible — but enough for a blush and a tremble, what a triumph for a mischievous brother-in-law.

"Decamp!" he intoned sonorously. "And in one hour return. Speak your thoughts freely to one another, but remember that every thought and all that passes must be disclosed when you return, still paired, in an hour. Remember also, *messieurs et mesdames*, that the pair that is one moment late shall be exposed to the derision of the Fellowship and condemned by public acclaim to a forfeit as punishment."

With her eyes opened a little to the danger by events of the morning the Queen was inclined to congratulate herself on the unusual good sense of her brother-in-law's choice for her. It had amused him at former *descampativos* to pair her with the giddiest and gayest of the cavaliers and there had been moments when it needed not only her dignity but her sense of humour to keep their absurdities within bounds. That was amusing enough at the time but with those fatal papers in mind even her daring shrank from it. But now — she looked with reassurance at Fersen's stately height and the serene self-control of his expression. Taken altogether the impression on her mind had always been one of latent strength and watchfulness — a curious intentness as of a man who could never be taken by surprise by his own passions or those of others. It gave her satisfaction to think of him as colonel of a regiment in the King's service and she had had a vague pleasure in seeing him at Court.

Beside him the Frenchmen seemed childish, feminine, impulsive, heedless, in their quick airy grace and laughter.

Naturally she had spoken with him often and always in her mind a little clear light surrounded his figure and distinguished him from the elegantly dressed horde about her. A brave man — and with resources in himself, if she did not mistake.

They walked together, he, hat under his arm, down the long sun-dappled glade, watching the rest of the flight of butterflies disperse, man and woman, some knee-deep through fern to the forest, some through trim garden beds to the lake. There was a far-off sound of high-bred voices chattering their charming French. It died on the air and left it unusually silent.

She led the talk with some interest to Sweden, piloting him to the little Pavilion of Flora where she desired to sit and pass the hour in peace, for indeed a sort of weariness — the reaction of the morning — weighed her soul and body.

He answered with the utmost courtesy, and a frank smile, growing more animated as he spoke of the far North. Would it never be possible that their Majesties should return the visit of the Northern Royalties who had been so graciously received at Versailles? She had seldom seen him smile before, she thought, and liked it. A smile that hid nothing but kindness.

"Oh, monsieur, there is little hope of travel for a queen of France. You know that. And now, there is such a spirit of unrest that the King cannot be absent. But I — you know how weary I get of my cage. To wander by the bays and fjords of Scandinavia and hear the legends of the North, would be my joy. But I never shall. The people would put some hateful gloss upon it. I have too many enemies — God knows why."

That was her imprudent way; with people she liked instinctively her lips were never guarded. It was her charm and danger, for every one received it as a special confidence and hoped for more — the more artful tempting her on to disclosures which might serve their turn, the more honest for pleasure in the frank eyes and lovely lips that spoke together.

Fersen could not resist the spell.

"Enemies, Madame? Your Majesty who is kindness itself? If such grace and generosity can have enemies there is no hope for any of us in this wicked world. And yet — it is true. You have enemies."

There was not another man in the gardens that day who would not have sworn on his knees that she was deceived. Enemies! For the most beautiful and beloved woman and queen in the world? Never. The contrast, the truth, impressed her instantly, and as they entered the small pavilion with its marble bench below the white Flora weaving her garland, she bid him sit beside her.

"If you could know how strange it is to hear the truth," she said. "Speak on, monsieur. Tell me why I have enemies. I cannot understand, for though I would not speak highly of myself I — I have tried to please. What — you will not speak? You shake your head? That is what it is to be a queen. If one's courtiers saw one running in the dark to a precipice they would never stop one. They would say, 'Oh, Madame, for others there might be danger; for you never!' I tire, tire, *tire* of it all!"

"I also, Madame!" he said with sudden feeling that surprised himself. "It is hard indeed if one has not only heart but intelligence like yours. But — recognize their side also. Few royal persons desire the truth, and when it is offered it is not always well received."

A deep flush rose in her cheek, her eyes dropped. Only that morning she had driven a true friend from her because she had dared to speak one unpalatable truth. For all the world she would not have had him know that fact. How petty, how contemptible it seemed now in the calm sincerity of his expression. What if she sounded him, and compared his point of view with that of Thérèse de Lamballe? From him — she could not tell why — it might be more endurable.

She veiled her eyes with the most delicate air of pleading.

"Monsieur, if I ask you a favour, will you refuse?"

"Madame!" His look was enough.

"Then tell me how you view my position at the moment. You are a foreigner. You can speak more freely — perhaps judge more clearly. Am I popular among my people?"

"May I be pardoned, your Majesty, if I decline to speak?"

His voice was unruffled, but some deep feeling lay beneath it. He rose and stood before her.

"Not 'your Majesty' here in the gardens. Only 'Madame'. No, I cannot pardon silence. I need truth and a friend's counsel. I feel you to be a friend. Speak."

He stood as a soldier under orders, his eyes on the ground.

"You honour me, Madame. No, you are not popular. There is great danger in my opinion. The Queen, the mother of the Dauphin, should be in the heart of France."

"And I am not. I know it, and why? Continue."

"Partly, Madame, because monarchy itself suffered in the reign of the late King. You are aware of what the extravagances of the King on certain ladies cost the nation."

"And *you* are aware," she said with angry self-justification, "that we are the very reverse. The King has no vices, his one thought is the happiness of his people. I — I must dress like a queen, live like one for the honour of the nation. What other charge can they bring against us?"

"Madame, I am silent."

"I command you to continue."

With a painful effort he went on, stiff and straight before her.

"Madame, there is no doubt that Austria is hated in France. And there was Trianon — there were many other costly toys, dangerous with the hungry eyes of a people upon them. Little enough I know compared with the frightful waste of the late King's favourites but —"

She sprang to her feet.

"And you compare me with them? You, a foreigner, dare to insinuate that a queen of France has no right to the pleasures, the surroundings of her rank? That a Pompadour, a du Barry, may take what she needs, but the Queen never?"

"Because she *is* the Queen, Madame," he said, looking down from his height with troubled eyes upon her. "But I entreat your pardon. I have done wrong. I have done exceedingly wrong. I ask your pardon! It is also true that I am a foreigner though in your service."

There was the dart of icicles in her clear high-pitched tone and blue eyes.

"I asked what others thought, not what your own opinion was, monsieur, and since I was foolish enough to ask the fault is mine and you are not unpardonable. We will change the subject."

It was a queen's command but if she expected him to glide with easy grace from the rocks and quicksands she was disappointed.

There was a long silence during which her wrath slowly gathered. The man had no tact, no sense of what was due to a woman's feelings — a northern boor and no more. If he ventured again she would make him smart for it. After a few moments filled only by the sighing of the faint breeze in the boughs, he spoke again hurriedly like a man leaping desperately to confront a fear.

"Madame, your Majesty's mercy will permit me a word more. There is danger. The tone of comment in Paris and the provinces is appalling and often where one would least expect it. Should you not be warned so that you may at least take precaution? Should —"

She sprang to her feet, gasping with anger, flaming with cruel unreason: "You have insulted me with every word. And why? What gives you courage?"

He stood rigidly before her and replied in a voice so quiet that it fell on her fire like ice. But a strange light irradiated his face.

"Madame, I love you, and because I would die to serve you, I offer you the one poor gift in my power — the truth."

"Love?" she cried with sparkling eyes. "Hate, I think! Love adores, reverences, sees nothing but good. Love's eyes are blinded to faults."

"Love's eyes are clear as the sun, Madame, and because I love you —"

"You insult me! Oh, the Princesse de Lamballe was right when she warned me against these miserable *descampativos*. I have honoured you only to be repaid with blame and insult I never deserved."

He answered as quietly as if he felt nothing.

"The Princess was right, Madame. You should not be here alone with any gentleman. It is not fitting. But, were you Empress of the world you could not be insulted by the statement of a love that asks nothing, hopes nothing, will spend its utmost in watching to do you service."

He stood aside as if to make way for her to leave the pavilion. Without a look she passed him, walking at full speed through the trees. He attempted to attend her, but she waved him back with a cruel gesture.

He stood silent, pale, in the shade till she was out of sight, then followed at a distance to assure himself that she reached the Palace safely. Again he stood motionless until his watch pointed to the hour, when he turned and took his way to the tryst absorbed in thought.

There was a chatter and ripple of alarm over the sudden indisposition which had taken the Queen back to the Palace. Frightened looks were exchanged and two ladies in waiting set off at full speed to overtake her. Even the Comte d'Artois was alarmed, though he masked his fright with an innuendo or two which brought no smiles to the faces about him. There was thunder in the air and before long the group dispersed and melted quietly away, men and women whispering apart as they went, in a kind of consternation. That was the last of the famous *descampativos*. No one could give a reason, but they were ended.

As for the Queen, with winged feet she passed across the lawns scarcely knowing where she went and unconscious that the two women were in pursuit. Fortunately the Princesse de Lamballe was walking before the house, lost in sad reflection, when the sight incredible met her eyes of the Queen unattended, almost running, toward her, as if escaping from some horror. The Princess ran down the stone steps to meet her, fearing she knew not what.

"Madame — Madame, what is it? You are ill? You are frightened? Lean on me, I beseech you. Where are the ladies?"

"I will not stir one step," said the Queen, gasping for breath, and more strongly moved than Madame de Lamballe had ever seen her. "No — not one step, until I have implored your pardon and admitted the justice of every word you said today. You were right, and I have been most terribly and wickedly wrong. O that I had followed the example of Madame Elizabeth! Just now a man had the audacity to tell me — *me* — that I was wrong in being alone with him in the gardens. A man who should have knelt at my feet for the honour. It made me in my own eyes lower than the creature represented in those pamphlets. I felt I had deserved them. Forgive me. You were right to disobey a woman so unworthy. Take me back to Versailles. I should not be here."

The Princess weeping stooped and kissed her hand again and again. They stood side by side looking over the wide prospect steeped in sunshine for one sad moment.

"The revels of the Court are ended," said the Queen at last. They turned and slowly ascended the steps.

It was true. The revels were ended. The reaping of a bitter harvest sown by other hands now dust and ashes was begun. "The fathers have eaten sour grapes and the children's teeth are set on edge." She went in, clinging to Thérèse, pale as death, shocked by a fear to which she could give no name. The world was chill about her as with the coming of a cruel winter.

But after that Fersen was much in her thoughts. He came to Court as usual but seldom approached her. To other observers his manner was unchanged. To her it appeared there was a new tenderness as though he grieved to have inflicted a wound and as her anger subsided the feeling that she had sinned against some high truth strengthened her self-reproach. That also was a thing to brood over as the sky darkened. She would have given very much to undo what she had done, unsay her foolish cruel words. But that is beyond the power even of a queen.

Chapter XI

NIGHT in the gardens of Versailles, a night of mellow moon and heavenly stars lamping low over an earth of passionate loveliness. Night gliding soft-footed by the waters, stooping to mirror her jewels, as beautiful there as in midnight skies. Night drawing mysterious veils of shadow over lovers whispering beneath the rigid canopies of great cedars or in groves where scarcely a moonbeam pierces — the profound stillness broken only by a rustle, a muted murmur that makes the secrecy of the vast silence deeper.

A man stood in the grove of Venus, moonlight falling through the leaves upon his black domino, waiting — waiting. Down the long alley he caught glimpses of marble figures of divine beauty bathing in moonlight as in water — surely no night in Greece itself was ever more exquisite, more charged with subtle meanings that send the blood trembling through the pulses to crave the touch of hands fevered with desire, and the answering passion of lips beloved. The Cardinal, transfigured into youth again with all its joys and fears.

There was no one near him — he waited and longed. Could it be possible that she would come or was it nothing but a dream to dissolve in the grey breath of dawn? Jeanne de Lamotte-Valois had at last brought him a timid, most reluctant assent, but still an assent. He should see her for one exquisite moment and hear from her own mouth that he was forgiven, that he might hope — what? Ah, *that* she would not say — what messenger would dare to promise for the Queen? — and even at the last moment Jeanne had tried to dissuade him, almost indeed with tears.

"It is not for me to stand in the way, Highness, and indeed I am not certain that *she* would now consent to delay. She trembles like a young girl over the thought and anticipation. But still if you wrote to her wisely she might — she might consent to postpone the interview! Consider the fearful danger! I am no coward but indeed. I fear! I was in hope she was drawing back and becoming more prudent."

Her face was pale as she spoke and de Rohan noticed her hands trembled but nothing on earth would have stopped him with the fruition of all his hopes in sight. He laughed aloud.

"Are you mad? Would any man wait at the open door of heaven? No, my friend, I take my risks and bless you for the news you bring me."

And now at last he was here and waiting and any moment might bring her to his arms.

The fountains had ceased to play but his ears were full of their music. Were light footsteps brushing through the grass or was it the dropping of liquid crystal from the uprush of imprisoned waters? How could he tell whose own breathing deafened him? Or that brightness through the trees — was it the Queen-moon curving to her kiss of the happy Endymion or the flutter of a woman's white dress drawing nearer? No young lover could have trembled more passionately.

Could he speak if she came? What should he say?

"Madame, I have loved you ever since I saw you at Strasburg a little lovely Archduchess with a child's innocence of blue eyes and rosy lips."

And what would she answer? Draw herself up to her full height and freeze his hopes with those cold queenly looks he knew so well, or melt divinely into his arms — the dream at last come true? No — impossible! She would never come. Yet Jeanne de Lamotte — she the good angel who had brought him letter after letter in that precious writing — had left him only a little while ago saying gravely: "I fear she will come. She has promised. She owes you much for your devotion to her wishes. And perhaps — though I scarcely dare breathe it — there may be a dearer debt than this. She too suffers. Yes, I fear she will come."

And even yet the Prince de Rohan doubted, though in a case against his heart his fingers touched the letter of her promise. Again and again he touched it to reassure his fainting heart.

"It will kill me if she fails," he told himself, and for the moment believed it, for when ambition and desire — the two strongest passions of the world — unite their strength a man is thrust before them like a leaf on a gale.

Silence except for light movements in the grass and leaves. Nothings that made his heart throb until he laid his hand on a bough for support.

Hush! The grass is stirring as though at the coming of a light breeze in spring. It quivers — it trembles. The scent from a drift of violets breathes upon his lips — the boughs part softly. It is not moonlight — no — nor a shower of cherry blossoms — it is a woman's white dress. God! — if it were she!

He stood transfixed, still as a man of stone, for she came gliding nearer, nearer, looking fearfully about her, starting at the light noises of her own small feet. Should he have moved to welcome her? He had no power to stir.

She wore the flowing white dress of her hours of ease at Trianon. How well he knew it from the furtive glimpses he had from time to time. A soft whiteness of lace was folded across her lovely bosom, and she had the shepherdess's straw hat tilted forward a little to hide her face from the too prying myriad eyes of the stars.

But she came nearer, while he trembled with ecstasy. Even if she passed him by as she surely would still she had come for his sake. That was much — infinitely more than he had dared to hope.

She came along the little track in the grass, and now — so close that he could catch the fragrance of her hair. She was delaying, pausing — there was a queenly rose in her breast, languid with perfume. A white hand fluttered towards it — a nobly carried head bowed as with delicious shame. She lingered — she whispered — "You may hope — " What? — was that all? But enough surely. "You know what this rose means. You may hope that the past is forgotten!" And in earnest of that pledge the rose was detached from her bosom and dropped into his hand.

He woke from his trance of ecstasy — he put out beseeching hands. She curved towards him. There was a rush, a crash through the trees which in his ears sounded like a crash of doom.

It was Jeanne white with a passion of terror.

"Footsteps are coming this way. Monsieur and Madame d'Artois and others. Oh, my God, fly, fly! or all is lost!"

The white figure was gone, only the rose remained and Jeanne violent with fear dragging at his hand.

"Is she safe? We dare not let her go alone!" he gasped, trying to pull his hand away. But Lamotte would hear nothing.

"Silence, if you love your life and hers. Of course she's safe. It is we who are in danger. Come! Not a word! Come, I tell you!"

They fled behind the cedars along the grass to the nearest way out only stopping to breathe when they must, and reached at last a great gate where a carriage waited to take them back to Paris. A man was on the box, another at the door. Spent and breathless they were dragged up the steps and de Rohan fell back on the cushions in exhaustion. He was of neither an age nor figure to race even through the groves of Paradise for the sake of a vanishing lady.

"I couldn't do it again," he almost sobbed at last, "not if my life depended on it. It's a fearful strain on a man's heart. But we soon distanced the footsteps. As a matter of fact I never heard them."

"Thank heaven, I did — and saw them too or we should all have been on our way to the Bastille now. Didn't I tell you it was a fearful risk, and yet your courage would not let you refuse it. You are the bravest man I know. And, oh, my friend, how she must love you to have done what she did tonight! I will own now that I believed all the time her heart would fail at the last moment. Are you satisfied?"

"Satisfied? There is no word in any tongue of men to express my pride and joy. This rose! There was never a rose like it since Eden. But is she safe? You swear it? It seemed the act of a poltroon to leave her."

"Highness, yes. Her retreat was secured, but who could have foreseen that those fools would come that way! Oh, my friend, you must be doubly cautious now that she has risked so much. Put yourself in my hands — and hers, I beseech you."

He expended his recovered breath in protestations. What would he not do? She had but to command.

"This!" she answered, drawing a little gilt-edged missive from her bosom, warm from its nest beneath her laces. He kissed it — possibly for the sake of both ladies concerned and read it by the flickering carriage lamps. The Countess waited, expectant.

"I am to go down to Saverne for a while, and she meanwhile will be strengthening my position with the King, who has been very fixed against me. She does not despair of a ministry for me. Oh, madame — oh, Jeanne, for so I must call my best friend — if you had done no other good in the world you have raised a despairing man to the pinnacle of happiness! I see a golden future opening for you as well as for me. You will not find me ungrateful."

She pressed his hand kindly.

"There is much more to come. So have patience. I know how you will count the hours at Saverne, but all must give way to the thought of her safety. You feel that?"

"Unalterably," he said and began to babble of the great things he would do for Jeanne and her "excellent husband" when the reins of power were in his hands, and then fresh rejoicings over the Queen's condescension and so forth combined with the jolting of the carriage to put him into a sleep from which he never waked until it drew up at the door of the little house which the friendship of the Queen had provided for her beloved friend, doubtless with an eye to happy secret meetings there in the future. So indeed the Lamotte-Valois had said.

Nothing but a parting word of good wishes could be uttered, but the Cardinal waved his hand from the window until the horses rounded the corner. Jeanne ran upstairs like a deer to the *salon* of the little hired house where two men waited for her — her husband and de Villette.

Her husband was now a better-looking man that at the time of their marriage, with the air of a higher class than he really belonged to. Knocking about Versailles and Paris it had been an advantage to pick that trifle up amongst others, her help had not been wanted, and practice had given him an ease of manner in a bow and opening a door which went well enough with the pseudo-title of Count which had been his wife's wedding gift. There was no question of love in the affair; they had for each other the toleration and quick sense of co-operation of hounds on the same trail. Why be unfriendly when the one end was in view? Attained, the next move would be decided by the needs of the moment. Still, in spite of a very lightly worn bond, there were moments when Jeanne regretted that she had married before meeting de Villette. There could be no question which was the cleverer and more courageous of the two men. It was always Villette who was ahead, planning, suggesting, daring; the other following obediently but timidly. It was Villette's interest to second hers now, but supposing they did not coincide later? She knew he would throw her over as lightly as any other of the women he loved *par amours* and cared so little to conceal from her. Well, and what matter! She of all women had no sentiment in business. She had presented him with the oyster and was resolved that together they should make a juicy meal on it or she would know the reason why. She knew enough to hang the man over and over again.

"I knew you would be here first!" she said, breathing quickly from the stairs. "Your cabriolet must have done two miles to our one. Had you any *contretemps*?"

"Not one, we drove *ventre a terre* all the way. Essigny cried with terror until your husband consoled her."

"Call her Olisva for God's sake," interrupted Jeanne. "Why use a name known as that of a disrespectable woman?"

"Why give her a name which any adroit detective can spell out as the anagram of Valois, madame? Oh, the incurable romance of women! — and to make her a baroness too! The name should have been as insignificant as possible. Well — we all have our weak points. Was it successful? I could not see from my cedar."

"A magnificent — a glorious success!" said Jeanne in her low, thrilling voice. "I declare to you both I could have mistaken her for the other myself in the moonlight and shadows. She walked with a dignity! — but then she has a beautiful figure — exactly like the — the other's."

"And you raised the hue and cry exactly at the right moment?" This was her husband, quivering with excitement.

"Exactly. I suppose she ran straight off to you?" Villette chuckled.

"Naturally. And Lamotte supported her tenderly to the cabriolet. I followed discreetly out of ear-shot. She was terrified."

"You don't mean to say she suspected what she had been at?" asked Jeanne seriously startled and looking angrily at her husband.

"Bless you, my dear, no! She thought exactly what I told her when I engaged her to play the part. I know her intimately enough to answer for that. I told her it was to win a wager for a Court lady who wished to play a joke on a certain nobleman, and God knows there are jokes enough of the kind at Versailles to make it a very likely story. Besides, what else was it? No, what frightened her was the unexpected rush and scurry at the end, but it was much wiser to leave it like that, for she ran like a hare in good earnest. We set her down in the Palais-Royal just now with the money in her hand and as pleased with herself as could be. 'I wish I had another chance like that!' she said as she tripped off."

"She may," Jeanne said, drawing the chafing dish toward her which held the little savoury *plat* for their supper, and lighting the wick.

Villette interrupted her decisively.

"She may not, madame. Never again. I would not run that risk for twice the worth of — you know what. It had to be, and it is done. The thing now is for us all to leave Paris for a while. There must be no appearance of hurry. Boehmer can wait. De Rohan is longing to get through with the business and delay will make him keener. And Lamotte must get Olisva (if you will have that absurd name!) out of Paris for a while, lest she should babble to the other women of the Palais-Royal. Do you give him permission?"

"I? Certainly. My husband and I understand one another perfectly."

"Olisva and the country!" sighed Lamotte resignedly. "What a combination! And you, my wife, where will you go? For there I shall go too when I can be rid of Olisva that we may hatch our plans in peace."

She reflected a moment.

"I shall go to Bar-sur-Aube — my native place — and I shall do it in style, so that the people who despised me in my days of poverty may know there was something in Valois blood after all. And" — looking at her husband — "you can find someone to take Olisva off your hands later and carry her off to Marseille or the ends of the earth, and then come to Bar-sur-Aube and let us be respectable or perish!"

"Right — a thousand times right!" cried Villette, rubbing his hands. "This little Countess of ours what does she not know! I declare it is a delight to work with a woman so far above the weaknesses of them all. It is like working with a man gifted with a woman's finesse and intuition. Lamotte, you should be proud of your wife! Well, let us be off and when we return — Then for the last act of the comedy!"

"Heaven send it don't prove a tragedy!" sighed the Count de Lamotte with the disregard of grammar that his fastidious Countess could never quite amend. "There is still the signed agreement from the Queen to buy the necklace — that must be carried through, and every fresh scratch of Villette's pen terrifies me lest de Rohan should smell a rat."

"Take a glass of wine to warm up your courage, my friend, and come and share this delicious *salmis* your wife has ready for us. Madame, I kiss your hands and feet for your action tonight. It was supreme — superb!"

Two days later the Cardinal's friends known and unknown to him no longer blessed Paris with their presence. And he himself at Saverne was beating against the bars and thirsting for Paris once more — beloved Paris that was near the fairest, most beloved woman in all the world! When would she relax her fears and permit him that bliss once more? — he whose only prayer was to be there that he might serve her in this costly whim of hers for a thing not beautiful enough — beautiful as it was — to adorn her lovely bosom.

At last — at last came the gilt-edged missive in the writing before which his heart did obeisance. It came to Saverne borne carefully as such a treasure should be by her Majesty's own gentleman of attendance, Monsieur Leclaux, a not unpleasing looking man with a somewhat dissipated cast of face, but capable and adroit of speech and distinguished in an undress Court uniform though in a private carriage to avoid general notice. Naturally not being in the prime secret, he had nothing but ordinary Court news to bestow upon his Eminence, and appeared perhaps a little surprised at finding himself on such an errand though he hid it discreetly. Doubtless he might imagine that the sealed letter contained some mighty affair of state. But his news was good. Her Majesty had herself placed the letter in his hands, enjoining speed and caution. No, she had added nothing else, but looked extremely anxious and beautiful. She had not done him the honour to say whether she expected a reply.

This brave gentleman refreshed himself handsomely with rich wines and meats at the cost of the Cardinal while the latter retired to devour the letter in solitude. It was written in a strain of melancholy tenderness. The royal writer blamed herself for the hopes she had permitted when fate so evidently was pitted against their fulfilment. But such affection as his would pardon such a weakness, and if he would be happier in Paris let him return. Though they might not meet, still they breathed the same air, and that would be a consolation to her also in her prison of rank and etiquette — and more to the same effect, ending with a slight but unmistakable allusion to the treasure which she would never wear without believing that its thousand lights reflected his thousand delicacies of sentiment and affection.

Inexpressibly soothing and delicious were those words! What could he do less than pen a few ardent lines breathing adoration and devotion and assuring her of his immediate return. And scarcely was the letter confided to the powerfully refreshed Leclaux — so charged with wine that the Cardinal felt grave hesitation in entrusting his protestations to such vinous hands, than his Eminence in his great heavily rolling berline was hard on the track of the galloping horses of Leclaux.

The coast now clear and a perfect understanding established the first person he sent for on reaching the Hotel de Rohan was Boehmer, for the agreement proposed by the Queen had reached him from Jeanne.

To Boehmer languishing in suspense, tormented by the incessant reproaches of Bassauger, that message came like a breathing gospel of peace.

For, ushered into the library where the Cardinal sat in such majesty as was possible to him, the first words which broke on his enchanted ear were these:

"The time has come, monsieur, to make the final arrangements for the necklace on behalf of her Majesty the Queen — the name to be kept a secret of life and death between you and me. The price is to be what you decided. It is to be paid for in five equal instalments, the first is to be paid to you here at my house six months from the present day, the remaining instalments every three months until the purchase is completed. The payments will all be made through me. Here is the agreement which must be submitted for her Majesty's approval and signature. On receiving it, you will deliver the necklace to her Majesty's gentleman Monsieur Leclaux in my presence. If all this is agreeable to you we will sign it together now."

What could the overjoyed Boehmer do but bow and smile and smile and bow again in quickest iteration. Hope had hovered over him rainbow-winged for a considerable time, but this was the bright bird alighting on his hand, for of what worth is the word of a Prince, Cardinal, Grand Almoner of France and much more if it is less than perfect assurance? They signed it together, all was agreed, settled and delivered, and comforted by a glass of generous wine the King's Jeweller took his glad departure, leaving behind him a no less joyful Eminence.

For he too had had his trials. Beauty, especially highly placed beauty, must ever be capricious, is indeed expected and encouraged to be so as an added charm — the tiny thorns that guard the rose's sovereign sweetness.

And some of her letters as regards the diamonds began to be of the "she would and would not" type, enchanting but bewildering. Indeed in the latest one received on his arrival she had commanded that the agreement must be submitted to her before it became effectual, conveying a hint that at the last moment she might possibly change her royal mind in a matter of so little consequence — "a trifle like this" were her words. A trifle possibly to a royal beauty, but to the Cardinal and Boehmer very much the reverse. And what on earth was he to do with the agreement or how get it to Versailles without Jeanne, though time might be of the last importance? He quaked on reading the pretty careless words — natural and charming enough in her — and prayed with truly religious fervour that Jeanne's return to Paris might be sure and speedy.

Joy and relief unutterable awaited him. That faithful friend never failed. For Boehmer had scarcely turned his back on the Hotel de Rohan before a clatter of horses' feet was heard in the street outside, and in swam the Countess, brimming with gaiety and happiness, radiant in lips and cheeks with country bloom. Heavens! Was anything ever so opportune? The agreement was in her hand in a moment. She laughed like a trill of bells.

"But I will take it to Versailles, my friend! Would I have you kept one hour in suspense if it can be avoided? No. You know me too well. That is not the way friends serve each other. My husband is still at Bar-sur-Aube and I am a free woman. What is to hinder me from driving down now and returning to-morrow? Give me a glass of wine and I will go."

No need to express the Cardinal's gratitude and bliss. He gave the choicest wine in his cellar and the little green oysters in which the soul of Madame Jeanne delighted and a sweet-bread, a delicate *salmis*, and a perfect omelette and more, and gave it with an outpouring of soul that added sauce to it all. The meal was not allowed however to delay the start for Versailles beyond a reasonable time, and never could the enchanted man forget the vision of the little dark arch face and shining eyes as she nodded and beckoned from the carriage window to where he watched from his with the agreement in her pocket and a kiss blown from charmingly rouged lips.

He slept that night in dreams of bliss sunned by those eyes with their brilliant glances and had scarcely finished his luxurious *déjeuner* when their owner was again by his side.

"Rejoice, Highness! — it is a day of gladness. She received me with friendship — more — with sincere affection, and her first enquiry was for news of you. Never have I seen her look more beautiful — her cheeks flushed with an exquisite rose, her eyes shining like blue stars, her lips, but no, I halt there. I must not make delay too hard for so faithful a lover. All anxieties are over. Look what I bring!"

From the little silk satchel which had so often conveyed missives in the safe hiding place of her bosom she produced a paper he knew, unfolding it with the gayest triumph imaginable.

There stood his majestic signature and the respectable one of Monsieur Boehmer following. But along the edge were now written these magical words.

"*Bon, Marie Antoinette de France.*"

Not much, but enough to change the April hopes of the Cardinal into full-flushed summer and to make Boehmer sing his "Lord, now lettest thou thy servant depart in peace" with every certainty of comfort when he should see it.

The Cardinal rejoiced. He thanked, he blessed the unwearied friend. He sent a message to Boehmer appointing the day and the hour, and enforcing upon him the command that he was to announce the sale of the necklace out of France if any unjustifiable enquiries should arise. On his own head be it if he did otherwise, but if he followed these instructions there could be no reasonable fear.

And then, the busy Countess taking herself off to look into household matters after her long absence at Bar-sur-Aube, his Eminence set himself to dream of the happy day when he first should see the diamonds sparkling where only they should be, and receive from brighter eyes that look of intelligence, secret between them, which should assure him of the Queen's gratitude and that of the woman also — each to be repaid in kind.

For the Prince de Rohan knew, or believed he knew the sex. A woman who has given so much as the Queen tells herself that it is no longer worthwhile to cry halt. She had denied him as yet — true! But wise was the man who wrote, "He comes too near who comes to be denied." The Cardinal understood that axiom as well as another.

As to the position of Master of the King's Household, he regarded that as his already. She who had tasted the convenience of having the help of a man who regarded her needs and wishes as the first and only consideration would assure success the moment she spoke her mind to the King. And when would that be? It puzzled him immensely to imagine the means by which she would attain her end. But when did a woman ever fail whose heart prompted her brain, and she a queen? No, he had no doubts, no fears. All that was past. He awaited fruition in a summer calm of hope and joy.

Chapter XII

SUMPTUOUS was the little supper prepared a week later for a guest dear to the heart of the grateful Cardinal, his beloved Countess de Lamotte-Valois, for the night of fruition had come, and what viands the round world could furnish were royal enough to testify his profound respect and devotion to the architect of his fortunes? Not that it is to be supposed there was a gross profusion. No, his Eminence was a gourmet of the most finished, and Madame Jeanne, though her taste had not been cultivated from the cradle like his own, was not far behind in delicate appreciation of the work of one of the best cooks in Paris.

It was served in an inmost sanctuary of the Hotel de Rohan, a small dining room hung with priceless pictures of that famous House on panelled walls lit by girandoles which had been the property of Anne of Austria. There was a tapestry presenting the Enchantments of Circe, which both the Countess and the Cardinal might have studied to some advantage, and against the wall was the famous clock, in rococo set with carbuncles and turquoise, which had come from the Medici collection and was the envy and despair of all collectors. The napery, glass, and porcelain were all perfection and the chairs set for the guests suggested royalty in their time-dimmed magnificence. The room shone like a jewel in firelight with sombre lights and Blooms.

Guests — not one guest alone — for when Madame Jeanne fluttered in in rose-coloured brocade she was attended by a portly figure whose appearance caused first surprise and then delight to their host. It was the Grand Cophta who condescended to enhance the glories of this world with those of the invisible.

It may be truly said the condescension was his own for there had been an interview with the Countess earlier in the day in which his intention was made clear.

It was in her own little house in the Faubourg Saint Antoine that he unexpectedly made his appearance that morning as she sat in a charming *neglige*, running over accounts in a little book bound in blue satin and cornered with mother-of-pearl, too elegant, it would seem, for anything so prosaic as figures. Yet what could be too elegant for the record of a

Cardinal's charities as almoner for a queen? For some time past the Queen in her letters through Jeanne had condescended to invite the Cardinal's help in her pet charities — a most natural and gracious movement to which he had responded with overflowing generosity, and that book contained the list of his liberality.

Not stated of course under that heading but fairly exactly set down. It caused the Countess a thrill to see to what a figure it mounted. The hire of the house she sat in at that moment represented a substantial part of it and when was charity ever better applied? The *negligé* of white and rose which clothed her *svelte* little shape sprang from the same beneficent source, and the satin shoes with sparkling buckles should have had their noteworthy place in the mother-of-pearl volume and no small one. It was her most private record. Neither her husband nor Villette knew of the Queen's charities.

So engrossed was she that she heard and saw nothing until Finette tripped into the room preceding the Grand Cophta — now in the ordinary dress of a gentleman of the period. His bow was sublime — it combined the worldly and the other-worldly in perfect proportion. "Madame, your most humble servant. It is refreshing indeed to see a lady of such charm engaged in study when others are sipping their chocolate in bed. I — who can read through the covers of a book — see it is the abstruse subject of figures which engages you."

Jeanne blushed a little and hurriedly closed it. There was no doubt that the Grand Cophta could sometimes be extremely disconcerting.

"But that was not the object of my visit," he went on, settling comfortably into a chair, "and now we are alone I will come at once to the point. Since the evening when your niece and I were enabled to consult the higher Powers on your behalf and that of Monseigneur I have heard many times from him and only once from you — that once being a charming little note conveying fifty louis as an acknowledgment of my services. You slipped it gracefully into my hand; the seal was a kiss. I own myself charmed but not satisfied."

"Monsieur, that sum was what you stipulated!" said Jeanne firmly. She scented danger, and instantly recovered herself, springing to attention at the touch of steel on steel. "What you demanded I paid, and there it ended. Though as you know I am always at your service if I can aid your plans for the good of humanity."

"At an end, madame? Have the goodness to remember you did not mention the importance of the interests involved. And did you think a mind like mine incapable of following up the clues given in the answers you dictated to me? Who was 'the woman honoured as she deserves by the greatest'? Whose was 'the gratitude of a great lady'? Could it have been that of Madame de Boulanvilliers who gave you your start in life? Ah, no! I know better."

Jeanne had grown a little paler and more intent but said nothing. Let the enemy show his cards!

"And 'the deed of courage and self-sacrifice' which was to bring fame and honour to Monseigneur? Did you think, madame, that he who gives me all his confidence, whose counsellor I am almost daily in the secret ciphers which pass between us would withhold his confidence from me? You were mistaken. He has told me all his hopes and fears and there has not been a moment when I could not have swept your cobweb to destruction."

It was a dangerously bold lie but the bid was successful. She knew the Archcheat's influence with de Rohan — who did not? — and believed him. She sat like a statue, but her mind was a confusion of whirring and revolving wheels of thought. She should have foreseen — should not have believed a word of de Rohan's protestations of secrecy! Had he told all? How much, how little? The meeting at Versailles? Did Cagliostro know her own position with regard to the Queen? Villette? She looked at him so steadily however that even he could not discern what line her thoughts were likely to take.

"What exactly do you know, monsieur?" she asked at last, with little hope of hearing the truth — unless indeed it paid him to be frank. "There is no use in fencing with intellect like yours."

"I think not, madame," he said with a superior smile. "I know all that the Cardinal knows and a little more, retrieved by my own assiduity. Your standing at Court, for instance. And I may mention that among the pretty women who have sought my aid for their complexions and figures, Mademoiselle Essigny was one. Ladies are apt to be confidential with those who aid them in matters of so much importance."

"*There* I certainly have no fears," answered Jeanne, with pale smiling lips. "She took part in a midnight frolic once with a party to which I belonged but naturally I don't associate with such women."

"Naturally, but knowledge like mine readily forms a mosaic of broken bits of glass and I think I can connect the frolic in which Mademoiselle Essigny took part with other matters. But no matter. Let us drop this fencing, madame, which wastes valuable time. You sup this evening with Monseigneur and have had a secret with him unknown to me. You have poached on my preserves and have been an efficient bloodsucker of money which would otherwise have flowed in my direction. The scandal will possibly ruin him. One of my most valuable sources of income will be dried up."

He struck swiftly again in another direction.

"Suppose I were to mention Mademoiselle Essigny to Monseigneur? I am perfectly candid with you. It is not my intention to have him involved in a scandal which will ruin him. That is, not unless I see my own advantage in it clearly."

His voice had become harsh and menacing. Greed and cruel determination moulded every line of his face. It was an astonishing instance of self-possession that she still met him with a fearless face though her heart within her was quaking. What would Villette, what would her husband say?

"Monsieur, I see I have been wrong. But believe me I did not realize how close the relations were between you and Monseigneur nor did I think that a man of your riches had needs as importunate as mine. If I had known that I should have acted differently. Forgive me. Let us be frank. It can be to the interest of neither to ruin the other, and believe me the matter of the necklace has now gone so far that the least dissension, the least slip will give everyone connected with it to ruin, the Cardinal among them. And remembering that aid you kindly gave me and the fifty louis I paid for it, I should be under the painful necessity of naming you as an accomplice."

For the moment he was nonplussed though he did not show it. That quick strike with the cat's claws took him by surprise and wrested a kind of unwilling admiration from him. Besides she was right — It might be highly unpleasant for him to find himself involved in any shady political intrigue of de Rohan's and land himself in the Bastille beside him and nothing gained. It would have taken higher credit than either Jeanne's or the Cardinal's to make an astute observer like Cagliostro believe that there was any hope of de Rohan's forgiveness at Court. The Prince had been too frank with him in the past to leave any illusions in his mind on that score.

But suddenly a new light blazed into his brain. The necklace? What could the woman mean? The necklace — Paris had chattered freely enough of Boehmer's masterpiece and it was known he had submitted it to the King and Queen and that it had been rejected. What if Jeanne were on quite another trail than the political one? What if there were money — diamonds — wealth? He was silent a moment, then cast on another scent: "Boehmer's diamonds! Well, I have heard Monseigneur's story. Had I not better hear yours?"

It was enough. The fish had swallowed his bait. If she had doubted the last doubt was gone. He would ruin her as carelessly as he would crush a fly if she could not make it worth his while to spare her. But it was clear that de Rohan could only tell him what he knew himself and therefore she would tell no more. Nothing should wring it from her.

Pulling herself together with a ghastly effort she told her tale with such arts of confidence as she could muster. The Queen must have the necklace. The Cardinal had guaranteed the payments. His reward would be restored Court favour and all it implied. And with lips that trembled through her smile she ended: "And when he is supreme with the Queen as he will be you can make your own terms with both. I shall not object, I assure you, my friend."

He looked at her dangerously.

"A very pretty story, madame, worthy of any woman. But how does Mademoiselle Essigny come in? And how do you explain the result of my enquiries as to your standing at Court? I heard of much — many useful little matters, but nothing of any acquaintance with the Queen."

"That is not known," she said white as death. "It was essential that it should be secret. That is obvious. As to Essigny — it was a frolic. Nothing more."

He took a moment to reflect, then suddenly dropped the mask and lunged like a swordsman.

"I have heard the lie — now for the truth. You are after the necklace, and fool as the Cardinal is he is no thief! Take ten minutes to reflect. Then —"

"Then what?"

"I go straight to the Cardinal and give him my version of the story. He will bless his deliverer. The game is played, madame. Checkmate!"

He took out his watch.

She knew it was checkmate but did not yet know with what a magnificent bit of bluff he had beaten her. For a moment she sat irresolute. It was part of her extraordinary courage and resource that she would never acknowledge herself beaten and in less than the ten minutes her mind, working like lightning, was made up. She had no choice. A man like Cagliostro might even be a valuable ally and any day they might need unforeseen help. In her own swift way she doubled on her tracks.

"You have beaten me, but I can say honestly it may be for the best. You have more brains than I and this business wants brains of the best."

"I am glad you acknowledge it, madame," he said with his false leer and bow.

She continued unmoved: "And I may need them. This may be really for the best, for the matter is most secret and dangerous. Sit close to me — I must whisper."

He was satisfied now that he had the clue and it was not worth her while to deceive him further, but his look pierced her very soul while she whispered her story concealing and neglecting nothing now that it was merely a question for him of which side would pay him best. Sitting stiffly back at last in her chair she looked at him as coolly as if she had been a free agent and he at her with unfeigned admiration.

"A wonderful plot!" he said slowly. "Wonderful indeed! I do homage, madame, to your genius, and I say — I, Cagliostro — that I should not have been ashamed had it originated in my own brain. *Mine*! I cannot state my admiration more highly. It is my deliberate opinion that together you and I might conquer the world. Were you only concerned in the matter —"

She interrupted, hope rekindling in her eyes.

"My husband and Villette are nothing. You and I can do what we will with them."

He scarcely heard her, continuing as if she had not spoken: "I know the value of the necklace. That has been common talk. It is better for us to sign a pact. What are your wishes?"

He fixed her with that peculiar steely light in his eyes which gave them such dangerous magnetic power when he chose to employ it, and suddenly, with the relief, her courage seemed to crack within her. For a moment her brain reeled. She felt like a bird trembling into the open jaws of the snake. Giddiness took her and she swayed forward in her chair. What recovered her — what breath of fortitude swept cool and bracing across her soul? She never could tell, but in a moment it seemed that he released her. She was strong again — a duellist, warily measuring her rapier against the other.

"I will concede whatever you ask," she said firmly, "because I must. I will not play at any other reason. State your terms."

"The half of the proceeds of the necklace. And that will be little enough to reimburse me for Monseigneur's injured fortunes. You are a brave woman, and I honour courage or my terms would have been higher. Sign this paper and all will be well. And tonight I will sup with you at the Hotel de Rohan and support you in all you say and do. I never fail my friends."

He took her pen from the little gilded and tortoise-shell bureau and wrote a few brief words on a sheet of her own paper.

She looked through it with care and said coldly: "No compliments, monsieur; I sign because I must, but my agreement shall he faithfully kept. What is your motive in *espionage* tonight?"

"To see the necklace which I have not seen. To be in a position to recognize your accomplice whom I do not know. You see I am frank. I will be your friend if you will permit me. And a powerful one."

She reflected a moment and said: "I accept that. I will trust you. Call for me tonight in your carriage. And now, lay aside enmity and if there is any point in which you can advise me I beg your advice. I have done very wrong to neglect you so long, monsieur, you who pull the strings of half Paris. It was a mistake in strategy."

"Sign, madame, and I am at your service."

She signed and he took the paper, folded it and put it in his pocket, then smiled at her almost with gaiety.

"And now, madame, I must offer my little secret, for friends must have no concealments. Monseigneur has not revealed your charming little mystery. He longed to tell me, in fact came so near a confidence several times that it naturally set my wits to work with the result you know. May

I beg you to remember in future that it is safer to trust than to mislead Cagliostro?"

If the pen had been a stiletto she could have driven it into his heart as she realized his triumph and her own folly. But her husband and Villette should settle that score for her later. She had never been so dangerous as when returning his smile she took his hand and pressed it gently between hers.

"Ah, Monsieur le Comte, what chance has a poor little woman against wits like yours? Spare me! Don't make me feel more humiliated than I do at my own failure in common sense, and advise me, you who know everything. I hail your victory! Do you see any dropped stitches in my work? Criticize freely."

That took him on his weak side — his vanity, and he laughed and purred like a great cat. Yes — yes, he would advise. The first thing was that she should let Monseigneur know that circumstances had forced her to confide in the Grand Cophta. Nothing would please him better; Cagliostro could be certain that he would rejoice in his counsel.

The talk then took a friendly turn, he advising her to get the woman Olisva safely out of Paris and down to Marseille lest any of her irresponsible chatter should do harm. True, she did not in the least know for what she had been employed — Cagliostro could answer for that — but still things leaked out and if by any chance it reached the Cardinal — No, she must be got off to Marseille. She did not mention that it was already done.

"A dangerous gossiping woman," he said. He enquired how the necklace would be disposed of, and Jeanne informed him that in spite of her pleading to the contrary her husband and Villette proposed to take it apart in Paris ("Which will be a work of considerable time," she added) and then disperse it and go off to sell the stones in London and Amsterdam.

"Therefore you will have plenty of time to make your arrangement with them," she ended, and with so perfect a mixture of truth and falsehood that even Cagliostro was deceived.

Still, below the smooth surface was the wariness of two wild animals in the jungle. Not a glimpse, not a grain of confidence from either: cold feline amenities — the glove with a dagger behind it.

He left with a bow and a kiss on her pretty hand which deceived neither her nor himself and after the door shut she stood fixed with a knot of bitter thought between her brows, her mouth a hard thin line belying the smiling curves of her lips, staring at the wall too absorbed even to think of her defeat. It was the future which concerned her. If Cagliostro had seen her in that moment he would have valued his life at considerably less than the half-value of the necklace. Next to that her chief thought was gladness that his blow had been delayed. The fool! It would be easy now. Slowly relaxing, she took her pen and wrote to the Cardinal:

Highness, when I come tonight I shall bring with me the Grand Cophta to whom I have judged it absolutely necessary to reveal our charming little mystery that we may have the inestimable value of his advice. You, who know it more precious than gold, will not reproach me. Already he has seen a future beyond my imaginings and we walk in security. Always your devoted J.

That would reveal nothing if it should go astray. She despatched it and sat down once more to sombre thought.

PART III

Chapter XIII

BUT when they entered the supper-room of Monseigneur, who so glad and gay as the butterfly of a modish little Countess in rose silk with puffs and panniers and lace ruffles disclosing arms rounded to perfection. Dark hair tossed to a most distinguished height above her brow and powdered as a background for roses and plumes. She wore a wonderful Chinese ornament in the front of her stiff bodice of rosy cornelian cherries dropping from a twig of green jade leaves and had the wit to perceive its exotic beauty. Her white hands were heavy with rings and the ivory of her naturally pale complexion was brilliantly lit up with rouge on lips and cheeks. Had not the heart of his Eminence been pre-occupied — That thought also occurred to Cagliostro whom nothing escaped. The very essence of his trade was observation. They had supped to repletion and soft wax lights were lit in the royal girandoles when Cagliostro said suddenly: "Madame, I know well that it can give nothing but pleasure to Monseigneur to hear that his friends are one in heart and that I possess your full confidence. Tell him that you also have sought my counsel and I have aided you."

"I have told Monseigneur," she said smiling brightly, "for I now perceive what has been the guiding star in my own mind through so many difficulties. Indeed, Highness, there was nothing to tell for nothing could really be hidden from the Master of Wisdom. I had but to connect the story. Never again shall I move without the Grand Cophta."

Louis de Rohan was enchanted. The whole time he had longed for Cagliostro's supernatural support and wisdom and Jeanne's submission was the last touch in her conquest. Joy rose in a full tide within him. He clapped his hands together.

"If I could but know that the lady of my heart also approved, my cup would brim! Ah, my great friend, the day may yet come when I sit at the helm of State inspired by your wisdom and then she too may seek inspiration from those lips which never fail in truth or wisdom."

"For the sake of France may it be so!" echoed Jeanne devoutly.

The Grand Cophta leaned back in his velvet chair. It seemed that a strange somnolence was stealing over him. His eyes were closing, the light dying out behind heavy lids. A voice unlike his own — dull, remote, charged with mystery hovered on his lips, and very singular was the effect in that sumptuous room with the two waiting, listening figures held in suspense before him.

"The love of a queen! I look into the past and see in the stately chambers of the Tuileries a royal woman beautiful exceedingly, strong to rule the state in spite of the *Salique* Law that sets her in the background. The great Cardinal Mazarin approaches. It is in his arms and from his lips she has learnt statecraft. Love and wisdom united sit on the throne of France. Oh, the greatness of the cardinals who have ruled France — Richelieu, Mazarin! I see a third added, a name written in stars across the firmament of fame. Eternally splendid and more illustrious than any of his predecessors. Not that of the weak King who crawls at his wife's footstool, but a man to rule both Queen and Kingdom — the greatest of the cardinals — Louis de Rohan! I see Love the happy ruler of Versailles and the Tuileries and a queen's heart at rest."

His voice died away as if in dream, while the Prince, enraptured, stared at his transfigured face. The power of conviction was certainly Cagliostro's and he used it to the full at that moment.

The minutes drifted by in silence. Gradually he stirred and raised himself in his chair to look at the Cardinal's beatified eyes beaming on his.

"I have dreamed. Forgive me. I am ignorant of what I said and —"

A lacquey at the door, a sonorous announcement.

"Monsieur Boehmer," and dreams fled to their appointed place as the King's Jeweller entered, his florid blond face radiant with delight. He was dressed as for a ceremony and indeed felt it to be no less. The Cardinal rose with a certain solemnity.

"I present you, Monsieur Boehmer, to the greatest man of the age — the Count Cagliostro. He, who is in my confidence, has deigned, as has Madame de Lamotte-Valois to be present at the handing over of your magnificent work of art to her Majesty's gentleman. Permit the Count to view it. Madame has already seen it, I believe."

Bowing profoundly, Boehmer opened the case. He had heard all the fairy tales which circulated in Paris of the Count's magnificence and power and was deeply impressed. Here indeed was a possible customer to be conciliated. He lifted the jewels from their bed of satin and with an obsequious air advanced to Jeanne: "Permit me, madame," he said and fastened them about her neck. "Nowhere but in one place can they be seen to better advantage!" he added elegantly and stepped back to admire.

She stood opposite a long mirror and her own eyes were dazzled by the myriad splendours that darted tongues of fire about her. Magnificent as an Indian idol robed in jewels she stood before them and as intoxication seized her for a moment she felt the necklace was her own — never again to be parted from her. The sumptuous figure shone on the background of the rich dimness of the room with gleaming points of light caught on its gilded chairs and the glow of jewels in the encrusted clock. But all lent their tribute to the necklace — all light was concentrated there and as she breathed, her bosom billowing the rows and tassels and pendants, it shot vivid angry unnamable splinters of light about the air and dazzled the watchers.

As she stood almost in ecstasy there was a step — a knock, a hastily vanishing lacquey behind a closed door and a man with the grave discreet demeanour of those who attend the great entering with dignity.

"*De par la Reine!*" It is Monsieur Leclaux known to the Cardinal on a former occasion as the messenger of bliss and now more welcome than ever.

The Countess hastily disengaged the necklace. It was unseemly that any subject should be wearing the Queen's property.

"I blush and apologize!" she said humbly, placing it in Boehmer's hands. With a solemnity which reflected itself on the others the room became still as death as the jeweller replaced it in the beautiful case and laid it in the hands of the Cardinal. He stepped forward with the majesty of a Rohan and a prince of the Church.

"Monsieur Leclaux, I have the honour to place in your keeping the diamond necklace which her Majesty has done Monsieur Boehmer the favour to purchase from him. It is the hope of her humble servants in this room, headed by myself, that for many happy days to come it may worthily adorn the most beautiful and gracious of queens."

"Monseigneur, I will do myself the pleasure to represent your words to her Majesty and I thank you for the trust reposed in me. Madame, Messieurs!" — and at each word a bow nearing the door. At the door a final and inclusive one. It opened, closed; the retreating footsteps of Monsieur and the lacquey on duty outside were heard.

The necklace was gone from among them. Boehmer stood radiant, his face transfigured with joy.

"And I may tell you now, my good Boehmer," said the Cardinal overflowing with graciousness, "that I myself — myself — have seen her Majesty and that she expressed her full approval of the transaction."

Indeed it overwhelmed the man. He bowed, rubbed his hands, would have kissed the little feet of Jeanne if he had had a chance. It was with difficulty indeed that he got himself away from the splendid company of his benefactors. And then with laughter and joy the three congratulated themselves on an immense triumph.

That night when she returned to her house only her husband was waiting for her.

"Villette played his part splendidly!" she said, panting a little after the excitement. "It was a wonderful sight. I never was afraid for a moment."

"He's making for the frontier now as fast as horses can carry him. And I shall be off in an hour. We meet at Amsterdam. Don't you lose a moment either if you value your life. Get off to London tomorrow morning." She shrugged her shoulders in high disdain.

"You coward! I may bleed the Cardinal a bit if I stay on. The first payment isn't due for six months and everything will be quiet until then. But you may as well know there's a cloud in the blue which is no fault of mine; sheer bad luck!"

She told him hurriedly of Cagliostro's move and he simply laughed aloud. He would be a clever fellow indeed if he could get a single sparkler of it now. Let him whistle for it.

"I know," she said, "but he's damned clever. The miracle is that he delayed to strike. Leave a diamond with me for him or there'll be trouble. No — You don't suppose I believe you let Villette make off with the whole? I know you better. I'll keep him in good humour and when it all explodes I'll write from London and accuse him. Did the old humbug think he could cheat *me*! Lucky if we spare his life!"

Lamotte looked at her as he grudgingly unfolded one diamond from the rouleau in his pocket — a small one, but of the best.

"Damn him!" he said, and added, "Give us a kiss, old girl. I never saw you look so handsome. And you have done wonders. Made all our fortunes! Don't be a fool and take any useless risks. Now, I'm off."

He kissed her on the cheek and was gone.

The necklace no longer existed. Never again would it grace the neck of queen or courtesan. The two had hacked and twisted the stones from their choicest settings and a huddle of brilliance in four rouleaux disposed about their persons was all that remained of the Queen's necklace.

Six months. Had she underestimated Cagliostro? At all events that diamond never reached him though the most brilliant promises did so. Greek met Greek to some purpose in the little house in the Faubourg Saint Antoine.

He called on her next day greedy to hear what had been the fate of the necklace. She told him with what appeared to be simple truth that they had been obliged to decide hurriedly that no delay was safe and it must be taken apart at Amsterdam whence she would have full details to give him; that her husband and Villette had been bitterly disappointed by his claim but recognizing the immense services which he could do them in his unique position had agreed to the division, and that the full accounts would be sent through her as the diamonds were sold.

"You are aware, monsieur, that that must be a gradual business. It would awaken the suspicion of Boehmer and everyone else if we flooded the market with diamonds, and such jewels as they are. And I am to tell you that we have ascertained that Madame de Souza, who has magnificent jewels, is one of your most devoted clients and to ask you whether you would consider a partnership there. In which case I who am on the spot could perhaps represent my friends. My husband says her rubies would be worth a fortune in London and he could easily dispose of them with the diamonds."

Cagliostro reflected. "Your proposal, madame, merits consideration and when the time draws near for my leaving Paris may develop. At present, it is impossible. But I regard the suggestion as evidence of comradeship which shall not be forgotten. I have the honour to wish you a good evening. You will inform me when there is news."

"Indeed, yes, monsieur, and without a moment's loss of time. You, in return will keep me informed of any undercurrent of events which may affect us?"

It was agreed and they parted in as much mutual distrust as two human hearts could hold without bursting. Yet for the moment she could plume herself on having worsted the Grand Cophta — an achievement few indeed could boast of.

Chapter XIV

Six months later Madame Campan returning from a visit to Paris, entered the Queen's boudoir with so light a step that her Majesty noticed it and asked for an explanation with the weariness that darkened her as the clouds darkened over France.

"Good news would be welcome, my kind Campan," she said sighing. "Nothing but evil reports and terrors come our way now. In the distance the muttering of storm, and all the pleasant days done. Autumn in the air and the coming of winter. But what have you to tell me?"

"Only a little thing, Madame, but it will please your generous heart. I met Boehmer near the Rue de l'Enfer, and lie was walking so brightly and briskly that I stopped the carriage to speak to him. 'And what of the necklace?' said I. For I never see him without thinking of that. And his whole face was an illumination. 'Sold, madame, sold long ago!' he said. 'And how?' 'Why, to the Sultan of Turkey for his first Sultana!' Did your Majesty ever hear anything so surprising? But I congratulated him warmly."

"Yes, I am glad," said the Queen with another sigh. "He was in great trouble about it. It is news to me that the Sultan buys his diamonds in Paris, but Boehmer was lucky to find any purchaser. There will not be much traffic in diamonds in France for the next few years, I fear. If you see him again tell him I congratulate him. And now help me to prepare for Mass."

It was the day of the Queen's public passage through the long gallery of the Palace at Versailles and by the famous hall of the OEil-de-Boeuf to Mass, and there it was the custom for the crowd of well-dressed people to assemble and see her go by in all the pride of loveliness and royalty. It seemed to the Cardinal that though attendance at Court was forbidden to him it could do no harm if amidst a mob of onlookers he dared to feast his eyes on his liege lady. There might — there *must* be some look of secret intelligence which he only could detect in those bright world-compelling eyes. And he needed assurance. The time for the first payment drew near, and though she could never fail in her queenly word and he had no anxiety on that score, another trouble darkened his sky. Long before this he had hoped to see the overthrow of his enemy de Breteuil from his post as minister. That at least he might hope as paving the way for his own elevation. But no. There sat the Baron de Breteuil still impassive, and the Queen delayed. It is true there still occasionally came those precious letters on gilt-edged paper, but seldom and somewhat changed in tone. He must believe she was sad, depressed at the cruel obstacles which lie between them. That was the Countess's explanation — and what other could there be?

He consulted her eagerly as to his proposed waiting in the OEil-de-Boeuf. Would her Majesty approve? The kind Madame Jeanne promised to ask, telling him for the twentieth time how in secret the necklace is worshipped, hung about the royal neck, gloated over by daylight, lamplight, any new effect to set off its myriad radiances. The heart of Marie Antoinette would be hard indeed if it did not open to the man who had put it in her hand. And as to any anxiety absurd! The Queen is in the hollow of his hand. Does he not hold her signature to the agreement for the necklace? Is not the rose warm at this moment in his breast? What more can the most timid and suspicious man in the world wish? A queen has very different risks to face from those of an ordinary woman. On her hang King and Kingdom and the future of her children. What good could it do the Cardinal if she plunged to ruin dragging him with her?

"For heaven's sake do not tempt her too strongly by your unhappiness, for she is a most unusual woman in the strength of her affections. I can picture her casting all away for a lover. Be wise for her. You are neither timid nor suspicious, my friend, but the bravest, most romantic Paladin in all the world. Ah, if you did but know her royal heart as I know it! and her passionate recognition of this! Wait. Your good time is at hand! As to waiting in the mil-de-Boeuf that you may safely do, and I have her promise that she will distinguish you with a smile and bow into which you are to read all she dares not say."

Therefore behold Prince Louis de Rohan full of palpitating hope, stationed among the crowd in the OEil-de-Boeuf to see the procession of the royal beauty!

Heavens, what loveliness! He itemized her charms after, but could not at the moment for watching the motion of her eyes. She was full-hooped, magnificent in a rich shimmer of gold brocaded in silver billowing sumptuous about her. From this widespread pomp rose the slender grace of her waist, and the glorious shoulders. Milk-white in the setting of gold. Her complexion had the Teutonic cream and rose in fullest perfection melting into the carnation of the sweetest lips ever seen and the sweeter to pride like de Rohan's because it was impossible to look at the budding lower lip — and forget the royal House of Hapsburg from which she came. That was its sign and seal of race — the Hapsburg lip. What centuries of pride and worship had shaped its velvet fullness! But her eyes — her eyes! Would she look at him? His heart choked in his throat.

Yes, by the grace of God! She wreathed her head, turning slightly with her own ineffable grace, and bowing, smiled a little as she passed on, leaving a violet-scented air behind her troubled like water-eddies after the passage of a stately ship.

Released, his heart raced, and he leaned against the wall to recover, his eyes filled as with sun-dazzle by the image of her beauty. He had a little forgotten its poignant edge. Her hair — that exquisite ashen blonde. There had been great pearls twisted in it and faintly coloured roses, and he could remember row after row of pearls lost in the warmer white of her breast. How beautiful — how beautiful! The Countess pulled gently at his sleeve.

"We must go, my friend. You dream. She made a sign, did she not?"

He could only bow his head in speechless delight. Yet if not so utterly dazzled and bewildered, he might have reflected that passing queens make a ritual of bright cold smiles to waiting crowds as of a remote moon smiling from highest heaven on tossing waves that catch the radiance a moment and presently are dark. He would not have believed it had he heard the truth that she never even guessed at his presence.

There were frequent suppers at this time at the Hotel de Rohan — brilliant little gatherings at which Jeanne de Lamotte sparkled enchantingly, whispering hope always in the Cardinal's sometimes desponding ear and receiving in return gifts which made it well worth her while to linger in France. The Queen's charities were also, it seemed, increasing. Certainly queens should be charitable and the Cardinal financed her Majesty lavishly as became the Grand Almoner of France. Lamotte wrote pressing her to show a clean pair of heels while she could but after all it was she who moved the springs — who so well as she could decide when the moment had arrived for England? The news from her husband there and from Villette at Amsterdam and later Geneva was excellent. No troublesome enquiries had been made, and from one jeweller in Bond Street alone Lamotte had taken ten thousand pounds. Money would not be wanting when the time came for her retreat.

And there were other reasons. Paris had its charms. Exile from Paris to a Parisienne is exile indeed, and she was knitting other bonds which might be useful in stormy days to come. Not only so, but she feared the Queen's anger less every day. When the inevitable should come what could the royal wrath do? The feeling against "the Austrian" as they called her in Paris was terrible. Vile stories of her doings were daily circulated and did not lack the Lamotte's speeding tongue. Nothing was too gross for belief. Vices which would have disgraced a Messalina were attributed to a woman whose pride alone would have kept her pure. And every suffering of poverty, of taxation, of bad harvests were attributed to the wasteful extravagance of the Queen whose yearly expenses would not have covered a month of the du Barry or Pompadour. The prevailing tone was this, "The King is a good king enough but the slave of the Austrian. Down with the Austrian! Bundle her back to Vienna!" Had it not been that the noble families were ranged on her side the outlook was frightful. De Fersen knowing less than half what the sewer-rat Cagliostro knew at times felt his heart sink within him.

No — Jeanne de Lamotte assured herself daily that she could probably strike the Queen harder than the Queen could strike her when they were face to face. And for their own sakes the Royalties would never dare to expose the Cardinal, for the de Rohans with their allies the Condes and others of the great clans of France were too powerful to be disgraced — the Cardinal of all men — with the power of the Church behind him!

And there was another reason for lingering — Cagliostro! For the present he must be kept in good temper, but very soon she would not fear even the Grand Cophta's revelations. With her powers she might well hope to see him in the dust. But she bought a handsome snuff box set with diamonds with a slice of the Queen's charity money from de Rohan and presented it to him as an earnest. She showed him accounts of the sale of the diamonds with his share allotted, hidden away safely in London, a share calculated to make the austerest mouth water and increasing daily, and they met on the pleasantest terms in the world at the Hotel de Rohan and one or two choice little suppers at her own house where the charming hostess's health was drunk in the Cardinal's best wines.

If there were even a moment when she hesitated and doubted whether it were not time to spread her wings for the North, letters from her husband pointed out the necessity of keeping everything quiet in Paris and attracting no notice until the last moment. As a matter of fact he was enjoying himself so much alone that he suffered no particular anxiety on her score.

But in the midst of all this weaving of cross-threads, the 30th of July approached, the day in which by her agreement the Queen must make the first payment for the necklace. And still no letter came clearly denoting her readiness to pay! De Rohan could not, would not, doubt, though in a matter of such terrible consequence even a royal beauty might be supposed to see there was a necessity to consider other things than her own convenience. He found himself wishing often that business could be combined with Majesty.

On the 19th of July hope however showed a momentarily smiling face. The friendly Countess arrived that evening at supper-time diffusing rays of joy about her and with a letter — A letter with money in it, but how much she did not know. The Queen had presented it with a smile, saying, "Take this to Monseigneur. It will please him."

"Give it to me here this moment, madame," cried the Cardinal. "Much more of this anxiety would make an old man of me. I live in a perpetual suspense, and were it not for the support of the Grand Cophta and your own there are days when I should be tempted to throw up the whole thing and retreat to Saverne."

He tore the letter open but not with a lover's passion — far otherwise indeed — and read it hastily, his brows black with storm.

"My God — She sends the interest of the money — some eighteen hundred livres and declares that it is not convenient to pay the principal at present. What am I to do with Boehmer? Fool, fool, that I was to trust myself in the hands of a woman! I have no money to pay him and would not if I could. Go back and tell her that she must and shall keep to her written word."

The Countess interposed mildly.

"My friend, have I not dared everything for you, and can you doubt that she will eventually pay? The Queen of France can command a larger sum than the worth of a necklace! It is only a question of delay. Send for Boehmer here — now, and let us discuss the matter with him. I will never desert you, and the matter is as sure as tomorrow's dawn."

Frantic with anxiety he could only take her advice and despatch a carriage for Boehmer, who came palpitating joy and hope. The Queen was better than her word as became a royal lady. The payment would be made on the 19th instead of the 30th. That was his happy certainty. Ushered into the library he found the Prince and the Countess seated with grave business faces instead of the warm congratulatory aspect he had expected. The Prince motioned to a chair.

"Be seated, monsieur. I have had a gracimis letter from her Majesty in which she encloses —"

Oh, how the eyes of Boehmer sparkled! What rays of delight they shot about them!

"Encloses the interest of her debt for the first payment due on the 30th July."

"The interest, Monseigneur! But —"

"She states that it is not at the moment convenient to pay the principal. But of course —"

Boehmer was on his feet, grasping the back of his chair, white with alarm.

"Monseigneur, I regret the necessity, but you will have the goodness to represent to her Majesty that the interest is useless to me. I cannot accept it. Does she forget that I have payments to make for those diamonds? I told her so when I discussed it with her and she refused to purchase. No, Monseigneur, it is impossible — I decline — I object — I —" He was stammering with fear and rage. Jeanne interposed deftly.

"You cannot, monsieur, doubt the word of your Queen and —"

"Madame, the Queen is the Queen but business is business. I have had trouble enough over this necklace to drive a man to suicide, which indeed I have threatened more than once."

He was really a pitiable sight. His florid blondness was livid, his hands, grasping the chair, shook in spite of their hold. The sudden jerk from security to misery was torturing every nerve. The Cardinal's anger and alarm grew with each word. He sat staring speechless, his mouth gaping, eyes fixed. Jeanne again interposed, dulcet, soothing.

"Is it ever wise to refuse money, monsieur? Is this interest a sum to throw into the Seine?"

"By no means, madame. But you are aware of my position. And if I must say it, the Queen's word was guaranteed by Monseigneur."

"My good man, I have no money to play pitch and toss with. All the world knows that!" the Cardinal ejaculated, trying to collect himself. "But for heaven's sake compose yourself. All is not lost because of a delay. Pocket the money on what terms you will, but pocket it, and give me an acknowledgment and Madame de Lamotte shall awaken the Queen to a stronger sense of business obligation. After all, women are like that, and a spoilt beauty perhaps more than another. We need not talk as if the sky were falling because a woman is a woman though I own it shall be my last dealing with one on these terms. Here, take your money, give me the acknowledgment and go."

"But, Monseigneur —" Jeanne put in her word with eyes of troubled sympathy. "I have a suggestion to make. Does not the Farmer-General Saint-James, sup with you tonight? Would it not be possible in the strictest confidence, to give him a hint that the loan of four hundred thousand pounds would oblige her Majesty? He has the control of taxation, and I am sure that in a temporary need —"

The Cardinal almost shouted for joy.

"Excellent woman! You have the best wits of us all. Saint-James is a friend of mine, and I verily believe would do anything for her Majesty. Take your money with a good heart, Boehmer. We shall see our way out before the 30th July."

Very far from taking it with a good heart, Boehmer signed his name sullenly to a paper declaring that he took the sum not as interest but in part payment of the debt. It might be very well with regard to Saint-James but he had had so many promises, so many disappointments that his ear had grown callous to hope. He wanted his money, no more, no less. His own creditors were pressing. And what to say to Bassauger? He went away dragging feet heavy as lead, carrying a half-broken heart.

That evening after supper Saint-James was ripe with wine. His narrow atrabilious face and quick eyes glowed with its generous warmth and it was not displeasing to him that the Cardinal had asked him to delay after the other guests were gone for half an hour longer with himself and the charming little dark-eyed Countess who seemed so much at home in the

Hotel de Rohan. Well — that could be easily understood. The Prince's tastes in that respect were princely. But she brightened the air about her with her quick little sallies and retorts, and the friendship of the head of the House of Rohan must always mean much to a Frenchman.

"*Roi ne veux,*
Prince ne daigne,
Rohan suis."

A man is always to be reckoned with whose ancestors could despise kingdoms and princedoms, and to whom to be Rohan was sufficient!

Monsieur de Saint-James had developed into urbanity itself in a silk coat and stockings when very delicately and in a manner half-careless, half-quizzical, the matter was opened by the Cardinal under the seal of closest secrecy. Women are so! — What would you have perhaps more especially. He happened to know that her Majesty had need of a large sum of money to pay a debt — a debt for a matter in which she had every right to please herself, which indeed originally had the King's strong approval. She had refused then and regretted it later.

"But you are aware, my dear friend, that in all circles a wife may sometimes consider it more prudent to tell her husband of certain expenses after the debt is paid. And if from the public finances the sum could be advanced —"

"Doubtless, Monseigneur, doubtless. But do we do right in discussing dull business matters before this charming lady, made only to think of roses and jewels — and love-letters!"

He darted a keen side glance at Jeanne, really surprised at the Cardinal's want of *savoir faire* in opening the Queen's secrets before his *belle-amie.*

Jeanne sat, masking the closest attention with a smile. "Monsieur, you may trust my discretion. This lady is in a certain great person's closest confidence. Has no breath of this reached you?"

Monsieur de Saint-James could not honestly say that it had, but unwilling to appear ignorant of any inward details of Court life he merely smiled and bowed with double courtesy and begged the Cardinal to proceed. When all was said he spoke with the politest emphasis: "Neither Monseigneur nor madame can doubt that in my department as elsewhere the Queen's word is law in so far as human power goes. And the pleasure to myself does not even need stating. But it is obvious that with a sum of importance I must have her wishes personally expressed. In short, an interview —"

"I have no doubt it can be managed!" cried the Cardinal. "That is, with due caution and preparation. Eh, Countess."

"Doubtless!" said Jeanne modestly. "If I am given time I do not at all despair of bringing her Majesty to see the solid worth of Monsieur de Saint-James's offer. Meanwhile, inviolable secrecy!"

It was agreed, and they parted on such charming terms that fairy visions of a new Olisva and the addition of, say, sixty thousand pounds more to add to her well-gotten gains flitted through the busy brain of the Countess de Lamotte-Valois. But she dismissed them as impracticable for the moment, and on returning to her little house devoted an hour or two to sorting and packing her jewels in case a hurried exit became advisable. A sensible woman will be prepared for any eventuality.

It was with an air of despair at the caprice of royal women that she informed the Cardinal a few days later that the Queen, though she had not wholly rejected the proposal of Saint-James, had shown herself much piqued at what she termed the desertion of the Cardinal.

"I had wished the secret to be his and mine," she said. "If he wishes otherwise, so it must be. But as a matter of fact I have other money to offer in payment of my debt before a month is over, and I shall not use Saint-James. It would be degrading. It has chilled me that Monseigneur should speak and feel like this."

Protestations from the Cardinal. It was Boehmer, that exceedingly rapacious and low-class individual, who had expressed himself so unbecomingly; never he! And the proposal of Saint-James had but been made to relieve her Majesty of the faintest flicker of anxiety. But all must be as she willed. Still, he was far from being at ease. He was not of an age, as he thought in the secrecy of his own heart, to stand these terrors. Ah, if he were twenty years younger, if he could recapture the grace and lightness of his princely youth, the Queen would have little to complain of in her lover! He would have been that and more long before this.

It was a relief to pour out many of these reflections to his faithful friend. She would repeat to the Queen only what could advance his cause, he knew. She understood his heart.

Meanwhile Jeanne quietly packed her jewels and her other valuables, despatching a small case or two to Bar-sur-Aube which contained old family books and papers — so she said.

Chapter XV

THE days went heavily at Versailles, darkening slowly and mercilessly down as days darken for winter. The gaieties and merry festivities of the Court were slowly dying down the libels on the Queen had become so atrocious that she walked in terror now lest her simplest action should be misconstrued. It was noticeable also that there was a gradual withdrawal of fair-weather friends. The clan of the Polignacs were less assiduous in their attentions to the Queen and the warm friendship between herself and the Polignac Duchess which had given rise to so many calumnies cooled in consequence. Not on the side of Marie Antoinette. It was a part of her nature to cling with passionate intensity to the few people near enough to her to be loved. She had done everything for the Duchesse de Polignac, had made her Governess of the Children of France, had heaped her husband and dependents with favours, and all she looked for was fidelity — no more. She could not believe that times and hearts could change, and it might be that the pride of the Queen buttressed the belief of the woman. What? Friendship desert a queen of France who had stooped from her state to take a lesser woman to her bosom? No, indeed that was not credible! Yet after a while she too must observe that the pleas of absence from Court on the ground of ill-health, straitened means, and so forth grew more and more frequent, and without a sign she drew back within the stately limits of queendom and suffered in silence. She was indeed a very solitary soul at this time, for though she respected, and in a fashion loved, the King his was not a responsive nature nor were his initiative and energy to be compared with her own. She felt it, though in the gathering dangers she scarcely dared admit it even to herself.

His inactivity during a reception to the popular political leaders, of which so much might have been made, so splendid a bid for popularity, if he had not stood there heavy and silent as much a wooden block as a king, wounded her heart to the quick, and the pent-up grief and shame broke out to Madame Campan as they were closeted together and she sat reviewing the wasted chance.

"What did you think of the King's demeanour, madame?" she demanded. "What impression would it make on the Deputies?"

The woman answered as in duty bound, her eyes cast down to the carpet.

"Nothing could have been more gracious, madame. Your Majesty has every reason to be satisfied."

She dragged the great rings off her fingers, the bracelets from her arms, panting with haste and nervous excitement.

"How dare you say so! He never spoke — never, not once — except a cold greeting at going and coming and bows that a machine might have made as well. What possesses him — when all may depend upon it? Oh, my God, if it had been I! I would have charmed them, every one. I would! I could!"

Madame Campan knew that every word was true, but what could she say? She tried for a smile.

"Your Majesty could charm a bird off a bough! Who else is so gifted?"

But the Queen was past flattery. Her wounded heart throbbed on her lips, pride and shame contending: "You are not to think the King lacks courage!" she said, almost gasping. "No, indeed. He does not. I deny it. But it is passive courage hidden under the most dreadful shyness. Who should know but I? He distrusts himself in everything. He is afraid to command, afraid to speak — especially in public. His education was fatal. What would you have? Treated like a child by the dreadful old King: — a child, and he twenty-one and heir of France! My God, what madness! And now he can't help it. Why, today, a few kind hopeful words addressed to those men would have been worth diamonds, but he could not — could not utter them!"

She halted in a silence as passionate as speech. The room seemed to vibrate with it, and Madame Campan, dreadfully embarrassed, could not tell what to do. Her own near relations were all in the reforming party and her position was extremely delicate in spite of, perhaps because of, her affection for the Queen.

"If you were to counsel his Majesty, Madame," she began with hesitation.

"Counsel!" said the Queen bitterly. "I who need counsel myself! And how can I move him? It's his nature. His manner of dumb endurance simply encourages the people to fresh outrage. As for me I could do anything — anything. I could ride at the head of the troops if it were wanted. But if I did —"

"If you did?" asked Madame Campan, looking at the glowing beauty of the face before her and wondering if such charm and eloquence could at all move the hard hearts ranged against her. Such things had been — might be again. The Queen spoke bitterly: "No — I know my place better. I can hear the yells against the Austrian and the rule of a woman, and how can I thrust the King into the background? A Queen who is not a regent can do nothing. She must be passive and prepare herself to die!"

The blood flushed into Madame Campan's face. There was a warning she was in duty bound to give and yet had not dared. It had been weighing upon her like lead since the day before and she had trembled under the responsibility. Now, the Queen's last words gave her the opening.

"To die, Madame?" she said slowly. "Has your Majesty any reason for saying so cruel a thing?"

Marie Antoinette answered with indifference: "Not I! What does death matter? I am ready enough, God knows, when it comes!"

Suddenly Madame Campan knelt and taking her hand pressed it to her lips.

"But those who love your Majesty are not ready. I have a warning, a shameful warning to give, and I beg your Majesty neither to despise nor misunderstand it."

The Queen's hand lay cold and passive in hers.

She lay back in her chair as if borne down with utter weariness.

"Go on, madame, what is it?"

"Madame, your Majesty knows the carafe of *eau sucrée* which is left for your use in the outer room. I have seen you a hundred times drink a glass. You must do so no more. The water must be prepared in here by one of your ladies and no otherwise."

Silence. Then as the meaning penetrated her brain and hot tears fell from Madame Campan's eyes upon her hands as she kissed them again and again, the Queen laughed aloud — the saddest laughter in all the world.

"And is that all?" she said. "Folly! It will never happen. The age of poisoning is passed. They will kill me indeed but with calumny. It is a much surer and less dangerous way. Get me a glass of the *eau sucrée* now, my friend. I am thirsty!"

She sat and drank it, smiling at her own cruel thoughts as if she defied them, and Madame Campan could say no more.

"Leave me, my kind friend. It does me good to sit alone and dream my dreams!" she added. And in a moment — "Believe me they are not all sad. Why should the wife of the King and mother of the Dauphin despair? We have as many friends as enemies when all is said and done."

That Madame Campan doubted, but, naturally a reserved woman, she moved quietly away into the outer room and closed the door upon the Queen.

She insisted often now on solitude, and at last in her melancholy musings it became almost an interest to watch how the women about her responded each in her own way to the test of trouble. Masks began to be discarded and some appeared very different from what she had hitherto believed them. It had seemed a world filled with happy people who never were ill (for that was not respectful to Majesty), never grumbled, were always cheerfully ready for any service however irksome, always crowded eagerly to sun themselves with delight in the beams of the Queen's loveliness and grace, the King's majesty and power. But now some of them began to reveal themselves as human beings who had their own ends to serve and no objection to showing it occasionally. Yet it would be difficult to put the subtle changes in words — though they were there.

The full tide reflecting sunshine, moon, and stars was ebbing, and ugly places and creeping creatures hidden before were visible now in the light of day. All things grew sadder to her one by one.

One afternoon late in July she sat in her boudoir at Versailles looking out into the gardens where even the crystal jets and mists of the fountains could not cool the air or restore freshness to the faded green of the grass and trees about them. The heat of the summer had been exhausting. Complaints of drought came in from the provinces and all the world was steeped in sick languor.

Marie Antoinette sat by the window, looking wearily out upon the shimmering heat that rose along the roadways. A table stood before her loaded with papers, and she leaned her aching head upon her hand but had no support on which to lean her aching heart. Not even that of memory.

The papers before her were another series of gross libels upon her printed in Paris for distribution throughout the country, shameful and torturing for any woman to read. And she knew but too well that any measures of repression taken under the King's direction were frightfully unwise and could only spread the mischief further. Indeed she had begun to doubt the wisdom of repression in any circumstances.

The worst that lay before her had been bought up by the King's orders, and his advisers could find no better way of destroying the masses of paper than by sending them to be burnt at the royal potteries at Sevres by hundreds of workmen, many of whom were infected by the revolutionary spirit of the day. Madness! and she could not make him see it, could not make him see anything.

She almost despaired as she sat, looking upon the hideous pile before her.

But was any of it so far true that she could blame herself for the ruin she saw looming in the distance? Was it not time she held a bar of justice in her own heart and there arraigned her past life before the sternest of earthly judges, her own conscience?

"Marie Antoinette, Queen of France, stand forth to be judged."

That was the summoning voice. And with hidden face she addressed herself to the task. A task which others were to take upon themselves later. The little Austrian Archduchess, the bride of fifteen, had she sinned past forgiveness, coming with her eager hopes and fears to France? Would any other child have done better, faced with the impudent splendour and influence of the du Barry, the dotard dissolute King, and the coldness of her own husband? Surrounded by enemies, plots and intrigues she could never understand, much less parry, had she failed in duty there? That she had been foolish, reck-less, headstrong, in her choice of pleasures, she was compelled to own. Was it for her to break through the immemorial rules of French royalty and ridicule every barrier set up to safeguard her position. She had argued the point with Madame de Noailles, the dull "Madame Etiquette" again and again, and having taken her own way must also take the consequences. They came quickly enough. Madame Etiquette had never forgiven the nickname and the slights, and having her party like every one else at Court they had acted for her when the moment came, and the result was the first of the libels on the Queen.

For when the old King died, a Court of Condolence was held, where many of the antiquated duchesses and marchionesses who had been beauties forty years before came up from their provincial mansions to Versailles to "make their compliments of condolence" to the young Queen. They were decorated in the fashions of their prime, terrible bonnets with black blinkers to protect passers-by from the blaze of so much beauty, and the rest of the dress black, sombre, and stiff to match. And as the girl-queen was gravely receiving their profound reverences she had the misfortune to catch sight of the gay little Marquise de Clermont Tonnerre, sitting on the ground to rest herself behind the secure fence formed by the Queen's hoop and those of the ladies in attendance.

There the little ape sat, twitching the dresses of the ladies in attendance and playing off all her tricks and grimaces as one dowager after another appeared with her tremendous curtsey and face of fixed melancholy shaded by blinkers, until at last a choking titter ran along the line and the Queen herself was obliged to put up her fan.

The mischief was done. The old ladies were profoundly indignant at the mockery and the shocking levity of the Queen "in face of the nation's grief" as they called it. And next day a song known as the Fal-la-la was winging all over Paris with the burden:

"Little Queen, you must not be
So saucy with your twenty years!
Your ill-used courtiers soon may see
You cross once more the barriers,
With a Fal-la-la-la-la."

That was the recurrence of the old grievance. They wanted her packed back to Vienna. And a strengthening Court party wanted it now. It was said to be the party of Madame Etiquette which had set it going, and that was the beginning.

"We are too young to reign," she and her King had said when the old King died. He was scarcely twenty. She nineteen. Yes — too young — too young by far!

Cruel enough; but as her heart went sorrowing through the past she blamed herself with crueller candour. She had never played her great part as she should have done. She had only remembered she was young and that youth passes on winged feet. In the French Court for a Queen to be young partook of the nature of sin. Other women might have the right to rejoice in their April, but not she. But she had rejoiced and had done and permitted things which she knew now were fatal.

Those terrible *descampativos*! She recalled the words, the look of de Fersen — repaid only with anger — and she writhed in a flame of shame. There was true love at her feet doing true love's noble service and she had driven it from her — such love as even a queen might have accepted with pride in its selfless truth. What was he thinking now, what doing, in this dreadful justification of his warnings? O that she could recall him, could ask for his advice as humbly as a queen might dare!

And the Princesse de Lamballe — Thérèse — she had also warned her tenderly and truly. What had been her reward? To be left in the outer cold for the sake of the faithless Polignacs now hovering for departure like swallows that seek the sun! Thérèse came very seldom near her now. Could it cause surprise?

Then there was the high play, the gaming the King hated and feared, custom though it was of the old Court. If she had seconded him it might have been done away with, but she would not heed. And the sight was permitted to the public of a banker and his second in command seated at the Queen's own card-table in the great room at Marly to provide money for the high play in which any decently dressed gentleman-adventurer who cared to come in might join by asking the ladies to bet for him on the cards, the women themselves flushed with greed, the laps of their satin gowns soiled with the loads of gold they held.

Little wonder that the tales ran north and south of the Queen's passion for play, with the addition that she had once played thirty-four hours at a sitting. It was not true, but it was believed. The people's money wasted in dissipation! — that was the cry. It did her fatal harm.

She sickened now in thinking of those flushed faces and grasping hands and the Queen in the midst of them flushed and excited also, and de Fersen's eyes gravely intent as he stood tall against the gilded wall, not joining in the play but curiously watchful and quiet.

And worse — worse — those outdoor night concerts in the gardens of the palaces, harmless enough in themselves, but disastrous in their results. There for a moment her sad thoughts lingered as on a lost beauty. The full moon hung in great trees, stars glittering on the long waters, soft music, sweet voices dying of their own delight — how she had loved it! True, she herself had never left the lit terrace, but other women had wandered away into the dusky gardens, and the people who thrust themselves in to hear, who had mingled familiarly with the Royal women on the terrace (once she remembered a young clerk pushing his way with a petition to a seat beside her on the bench she sat on) — what tales they must have carried away and invented to inspire those horrible papers! Well — there too she had been warned. The King would never appear at the concerts. She continued them on her own responsibility.

Madame Campan and others had told her that stories were afloat and she had laughed in scorn.

Laughter, scornful or otherwise, was a thing she was not likely to transgress in any more. That day was done — with much else.

Extravagance — no. There she could not plead guilty. Spendthrift waste never meant anything to her — she who refused the large addition to her income which Calonne, chief of the national finances, offered. She had refused the diamond necklace. She had —

The door opened and Madame Campan entered with a letter, scattering her thoughts to the four winds like ominous black birds soon to reassemble.

"Boehmer — something to sell, I suppose," she said, glancing at the signature. "But I have neither money nor inclination to buy. Well — let me read it."

She looked down the page in astonishment then looked up.

"That man is mad. What on earth can he mean? Listen to this —"

MADAME,

Your humble servant desires to express his deep satisfaction in seeing the greatest of queens in possession of the finest diamonds known in Europe. Having been the humble means of procuring them he entreats your Majesty not to forget your humblest and most obedient servant.

BOEHMER.

"He is most certainly mad!" she exclaimed. "What finest diamonds? Certainly I have the Sanci, the Regent and others, but that is no business of his. He must have some hallucination about diamonds. I half-believed that last time I saw him. They should have him watched."

Madame Campan, casting about in her mind, interposed.

"Madame, I believe I have it. He is referring to those splendid diamonds you bought for earrings so long ago. He may have more of the same sort."

151

She referred to six magnificent pear-shaped diamonds which had been set as earrings soon after the Queen came to the throne and bought and paid for at a great price.

"Ah, that must be it. And he hopes for favours to come!" said the Queen carelessly. "Well, if you should see him, tell him I have no wish for more jewels. The taste has left me. I have very different things to think of now and only wear what I must. But I firmly believe that Boehmer's brain is touched. I have thought that for some time."

She twisted the paper and lit it idly at a wax taper standing beside her.

"It's not worth keeping," she said, then added: "That man has always some mad scheme in his head. Tell him, if you like, that I shall buy no more diamonds so long as I live, and that if I had money to spend I would rather add to my property at Saint-Cloud. Impress this on him and it may put a stop to his visions."

"And shall I send for him, Madame?"

"Certainly not. That would be making it of too much consequence. It will do when you see him. Call my *lectrice* to read to me a little. My very soul is weary."

*

Four days later Madame Campan left Versailles for a brief visit to her country house, sad at heart in the gathering storm, uneasy at she knew not what, terrified at the rumours reaching her from Paris. She herself needed a little respite that she might gather her forces to support the Queen. How quiet the little green lawns at Crespy, the little singing rivulet that spilt itself musically down fern-fringed rocks, the quiet ways of the house and simple faithful old servants! There one could talk and sleep in peace with no fear of spying eyes and listening ears as at Versailles. She would go back stronger. She too was very weary.

On the fourth day as she sat on the lawn under a great tree, her faithful Marie came slowly over the grass, sedate in her great white cap with handsome gold pins and a spotless muslin folded across her bosom.

"Madame, a gentleman from Paris requests the honour — Monsieur Boehmer."

"Boehmer?" She sat up in astonishment, dropping her book. Then remembering. "Yes, bring him here, Marie. I wish to see him."

It would be a good opportunity for doing the Queen's errand and stopping the man's folly once for all.

He came, following Marie through the trees, and she saw at once that the high-flown gaiety and good spirits had collapsed. He was pale and anxious, and the Queen's often repeated suggestion of madness recurred as she bowed slightly from her chair. She looked round rather nervously for Marie. Could that be the real explanation of his mysterious behaviour?

"Monsieur."

"Madame" — with a low bow.

"Be seated!"

"A thousand thanks, madame. My visit must be brief and I prefer to stand. I apologize for intrusion, but it is of the first consequence that I should know if you have any commission for me from her Majesty. Has she any commands for me?"

"She entrusted me with none. But I have a message if it can be so called."

He started eagerly.

"Oh, madame, now! This moment!"

She repeated it word for word, and the light died out of his eyes. He interrupted sharply.

"But the answer to the letter I wrote her — to whom must I apply for that?"

"To nobody. Her Majesty burnt your memorial without in the least understanding its meaning."

The man's face worked nervously.

"But, madame, that is impossible. The Queen knows she has money to pay me."

"Money? Monsieur Boehmer? Your last accounts against the Queen were discharged long ago."

"Madame, you are not in the secret. A man who is ruined for want of payment of four hundred thousand pounds cannot be said to be paid by the interest."

She stared at him aghast, her suspicion of madness strengthening with every word, then glanced behind her at the windows to see if flight and help were within reach. At last: "Have you lost your senses? For what can the Queen owe you such an extravagant sum?"

"For my necklace, madame — my necklace."

For the moment she was certain of his madness. She stared at him with startled eyes.

"Why, you told me with your own lips that you had sold that necklace at Constantinople. Do recollect yourself, Monsieur Boehmer. I am sick of the very name of that necklace."

"And I, madame," he replied grimly. "True. Yes, I certainly told you that. The Queen desired me to give that answer to all who should speak to me on the subject."

Suddenly a sense of the gravity of the matter broke on Madame Campan. She no longer believed she was dealing with a lunatic. There was that in his tone and expression which carried conviction of his own belief. Dim and terrible abysses opened before her, vague, uncertain and the more alarming. She rose instinctively and stood facing him, as pale as he.

"Monsieur Boehmer, do you know what you are insinuating?"

"Madame, I know very well. I make no insinuation. I state a truth. The Queen secretly desired to have the necklace. She regretted her refusal to his Majesty and she had it purchased for her by Monseigneur the Cardinal de Rohan."

"But you are deceived, frightfully deceived. I assure you with all my strength that I know for a fact she has not spoken to the Cardinal for years. Not since his return from Vienna where he offended her so deeply by his references to her mother the Empress. There is not a man at Court less favourably looked on. You must be frenzied."

"You are deceived yourself, madame. She sees him so much in private that it was to his Eminence she gave a few hundred pounds which was paid to me as an instalment. She took it in his presence out of the little *secretaire* of Sevres porcelain next the fireplace in her boudoir. And the money was given me in a letter from her Majesty by the Cardinal."

"And the Cardinal told you all this?"

"Yes, madame, himself."

"Then I say," cried Madame Campan, towering in wrath, "that it is a detestable plot against the Queen. It is nothing less. She knows nothing whatsoever of the whole matter. You have been most dreadfully deceived."

A heart of stone might have pitied Boehmer standing quivering there lost in a maze of perplexities.

"Indeed, madame — Oh, madame, forgive me, for I cannot tell what to do. I myself begin to doubt. I am in great terror. For his Eminence assured me that her Majesty would wear the necklace on Whitsunday. And I went to Versailles and she never did. My God, what am I to do? What does it mean?"

There was silence — the two staring at each other pallidly. At last he spoke: "Madame, for the mercy of God, have pity on a most miserable man and advise me. I don't even know where it is. They took it from me — they took it from me! O God!" A choking sob cut his words in two.

He stood now, the tears raining down his cheeks and perfectly unconscious of them, as was she.

"Madame, I beseech you!" he sobbed.

"But I myself am distracted! I can't tell what to say," she stammered. "I pity you indeed. But surely you are extremely culpable, you a sworn officer as the King's Jeweller! It was unpardonable of you to have acted, and in a matter of such consequence, without signed orders from the King or Queen or a minister. You have brought it on yourself. You have indeed! No, go, I will not be mixed in it. I utterly refuse to hear. I have nothing more to say."

For indeed a chillier terror was invading her mind with every word. De Rohan — the greatness of the names involved was too heavy a burden for the Queen's waiting-lady. But he persisted.

"Madame, can you believe me so foolish? I have in my possession notes signed by the Queen. I have even had to show them to certain bankers to gain an extension of time for the payments I myself must make. No, I have not been in fault. Mere loyalty compelled me to act as I did. Madame, it is a desperate man who implores your advice."

"No — no! I have none to give. It is too much for me. But yes, I may say this: Were I in your place I would fly to Trianon, the Queen is there now, losing not a minute. I would see the Baron de Breteuil, who is head of the King's Household and therefore of your department. Tell him the whole story, but be circumspect. You are moving amid great dangers. Reveal it to not a soul outside. Now, I will not hear another word. Not one. I will stop my ears. I wish I had never heard this. Go."

He turned and stumbled away without a look behind, lost and bewildered as an animal in the snares.

Released, Madame Campan flew to her father-in-law, as well acquainted as she with the ways of Courts, and told him all.

"I must go to the Queen instantly. It will drive her nearly out of her senses."

Monsieur Campan considered the matter in grave silence. His keen French face fixed itself on the problem steadily before he spoke.

"Daughter, there is more, much more, in this than we understand and you must not be drawn into what may well prove to be the scandal of the age. Wait. Go warily. Do not return until her Majesty sends for you, and keep your lips padlocked except to her. The business is not yours. Let it not become so. You advised the man right. The head of his department is the man to counsel him."

Meanwhile Boehmer had made his way to Trianon, asking to see the Queen, for Breteuil was not there. He should have known better. She said coldly to her attendant: "Tell the man I will not see him. He is mad. He troubles me."

The Cardinal! — what other way was left? He took the road to Paris.

Chapter XVI

To the Cardinal, closeted with the Lamotte, who was administering her usual soothing syrup to a much-perturbed mind, entered Boehmer, now hopeless of all good and grown desperate as the weakest of animals may grow in defending its one poor life. No longer had majesties, eminences and countesses any meaning for him, and he spoke out from his whole heart at last and with passion which rendered him eloquent. Words poured from him in a torrent of lava, and the Cardinal, stupefied, heard from the lips of a man so far beneath him in rank, furies, distrusts and suspicions which left him speechless, while Jeanne de Lamotte's fixed, searching gaze never wavered from Boehmer's face.

"I have been wickedly wronged and robbed, and the persons who did it shall suffer if they were the highest in the land. What? The Queen refuses to see me — me to whom she owes a fortune? If she were fifty times a queen I will have my rights." He shouted this, standing flushed and raging by the door, as if unwilling to trust himself within. "The time has gone by when honest persons can be treated as *canaille* and sent to the Bastille when they ask their rights. Nothing shall hinder me from seeing the Queen, and so you may tell her. I tried my best just now and failed."

A last gleam of wisdom kept him from mentioning Madame Campan's advice that he should see de Breteuil. Or it may have been blind rage, for of Madame Campan herself he had spoken.

"Naturally!" put in the Lamotte swift and alert.

"Since you were warned that she would not see you on any pretext you have only yourself to thank for whatever goes wrong now. You are aware that Monseigneur met her at Versailles. I myself returned only yesterday from there and to me the Queen declared plainly that if pressed she would deny ever having seen the necklace or had any dealings at all with Monseigneur. Why you cannot have a little patience, God only knows! You will ruin all concerned and do yourself no good. What will your word be against hers?"

What indeed? Boehmer was well enough aware of that, and for all he knew or cared the Countess might be speaking the truth so far. The Queen might be implicated and deny all. But more and more was it forced in upon him that here and from his Eminence and his Countess he would get no good, for in them he began to fear he knew not what, and that he had but wasted time with them. To Breteuil! There was the only hope of any light in the bottomless darkness. But not a word of that to them!

Roused and steadied by Jeanne's words the Cardinal at last broke in: "Madame is right, Boehmer. You have done a mad, a terrible, thing in going to Madame Campan without consulting us. She is the Queen's woman and no more, and certainly not in her confidence in any way. Sheer madness! Great God, what horrors may it not bring about if the Queen cannot silence her!"

The sweat-drops stood on his forehead. He turned furiously on Jeanne.

"I warned you that this *canaille* should never have heard the Queen's name, and you said you would stand guarantee for his honour! And this is your reward and mine!"

"Perhaps I did not rely so much on his honour as his fears," she answered with pale tight lips. "It is a brave man who drags the Queen into an open scandal and above all when she has trusted herself to him. Well, Monsieur Boehmer, and what do you propose to do next? Ask her Majesty's pages what they know about the necklace? Or suggest that the King has it in his pocket? *My* course is clear, Monseigneur. It is to go at once to Versailles and warn the Queen and do my best to avert the harm this fool has done." She flashed a lightning glance at him.

Even Boehmer was shaken for the moment. If she were a trickster could that have been her attitude? If her story was true, fierce wrath with his meddling was exactly what she must feel. If not true — could she dare? He hesitated. She saw it. And the Cardinal's belief in her was complete. She pounced on her advantage.

"If we are not all to be ruined together, listen to me. Give me three days for the Queen, and I will fly to Versailles and bring her to reason. She must consent now to see Saint-James, and if she does the money will be in our hands at once. Certainly the first payment and possibly the whole — straight down — and that would finish it. O my God, imagine the folly of this Boehmer! She refused to see Saint-James because she would not have another in the secret, and Boehmer goes to Campan! You will get your money, monsieur, sure enough, but you will do well to leave France for a time to avoid the anger of the Queen. *I* know her. This time on the fourth day meet me here and I will have the money in my hand — but not the Queen's pardon! No, not that. She and I must concert what is to be done with Campan. And for you, Monseigneur, this day week is the Feast of the Assumption and you are to officiate at Versailles. That is quite safe and natural, for it is in right of your office of Grand Almoner and will cause no talk. Afterwards ask to see the Queen. I know she thought delay best but I believe in my soul the time is ripe for a meeting now, and that she will bless you afterwards. If you displace de Breteuil, as I fully expect, you can arrange to complete the money for the necklace directly you are in power. Have Campan arrested. I shall speak of that today with the Queen."

The line she took was nothing less than masterly and they answered to it.

She was magnificent as she looked from one to the other, her dark eyes sparkling, every muscle of her face tense with will and intelligence.

Her acting had always this merit at least — that it carried herself away as well as her audience. Yes — that was how she would have spoken, looked, acted, had she been indeed the Queen's friend and Boehmer the pitiful poltroon she called him. She felt the part to her fingertips for if ever there were a woman of imagination Jeanne de Lamotte was one. In her garret she had dreamed, and for the true dreamer to realize his visions is always a certainty. The difficulty is to make others realize them also, and failing that — the dreamer wakes!

But she was magnificent. She swept the Cardinal off his feet; she utterly bewildered Boehmer for the moment.

"If I consented to wait one day more, madame —"

"You may consent or not as you please. Three days was what I said. If I can undo your work in three days or ever it is much, and I scarcely dare expect it. I go to the Queen!"

The Cardinal was on his feet instantly — a certain amount of hope reviving. He cast glances of scorn on Boehmer, who retreated to the wall bowing as she swept out.

"Will *you* be guided by my advice?" she asked de Rohan, turning her head proudly over her shoulder as she passed him.

"In all things, my dear Countess, in all things!"

"Very well. Then wait and if I have any special news or warning to give you I will send a mounted messenger from Versailles. Ask at my house. Otherwise, act as I said."

"But, madame," stammered Boehmer. "I was told — Madame Campan said her Majesty was at Trianon."

"Fool! She is returning for the Feast of the Assumption!" was all the Countess vouchsafed as the door closed behind her. Her carriage waited at the door and in a moment she was bowling swiftly towards her own house.

The mask dropped instantly from eyes and lips, but not a quiver showed fear. As a matter of fact she was not afraid. She had known the explosion must come, though even she could not predict when and how and she was prepared as far as possible. She had some time since arranged for a berline and horses to be at her door at the shortest notice night or day. As they dashed along, she ordered the man to go that way and scribbled a word or two to be left there.

"At my door in one hour. For Versailles," it said.

For Versailles. That was in case de Rohan or Boehmer should have her watched. It would confuse the trail prettily in other ways also.

Her own carriage had orders to be in readiness to take her to a reception next evening at the house of Beaumarchais whose "Marriage of Figaro" and "Barber of Seville" were filling the air with witty and ironical sedition and hints and slanders against the royal family which the Queen in her madness had laughed at with the best not so long ago, far indeed from understanding their implications. An excellent joke indeed! But sparks even of wit are best avoided in a powder magazine.

Arrived at her house Jeanne strolled in with the easiest air imaginable. There were only two women — the man, hired for grand occasions, was not on duty. She called her maid: "Finette, I must be at home until eight o'clock in the evening. Why should not you and Louison have a holiday until six and go to 'Le Mariage de Figaro'? You never saw anything so amusing in your life, and I have tickets for you. But be in as soon after six as possible, for I must be dressed for the *soirée* of Madame de Guemenée — that is, if my bad headache will allow me to go. No, no thanks. You know it pleases me to give you pleasure."

Sparkles and smiles all round.

"She may be an adventuress," said Finette to Louison as they tied on their rose-wreathed shepherdess hats in poor imitation of the Queen's, "but she's a good fellow all the same. I never knew her out of temper since I've been here, and she does treat her servants like flesh and blood when all's said and done, which is more than you can say for the grandees. But their time's coming, thanks to God!"

In a quarter of an hour they were out of the house and Jeanne surveying her line of retreat with the eye of an experienced general. She even smiled as she heard their tripping footsteps go down the stairs. Yes — it paid to be civil to one's *canaille* of servants. She had proved that over and over again if it needed proving as it did today. She turned to business then and looked round her bedroom and dressing-room. A few pretty trifles lay about her but the armoires and cupboards were empty. A fortnight ago she had told Finette that they were to be sent to a house she had rented near Versailles, and she had forwarded her large trunks down there — as Finette supposed. That they had taken a very different route was of no consequence except to herself.

Now she hurriedly packed her jewels, and the few garments left, burnt a heap of papers, put on her travelling cloak, made herself an excellent cup of coffee and sat down to wait for the berline. She counted the money in her possession while she drank, and with a smile. There was no need for any anxiety, even setting aside the loose jewels sewn into the padding of her cloak and in one or two other places of security.

When she rose for a final look round, she took her pen from the mother-of-pearl inkstand, wrote these words on a sheet of paper:

To MADEMOISELLE FINETTE.

I am called away unexpectedly to Versailles, but shall return tomorrow afternoon. Do not forget to see that Madame Duport has the yellow silk dress ready for me to wear tomorrow evening at the reception of Monsieur de Beaumarchais. If I should be delayed beyond this at Versailles return for answer that I am there and shall let my friends know directly I am in Paris again.

She placed that open on the table in the hall, and stood at the window looking out and waiting. A man passed on the opposite side with his hat slouched above his ears, as the berline clattered up to the door. She laughed, knowing Boehmer very well, for all the pains he had taken. She saw him slip across the road and address himself to the postilion and could have asked his question for him, so sure was she of what he would want to know.

Craning behind the curtain she heard the man's careless answer: "To Versailles, monsieur. My best thanks — Yes, a charming lady indeed."

Boehmer playing the jealous lover at watch upon his lady! A really humorous smile lifted her fine little lip as she tripped down the stair and opened the door, her small trunk in readiness.

"Good-bye, Finette. Be a good girl," she cried gaily to an imaginary audience and shut the door smartly behind her, never again to enter it as she knew very well.

Boehmer had disappeared, but since he might be lurking near she gave her orders in a clear ringing voice.

"To Versailles — to the Palace," and settled herself in the cushions, laughing again as the whip cracked and they set off at a round trot. Four days' clear start! She had never felt more at ease in her life.

For half an hour they took the westward route to Versailles, and then she dismounted at an inn much-frequented on the road, and disappeared, telling the men to wait. It was scarcely ten minutes before she returned pale and concerned, an open letter in her hand, her handkerchief at her eyes.

"I have had a despatch. My husband, the Count de Lamotte-Valois, is terribly ill at Bar-sur-Aube. We must turn southward at once. *O mon dieu, mon dieu*, the time I have lost — the precious time! My friends, drive like the wind. You shall not regret it. There are relays all along the road."

The poor lady — the poor pretty little lady! The horses sweated for her grief, and as the postilion remarked to the coachman he did not know that they had ever made better time through the suburbs. The people scattered to right and left and a dog and two hens fell a sacrifice to the anxious wife's haste to her husband.

The Cardinal sent that evening to know if there were any news for him from Versailles, and had for answer from Mademoiselle Finette — "No. Madame would probably return by tomorrow afternoon and was to attend in the evening the reception of Monsieur de Beaumarchais. If delayed at Versailles she would let her friends know when she returned to Paris."

Smiling a little as she did it, she enclosed the little note, being perfectly alive to the close friendship that bound the Hotel de Rohan to the little house of Madame de Lamotte-Valois, and it was greedily read when it reached the hands of Louis de Rohan, though it had not needed that to strengthen de Rohan's confidence.

His thoughts now turned solely on his visit to Versailles on Assumption Day. Again his hopes were high. At that moment the Countess must be closeted with the Queen and surely when she knew of Boehmer's madness she would perceive the urgency of the matter and consent to receive Saint-James. Then all the troubles would be over, and rewards, the sweeter for delay, would pour into his hands. Not that he would undertake such a business again for Venus's beauty with Juno's power thrown into the bargain. He was getting too old for that sort of foolhardy romance and it was nothing but the combination of love and ambition that had brought him through it alive. That despicable Boehmer! And yet — this last outburst of his might really be a blessing in disguise if it brought the Queen to reason. Without that she might have kept shilly-shallying on for another year without seeing Saint-James or taking any decided step. And what should he do for the Countess when all was finished? As minister, a good appointment for her husband would be in his power — and she should choose within reason, of course, but freely. And for herself, what special remembrance? Something charming and distinctive from Boehmer, if he behaved well for the rest of the time. That would kill two birds with one glittering stone. All these thoughts with a little re-reading of Jeanne's letters at various times, kept him happy and amused while she was speeding toward Bar-sur-Aube.

He had himself driven to Versailles the day before the Feast of the Assumption and, hoping to meet her on the way, directed his servants to watch for her carriage. No sign of her, but that meant little, though he hoped for a word before she returned. Still, she had said: "If you hear nothing all is well. Go onward steadily as I have advised." He would obey his best friend blindly. She knew the Queen's mind. He could not. So he mused in calming anxiety while the world was cracking about him. Little did he understand that in a game so close, so fine as that of Jeanne there are terrible risks to be taken. One slightest oversight and matters hurl together into confusion and chaos. She knew that Madame Campan had gone out of waiting but could not tell when she would return. In the ordinary way it would not be for a week or more. But there she was mistaken. On the very day after her interview with Boehmer the Campan was in the Queen's boudoir.

She had not intended it herself, but it so chanced that the lady who filled her place was taken ill and the Queen sent for her. She came so shaken with nerves that she was trembling from head to foot and on the verge of hysteria. The Queen noticed her nervous agitation kindly.

"Why, my dear Madame Campan, you are as ill as our friend! Are you fit to stay here?"

"Very fit, Madame" — her teeth literally chattering — "I have had an alarm, and your Majesty will excuse me. It will wear off in half an hour."

"An alarm? And what? With your horses?"

"No, Madame." She could not get more out. Her teeth locked on the words. The Queen laid down the book she had been reading and looked at her with mild surprise.

"Pray tell me. But before we begin tell me also why you sent Boehmer to me from Crespy? He sent in word that he had been with you and you had advised him to request an audience. You know my strong dislike to seeing the man."

"Madame, that was my alarm. He terrified me."

"Then I am right, and he was mad! I knew it, and he invented the idea of your sending him to me?"

"Madame, no. I advised him to come."

The Queen's quick perception told her at once that there was something to hear and to dread. She paled slightly and stiffened in her chair, head erect, eyes bright and fixed. Late months had taught her a cruel resignation.

"Explain yourself."

"Madame, I entreat your forgiveness for what will trouble you, but I know it is necessary you should hear. Boehmer came to me at Crespy and declared that you had purchased the necklace of him through another person and that the sum of four hundred thousand pounds was due to him from your Majesty in consequence!"

A faint smile touched the Queen's lips.

"I told you he was mad!" she said. "Was a more lunatic story ever invented? That poor man must be put under restraint. Is that all? You laughed at him, I don't doubt."

"Madame, I could not laugh. He believes it. He assured me that he held papers signed by you to that effect which he had been compelled to show to certain bankers to obtain delay from them for payments he must make for the diamonds."

The blood fell away from the Queen's face and left her ash-white. So many foul libels, so much torture, and now a fouler plot of which she could not gauge the depths! But with a queenly effort she held her forces together that she might probe it to the bottom.

"A lie. Through whom did the man say I had bought it?"

"Madame, the Cardinal de Rohan."

The first sign of relief was on her face at those words.

"There is no one mad enough to believe *that*," she said proudly. "The world knows he was forbidden my presence and the King's, and that I dismissed the porter at Trianon for permitting him to enter the garden when half the world came to a fête. If that is all I need not alarm myself. But send for Boehmer instantly. The thing must be put a stop to."

She would say no more on the point, but remained lost in thought and evidently deeply wounded in pride by the atrocity of the statement. Silence was a relief to Madame Campan whose tremors were renewed at the thought of being a party in any way to the investigation. A courier was despatched to Paris. Not a word more from the Queen on the subject until Boehmer arrived.

She wrapped herself in proud reserve very unlike her usual kindly ways with her attendants. "A cold white dignity," as Madame Campan expressed it, seemed to shut her into a world of her own, and what her thoughts were in that silence none could tell.

The man was ushered straight into her boudoir on arrival, and Madame Campan was the only person with her. There was that in the Queen's face and manner which might have chilled any man into awe, but that Boehmer was beside himself with fear and anger.

Commanded to state his facts, his manner, little as he meant it, was an outrage, so evident was his disbelief in her innocence.

"Willingly indeed would I have spared your Majesty's feelings but for my creditors."

"And what are your creditors to me?" she asked with frozen pride.

The story poured out charged with rage and offence. It was Marie Antoinette's first personal contact with disgraceful suspicion and it stirred her to the fury of a wounded lioness. Her cheek flushed, her eyes sparkled most dangerously.

"What? You dared to suppose that I — I could have any confidences with such a man as the Cardinal? You believed that I could deal through him with a tradesman for a thing I had steadily refused and felt no interest whatever in?"

It did not shake him. He stolidly repeated again and again: "Madame, there is no longer time for feigning. Condescend to confess you have my necklace, and let some aid be given me or my bankruptcy will bring the whole affair to light."

"To light? But that is my own determination. I desire nothing better. On your part, confess that this is a shameful plot. Who is the woman Lamotte you speak of? I never saw — I never heard of her." She flashed round to Campan. "Have you?"

"Never, Madame. I never knew of the existence of such a person."

"Surely, Madame," repeated Boehmer, "it is vain to deny what all the world knows: that she was one of your closest intimates. I believe she is hidden in the Palace at this moment. She declared she was coming straight to you from the Cardinal and I saw her set off for Versailles."

The Queen's condition was pitiable. She felt herself trapped by invisible yet unbreakable bonds, and that even a person so insignificant as Boehmer could believe her guilty of association with such as Rohan and Lamotte was a mortal blow to her rightful pride of place and womanhood. Horror and shame and fury passed like waves over her face and left her speechless. When it became unbearable even for an onlooker Madame Campan ventured to interpose, trembling: "Madame, if I may humbly offer my advice, this matter has reached a point where it should be in men's hands and strong ones. Send Monsieur Boehmer to the Count de Breteuil, who is head of his department — the King's Household — and then see the Count yourself. It is impossible but that it should be cleared up in a very short time when proper measures are taken."

The Queen looked at her for a moment with vacant unseeing eyes. Then, summoning her strength, "Go!" she said faintly, waving her hand with a gesture of dismissal to Boehmer.

He went out, his face scarlet, his head held high, and straight into the presence of de Breteuil.

Marie Antoinette rose from her chair and moved toward the inner room, holding herself together with an effort so tense that for the moment grace was dead and she moved with stiff short steps like an old woman. At the door she turned: "Did I not tell you that there would be no need for poison? They will kill me with calumny."

The other woman hid her face in her hands.

Chapter XVII

WHEN Boehmer was ushered into the presence of de Breteuil, his face scarlet and head held high, he little knew what a terrible page of history he was turning, little guessed the ramifications under the surface. Had fate led him to almost any other man — to the Comte de Vergennes for instance — personal motives might have been in abeyance and the public danger recognized. But de Breteuil was a sharp small-minded man devoid of all vision and in this revelation he saw only the chance of a life-time and ample satisfaction for a grudge of years' standing which he had warmed like a snake in his bosom against the Cardinal de Rohan. Even his downfall could not satisfy de Breteuil, for the Cardinal still held his high rank, still was courted and flattered by his sycophants, still had a kind of popularity among the people from his genial manners and his careless liberality in such cases of distress as were forced upon his notice. How could de Breteuil be satisfied when in the streets of Paris he met the gorgeous coach with its proud coat of arms driving through the street, de Rohan sitting stately inside and taking salutes of the people as a right. Indeed his popularity had grown of late, for his sharp-eyed secretary, the Abbé Georgel, was always stressing his ostracism by the Court, and to be persecuted by the Court was to be a friend of the people. The Abbé was very clear in his own mind as to the side on which his own bread and the Cardinal's was to be buttered in the future and with which party it would be well to be allied. As to Jeanne he never gave her a thought. Plenty like her had come and gone. In a year his master would not remember her name. The Fates, hearing, smiled.

As Boehmer opened the story before de Breteuil his face flushed with pleasure and a smile showed his teeth. Every gleam of his eager eye, every note of his edged voice as he questioned, showed egoism alight and alert in the background.

"And the Cardinal himself acted all through? You saw him? The woman Lamotte did not act as intermediary between you and him?"

"Monsieur le Comte, no. I saw his Eminence repeatedly. It is true that Madame de Lamotte-Valois acted as an intermediary in a way, but

Monseigneur was with her in it all. Many of my interviews were with him."

Even as yet Boehmer could not quite abandon his belief in that consummate actress. He saw the flash and passion of her as she swept out of the room on her way to Versailles and clung like a drowning man to the belief that some explanation must emerge — somehow, somewhere.

"And he signed the agreement?" de Breteuil questioned greedily.

"Undoubtedly, Monsieur le Comte."

Even Boehmer was startled by the look on de Breteuil's face as he struck his hand on his knee, crying: "I have him — I have him at last!"

That was the man with a dropped mask, but it was pulled over eyes and lips again when he turned smoothly and gravely to the trembling Boehmer: "Monsieur, the matter shall be dealt with. Allow me to say however that you did very unwisely in not opening the matter to me at once. Surely in your position you should have known that the Queen does not transact business of that sort for herself. These things are done through the Household Department. Depend upon it she has known nothing of the matter from beginning to end."

"But, Monsieur le Comte, what then is to become of me?" cried Boehmer in the extremity of terror. "I tell you I saw her writing. I had her instructions. Monsieur Leclaux took the necklace in her name —"

He could neither continue nor even stand upright any longer but collapsed pitiably into a chair. Not a gleam of pity however was on the face of de Breteuil. He bade him pull himself together, get home and put his story in writing, omitting no detail. It should be sifted to the bottom. That was all he could promise.

"And remember," he added, "that you yourself may be very gravely implicated. A suspicion may easily arise that you wanted to get rid of this dead weight of diamonds anyhow and counted on forcing the Queen to pay you to avoid a scandal. Be careful. Stick to the truth but omit nothing — nothing. Especially what concerns the Prince de Rohan and the woman."

Boehmer had risen again, supporting himself by the chair, and was staring at de Breteuil, haggard with horror at this new complication, when the door opened and de Fersen walked in, cool and tall, with a glance of surprise at Boehmer's condition. He knew him by sight as all the courtiers did and for de Fersen he had more interest than for others because it was known that as an old servant the Queen unbent with the man. He himself had never seen her since the fatal day of the *descampativo* except surrounded by her friends, coldly acknowledging his salute, high, unapproachable, a woman deeply offended, a queen coarsely outraged. Well, he could bear it, for his conscience acquitted him. No woman, no queen, should dare to resent a love which, asking, hoping nothing, offers itself only as a sword and shield to the beloved. And in his own heart he knew that the day for sword and shield was close at hand.

And here was this man fresh from her presence, half-fainting with terror. What had happened? Every instinct in him sprang to attention. De Breteuil was obviously angry at his entry, apologizing hurriedly.

"So sorry, my dear Comte. Shall I join you in the anteroom? I had forgotten our appointment. Monsieur Boehmer is here about some jewellery of her Majesty's. I shall be free in a moment."

He signed to the door, but Boehmer now almost out of his mind sprang to de Fersen, who had the reputation of being one of the Queen's immediate circle.

"Monsieur le Comte, I beseech you to represent to her Majesty that I am to be accused of stealing my own diamonds and I know not what other horrors. For Christ's sake, ask her to disclose the truth! I am like an ox before the slaughterers. Everyone has his own interest to serve and there is no pity anywhere. Pray for me to her Majesty. Pray!"

De Fersen, a shade paler, turned to the other: "I think, my friend, that it is desirable I should understand Monsieur Boehmer's grievance."

The other shrugged cynical shoulders. From his point of view the sooner the Cardinal's disgrace was published the better.

"Since it will be all over France in a week I see no objection to a gentleman's hearing it now who can hold his tongue. But for your own comfort's sake I advise you to keep out of it."

De Fersen made no answer. He turned to Boehmer — now so frantic with terror that he would have flung himself down a precipice if it had been a refuge from his pursuers. Out came the story. It had so fixed itself in his tortured thoughts that he could tell it with a certain brevity and conciseness and the more so because de Fersen's immovable calm was a rock against which he could steady himself. He leaned against the door, listening intently. Not a flicker of emotion or interest passed over his face. He listened like a mask — sometimes Boehmer imagined his own thoughts absorbed him, but if he faltered for a moment a quickly raised finger warned him to go on. He finished, tottering with faintness and despair, and de Fersen filled a glass with wine from a decanter which stood on the table.

"Thank you, monsieur. You have put it very clearly and I comprehend. Drink this and it will enable you to get home and do all that you see is needful. There may be a way out of this miserable tangle yet. Keep calm and silent. And believe me when I say that truth and innocence can never fail of a hearing before the Queen."

The unexpected kindness of his tone moved Boehmer to speechless emotion. He bowed humbly, forgetting the greater man altogether and crept to the door.

"A pretty kettle of fish!" de Breteuil said with acid enjoyment. "That fool has done for himself this time with a vengeance. No doubt he will be sent to the Bastille tonight!"

He was sure of de Fersen's agreement as of himself and the shock was like a blow in the face when he was answered quietly: "You are surely not serious?"

"Serious. You will find I am and the Queen also, if she has a grain of sense. I believe her to be innocent —" de Fersen made a quick gesture but said nothing — "and if so the world cannot know too soon what a scoundrelly part the Cardinal has played. It's her only chance of clearing herself. Good heavens, how her enemies will exult."

He halted for agreement and as none came went on: "Monseigneur must be shown for the sharper he is, the contemptible ally of that brute Cagliostro. You see he was there too when the diamonds changed hands. No doubt the fellow who received them was a tool of his and Monseigneur's. *Mordieu*! they made a pretty haul of it. The blasted impudence of the man is what takes me!" He repeated one or two of Boehmer's statements, gloating over them with a pleasure not lost on the other. Not a thought of the Queen except as a pawn in his own game. He took high ground. He spoke of saving her from herself, but the truth spoke louder than his own words and gestures, and still the other listened summing it up, analysing, resolving in silence until de Breteuil gathered up his hat and sword to hurry to the King.

Then slowly, and in his own reflective way, de Fersen spoke: "It is fortunate, I think, that I should have heard the facts before you saw his Majesty. Two heads are better than one and I shall be obliged if you will hear me."

He still leaned with his back against the door and it would have been unpardonable to thrust past him. The other flung himself carelessly into a chair and listened.

"It is perfectly clear to anyone who hears the story that de Rohan has been fooled. The woman has accomplices —"

"Impossible!" de Breteuil said angrily. "He told Boehmer himself that he had seen the Queen! Could he be fooled there? Unless indeed you think —"

De Fersen's look stopped him.

"If you consider you will see that part of the story is impossible and —"

De Breteuil cut him short.

"And why if he wanted to fool Boehmer and get his claws on the diamonds?"

"Because there's no motive. In no conceivable circumstances could the diamonds have tempted him. Consider — consider! He is a Rohan and remember the jewels of that House. He has spent freely, yes, but there has never been a moment when he could not have raised any sum on those alone. No no! Dismiss fatuities. He has been fooled. But I go further — if he had not been, if he were guilty, still the Cardinal cannot be touched. He too must be shielded."

De Breteuil laughed aloud.

"To shield the Queen? Good God, you must believe her in the plot also if —"

De Fersen made a movement forward and restrained himself.

"Allow me to finish. In the dreadful state of public opinion and hatred of the Queen, de Rohan will be made a hero. It will be said he is her victim and you will ruin her and he will escape scot-free. He is closely allied with all the great families in France — the Condos and God knows who! Will they bear it? They will move like one man. He is a prince of the Church. Will the Church stand it? He is popular with the people, will they forgive the Queen? Is not her position cruel enough without setting the Church and the nobility against her? I dare swear that her own pride and consciousness of innocence will resolve her to hunt the fool down to the last, but if you value the monarchy you will save her from herself!"

In his own heart the thought was of her and her only. What did the monarchy matter except in so far as it concerned her? But the spoken appeal was made to de Breteuil — a nobleman of France who might be supposed to concern himself for the Crown.

He made a gesture of ridicule.

"What? The people are to see that she dares not expose the Cardinal? A pleasant position for the Queen of France! I believe you must be as mad as Boehmer."

"I make one last appeal," de Fersen answered. "I tell you if you value either King or Queen that you are heading them straight to ruin. See de Rohan. Get his explanation first. Get the King to see him. Do not drive him to despair. No talk of the Bastille! Use him to sift the Lamotte and her accomplices. As I stand before God I tell you I am not sure that even they can be attacked — so precious, so delicate is the Queen's name at the moment. What matter diamonds and vengeance compared with that? Can I not make you see? The thing must never reach the public. Never!"

De Breteuil buckled his sword on and looked de Fersen straight in the face.

"We are losing valuable time. Your counsel would be mere cowardice and condemnation for the Queen. And who could keep such a scandal secret? She must face it like a brave woman and she will conquer."

"She will face it like a brave woman but she will not conquer!" said de Fersen. He knew de Breteuil's grudge against the Cardinal — all the world knew that! He could read the mean little signals of gratified spite fluttering in the man's face. Well, he could do no more.

"For the last time I ask: will you even wait and discuss it with de Vergennes? He is one of the astutest men I know and the case needs it all. Delay — I entreat you!"

"For the last time — no!"

De Fersen moved away from the door. The other went out, flinging it to behind him. When he was alone he stood leaning on his own sword which he had unconsciously unbuckled. His absorption was so deep that he might have been the statue of a knight keeping his vigil before the altar in eternal marble. Minutes ebbed by and still he stood.

At last he roused himself. Thought had taken shape in will.

He strode out and along the echoing corridors until he met a waiting woman whose face he remembered. He had seen her in attendance on the Princesse de Lamballe and now addressed her courteously.

"Has Madame returned from the country?"

"But yes, Monsieur le Comte. Her Highness returned this morning."

"Have the goodness to ask if her Highness will have the condescension to spare me ten minutes as soon as possible."

In less than ten minutes he stood before the Princess.

An hour later a message was sent from her to the Queen. She entreated the honour of an audience. There was no answer. Her Majesty was closeted with the King and the Master of the Household. It could not be delivered. Four hours later she sent again. Her Majesty was indisposed hilt would see her.

Never during the remainder of her short life was that scene blotted from her vision. The Queen, ashen pale, her eyes red and swollen with tears that rage had dried was walking up and down the room so rapidly that her white dress seemed to flash past the Princess's eyes. Her lips were moving as if she talked to herself, but no sound came from them. She did not even see the woman who stood waiting tall and sad by the door until at last gathering courage she put herself directly in the Queen's way. She stopped and put her hand confusedly to her brows.

"Thérèse! But you were away! All the world has gone mad since you were here, and I with it."

Very gently the Princess led her to a chair and dropping on her knees before her looked up into her face. Marie Antoinette closed her aching eyes.

"You know this horror?"

"Madame, I know."

"Then know also that for once the King acts with energy. I shall be vindicated in the face of France and the world. The archfiend will be in the Bastille in a few days."

"Madame, who?"

"De Rohan. Who else?"

It took all the high courage of Thérèse de Lamballe to speak as de Fersen and she had agreed. Afterwards she did not know how she had dared — could not even remember the arguments she had driven against the Queen's immovable resolution, for her own brain was numbed with the struggle.

She could hear herself entreating that he might be exiled, after being confronted by his shame.

"I hate the man as does your Majesty," she said passionately. "Yet there is some spark of good in him, and the blood of the Rohans does not willingly associate with the dregs of humanity as you are now driving him to do."

And nothing but the Queen's blazing scorn answered her.

"He chose his associates for himself," she interrupted haughtily.

"True, and he has been frightfully duped, but for a dupe there may be forgiveness, especially if politic. Forgive him. Get the threads of the intrigue from him. Make it his interest to be frank. Do not alienate the Church and the nobility. The people are already —" She broke off short.

The Queen replied with concentrated bitterness of emphasis.

"Why hesitate? The people are already my enemies. Well, alone I will fight. Alone I will die, if need be. I will not hear a word more. It is disgraceful even to listen to such counsels, and to utter them is a crime."

Not even that insult revolted the true heart of the Princess. Those who loved the Queen loved her well, for they had much to bear from her at that dreadful time and did not flinch.

Once more and despairingly she made her plea and in vain.

"What! and let the others escape too? Become their accomplice? Perhaps you would have me pay Boehmer for the necklace that all the world may say there was no shame to which the Queen would not fall to cover up her guilt. And you say this, *you*! I thought you were a clean-hearted brave woman. I know you for a cheating coward like the rest."

She bore that also, entreating, gathering every argument, knowing in her own inmost soul the frightful danger ahead. In all France there would be no pity, no sympathy for the woman who felt her wrongs to be so gross that the mere recital of them would rally every man and woman in France to her side. She looked into Thérèse's eyes with pitiful confidence.

"This monstrous thing will show them that the other slanders were lies too. Oh, Thérèse, it may even be a blessing in disguise. I have borne so much, but this frightful ordeal will end it. France will see my enemies driven into the open. She will rejoice with me. You will see. Oh, I could thank God almost! Not quite yet. But I shall — I shall! De Breteuil urges me and he is right."

It was agony to Thérèse. How she endured it she never knew. But she knew also the madness that led the Queen to her decision and struggled on — and in vain.

At last she saw the battle was over and she was conquered. She rose and stood before her Mistress, wearied out but with a strange serenity.

"God keep you, Madame. God guide you. Have I your leave to go?"

Marie Antoinette rose and stood also.

"Kiss me, my friend!" she said. "I wish I could share my courage and conviction with you. But I love you always."

She kissed Thérèse de Lamballe with cold lips, and the Princess looking back at the door saw her as it were in immense deserts of solitude, alone with Fate.

Chapter XVIII

LITTLE could the Cardinal guess what awaited him at Versailles when he proceeded there in all his pontifical pomp and with hopes far other than pontifical in his breast. His face, handsome and florid, became his magnificence well and none could guess what lay below the surface. Received with all due observance he betook himself to the gallery and the OEil-de-Boeuf where the splendidly dressed crowd waited for a signal to proceed to the worship which seemed only another aspect of Court life. The King and Queen would soon make their appearance and the splendid procession be formed.

Meanwhile little subdued cascades of talk overflowed everywhere; comments on dress, appearance, rumours, scandal — all the floating froth-talk of fashionable society bubbled and broke about him, politely subdued, but urgent, invading. Lost in his own preoccupations he scarcely heard it. Would she come soon? Would she look at him smiling, with the hidden meaning which he had read into her look the last time he had seen her pass through the long gallery? No, it would be better; it — A sudden lull in the polite hubbub. A message, a — What is it? It flies round the circle. The Cardinal de Rohan is summoned to his Majesty's closet.

"Lucky man! Wish it were I!" says one. "Oh, the nuisance!" yawns a lady. "Do but think of the delay! — and I have an appointment in half an hour." "I must say their Majesties might have a *little* consideration for their unfortunate subjects. It really justifies all the thrusts of Beaumarchais!" And so forth. Little waves of polite curiosity and irritation bubbled and splashed all round.

Meanwhile the Cardinal, his cheeks purple with agitation, his heart beating a double-quick measure, was ushered to the Royal Closet, and there marshalled inside by the official and so left. Entering too humbly to perceive exactly who was present none the less his bows were tremendous. At last, at last! — something inside his breast exulted — his eclipse was over, his summer-time begun! She had worked these miracles for him. She should have his life's devotion in return.

Cold silence. He raised his eyes in surprise. The King stood there motionless, his eyes fixed upon him, but without making a gesture to return his salute. The Queen sat in her chair, rigid and white. No smile, no greeting. Instinctively he halted, drawing back a little, his heart beating violently. Instantly the King spoke, and with a flash the horror was upon him, for the tone was enough, even without the words.

"You have bought diamonds of Boehmer?"

Was it his own voice in reply that he heard or a stranger's? It sounded small and flat in an immense void.

"Yes, Sire," it said.

"What have you done with them?"

Clinging to what composure he could, he answered mechanically: "I thought they had been delivered to the Queen."

"Who commissioned you?"

"A lady called the Countess de Lamotte-Valois, who handed me a letter from the Queen."

His voice stumbled and broke. The King was staring at him in dull amazement. De Rohan added lamely: "I thought I was gratifying her Majesty by taking this business on myself."

The Queen stiffened in her chair and spoke as coldly as drops of hail beating a window. Her voice too sounded to him small and clear in an immense place.

"How, Monseigneur, could you believe that I should choose you, to whom I have not spoken for eight years, to negotiate anything for me, and through the mediation of a woman of whom I never heard?"

For a moment he could not speak, though he tried to for manhood's sake. Words fluttered and choked in his throat. It was a full minute before he mastered them, and then only partially and halting between the words. For suddenly in one dreadful moment, her look had shattered his house of cards and blown it apart like autumn leaves. No reasoning was needed. It was gone. It never had been. He stood alone to face the storm.

"I see plainly —" he gasped — "I see plainly that I have been duped. I will pay for the necklace."

Silence. His voice staggered on.

"My desire to please your Majesty blinded me. I suspected no trick in the affair."

Silence.

"I am sorry for it."

Silence. It seemed that the room was whirling round him in bright spots of colour. Would they never speak?

He fumbled for his pocketbook, found it, opened it, and without a word handed to the King a letter from the Queen to Jeanne de Lamotte-Valois, giving him the commission to buy the necklace. Without a word the King took it, the Queen sitting rigidly by. He read it, then holding it by the edge toward the Cardinal like a thing unclean, said coldly: "This is neither written nor signed by the Queen. How could a Prince of the House of Rohan and a Grand Almoner of France believe that the Queen would sign 'Marie Antoinette de France'? You knew well that queens sign only their baptismal names. Have you ever written such a letter as this?"

The King handed him a copy of his letter to Boehmer. He looked at it, the confusion in his brain growing worse with every minute, and stuttered out: "I do not remember having written it."

"But what if the original, signed by yourself, were shown to you?"

"If the letter be signed by myself it must be genuine." Something seemed to break in his head. He no longer was able to think. He repeated aimlessly: "I have been deceived, Sire. I will pay for the necklace. I have been most grossly deceived. I ask pardon of your Majesties."

His misery made some impression on the King, who spoke with a more human touch. The Queen was an image of stone.

"Then explain this mystery. I have no wish to find you guilty of such disgraceful conduct. I still hope you may be able to justify yourself. Account for all these manoeuvres with Boehmer. What do these assurances and letters mean?"

The Cardinal, breaking under the strain and deadly pale, leaned upon the table for support, the Queen regarding him now as if he were a foul animal. He got out a few breathless words: "Sire, I am too much confused to answer your Majesty in a way —"

A gleam of the King's real kind-heartedness struggled through his anger.

"Compose yourself. Go into my cabinet. You will there find paper, pens and ink. Write what you have to say to me."

He showed some human feeling, the Queen none. She stared at de Rohan with eyes where the blue had turned to steel. It was natural enough, for deadly terror gripped her as well as fury, and the two struck her dumb with frozen hatred of the man who was the cause of this obscure strangling squalor that was winding coil after coil about her.

Left alone, the King turned to her and, taking her hand, kissed it tenderly.

"Don't be so silent, Antoinette. You are safe now. The man shall help us to disentangle the plot. I believe he was a dupe — not a rogue."

"For God's sake, show him no mercy!" she ejaculated in a stifled cry. "If you have any pity on me, hunt this man down. Could he have believed in those letters? He — a Rohan! He is the vilest of plotters. Arrest him."

They said no more, he lost in thought, she in her dumb misery. At the end of a quarter of an hour de Rohan returned, magnificent in his ecclesiastic robes, but with a skulking terrified face under his scarlet biretta. In his own way he was as far beyond the power of thought as Marie Antoinette herself. She raised her great eyes and fixed them on him dumbly once more. In a shaking hand he extended a sheet of paper to the King, who took it in silence.

It was hopeless. A mass of blots and erasures, unfinished sentences — utter confusion, and no more.

After looking at it in vain and finally laying it on the table, the King walked to the door and called into the anteroom, and in a moment the Cardinal's prime enemy was beside them, the Baron de Breteuil, Master of the King's Household, and there was joy in the sharpness of his glance at the fallen enemy.

What followed was incredibly simple. The King turned to de Rohan and said coolly: "Withdraw, Monseigneur," and to de Breteuil: "Is the guard ready? Arrest this man." The die was cast.

It was all over in a moment, and in a moment more the Cardinal, in charge of a lieutenant of the Body Guard, was stumbling along the great chambers and galleries, with an astounded fashionable world crowding and fluttering about him like a disturbed rookery, while the King alone with the Queen tried to support her, her head fallen back upon his shoulder, her mouth set like death.

Dreadfully embarrassed with the rank of his captive, the young lieutenant, dark, slim, and sworded, did his spiriting with the utmost obsequiousness, and this trifle revived the Cardinal's dying courage and enabled thought to penetrate his terror. All was lost, lost for ever, if they rifled his cabinet at the Hotel de Rohan, he suddenly remembered. Strange, he had not thought of it before. Then all *must* be lost, for in heaven and earth he could see no way of communicating unsuspected with his secretary, the Abbé Georgel. Would this young man — Could it be dared? God, what was to be done? He saw the aide-major of the Body Guard approaching to relieve the lieutenant of such an important charge.

In one instant the last chance would be gone for ever. He said in a thick whisper: "Lieutenant, where are they taking me?"

"Monseigneur, to the Hotel de Rohan and then to the Bastille. Under strict guard."

"Lieutenant, if it were possible that I could have a word with my heyduc — I believe he will be somewhere about. I need some personal comforts which they should make ready. A word — a word only, I beseech you. It is a very trifling mercy."

"Monseigneur, if you can indicate your man —"

He knew nothing than that it was a political arrest, and to a young lieutenant a cardinal is a cardinal and a prince a prince. And what harm could a servant do — all said and done!

"He will be in my livery. Tall, blond — from Strasburg. And would it be possible to lend me a pencil?"

It was possible and swiftly done and, saluting, the young lieutenant drew back on his heels.

The aide-major was now in charge instead, walking stiffly beside his prisoner. The young lieutenant had disappeared in the gaping crowd of plumed ladies and sworded men.

They were nearing the door of the Salon of Hercules.

There was his man, nervous, terrified at his master's plight, but there, thanks be to God, and the slim young lieutenant stood at his shoulder. The Cardinal halted and said in a clear voice to the aide-major: "Monsieur, have I your permission to give a brief instruction to be carried to my valet of articles I shall need in the Bastille? What I write is open to your inspection."

"Perfectly, Monseigneur, perfectly, if it can be accomplished without much delay. Accommodate yourself at this table."

Again a cardinal was a cardinal and a prince a prince, even with the aide-major! He wrote for a few seconds and held the paper to the officer who glanced at it blandly and waved it away. It was written in German, and it would certainly not become an aide-major to acknowledge his ignorance of that or any tongue before not only the bystanders, but his own men.

The Cardinal beckoned his heyduc and spoke in German.

"Take this instantly to the Abbé Georgel, who will instruct my valet. On your life."

He added in French as if recollecting his position: "That will save me much discomfort. Monsieur, I am now at your service."

The crowd parted before the heyduc as he sped along. He at all events could read German, and tore for his life to where the nearest horse could be procured, then hell-for-leather to Paris. The horse foundered and died when they got him to his stable, the heyduc in little better case staggered faintly to a chair when he had thrust the paper into the secretary's hand. But the deed was done, and before the prisoner was half way to Paris all the documents connected with the case had gone up in smoke, and the Queen's last chance of clearing herself had gone up with them.

There was a great parade when the lieutenant of police put formal seals upon all the Cardinal's papers, by order of de Breteuil, but the Cardinal could leave it with princely equanimity knowing that his correspondence with Jeanne and all else that concerned him personally lay in black ash before them.

One screed of paper unburnt they found with the august name of the Grand Cophta inscribed upon it, and since there had been not a few devilments in Paris of late in which his mystic finger was plainly discernible the thought struck de Breteuil that he might possibly be able to throw a gleam of his own peculiarly lurid light upon the intricacies of this transaction. And the Lamotte — where in the dark places of Paris might she have hidden her viperish head? Who knew but that it might be in the Grand Cophta's own sanctuary! She was known to have been an intimate of the guarded rites.

They went to his house in haste and arrested Cagliostro in undress array, as it may be called. A loose robe of purple velvet covered his portly form and slippers his feet, and on a table by his elbow stood a bottle of the Cardinal's wine and a book, not alas, dealing with the sacred Arcana, but with the light loves of the town — the flying foam of the gaieties of Paris — which was perhaps the reason why his spirits had left him uninformed of his approaching doom.

They arrested him on a charge of complicity in the Affair of the Diamond Necklace.

"But why me?" he enquired with his own brazen composure. "Why not the little Lamotte? She really knows more about it than anyone else."

"And what do you know of her?" the lieutenant of police enquired. "Any information that aids the course of justice will be to your own advantage."

"Why, I know that she was the prime mover throughout. And a thorough-paced adventuress. She presented me with a snuff-box set with diamonds as a return for a valuable service I did her, and when I had it examined every diamond was paste! What can you do with a woman like that?"

"Then she is not under your protection, monsieur?"

"Under mine! God forbid. She is at Bar-sur-Aube — if she has arrived there. She posted down, after a feint of going to Versailles. This first aroused my suspicions. You will find her there if you make haste."

"Doubtless, monsieur. But may we first ask what was the service rendered which claimed the gratitude of Madame de Lamotte? Was it by chance connected with the Necklace?"

The Grand Cophta smiled over his pinch of snuff. His composure was amazing.

"Why, yes, monsieur Pofficier. You may certainly ask. No secrets from you! I provided Madame la Comtesse with the Ivory Bloom of Eternal Youth. You must have heard the Parisian ladies speak of it. I, Cagliostro, who now address you, owe all to that miraculous balsam, and I gave it to the Countess for nothing in the world but the love of a helpful deed. The result was the ingratitude you see!" He gave an impatient spin to the snuff-box and sent it flying off the table, retrieving it smartly with a turn of the wrist.

"Now, *messieurs*, if you are ready!" cried the raucous voice of the lieutenant of police. There was a swing, a turn in the room, and they were marching steadily down the broad shallow staircase to the vast *porte-cochère* where the frightened domestics had assembled to bid farewell to their master.

"To the Bastille! Have the goodness, monsieur, to place yourself by Monseigneur," cried the awful voice, and again, "Arrest the woman at Bar-sur-Aube, *de par le roi.*" And in a moment more the Cardinal and Charlatan were both on their way to the Bastille, the grim old fortress that was still the heart of Paris.

The Cardinal sat staring from the windows of the carriage in a stupor of alarm. Cagliostro hummed a tune contentedly beside him.

"You are in good spirits, my friend," said de Rohan with a sickly smile, after enduring the music as long as he could in silence.

"If Monseigneur could share my knowledge, Monseigneur would be equally cheerful. And my song also interests me. It is the Fa-la-la.

"Little Queen you must not be
So haughty with your twenty years!
Your ill-used courtiers soon may see
You pass again the barriers,
With a fa-la-la-la-la.

"Such as it is I prefer my own future to her Majesty's," he added.

"And my future, my wise friend?" asked the Cardinal, with reviving reverence.

"Yours also is preferable to her Majesty's, Monseigneur. And I am considering with some amusement what the Comtesse de Lamotte's expression will be when they overtake her at Bar-sur-Aube."

"My friend, I beseech you to counsel me before we are separated as to my attitude to that accursed woman. What does your wisdom tell you?"

"That you were her dupe, Monseigneur. That I was so also in a measure, for unhappily I never brought the Celestial Wisdom to bear on it. But you and I are safe. You have powerful protection of one sort, I of another. A last word — do not imperil yourself to defend the Queen, for she will ruin you if it is in her power. As to Lamotte, she has no friends. Throw her to the wolves."

The Cardinal was silent. In a few moments more the Bastille was frowning above them, and the Cardinal was taken with some ceremony to his quarters, Cagliostro with none to his.

PART IV

Chapter XIX

EARLY in September the Queen sat under the great horn-beams in the gardens of Versailles with only Madame Campan in attendance. She was pale as the white dress she wore and her eyes had the weariness of insomnia with dark shadows beneath them, but beauty was still hers, pathetic and heart-piercing, beauty destined to endure to the end though pain was henceforth to be its companion. In her fresh youth life had seemed an assured series of triumphs certain to end in a blaze of sunset glory — the life of a great queen, daughter of the greatest empress of her time. What else could it be? Now, taught by destiny, she saw it as a race with a receding goal out of reach for ever, never to be attained — and realized that no triumph is allotted to any human endeavour. Even to pass through life without dishonour appeared now a task beyond mortal power, for the nature of things took its own way and was always cruelly the master.

She sat revolving these sad thoughts with the shade of the yellowing leaves coming and going upon her pale face. It was early in the morning and the craving for fresh air and quiet had brought her out to drink a little tranquillity from the pure chalice of the dawn. Madame Campan attended her, the only one of her women with whom at present she could discuss the horror that crushed her, for with one exception the greater ladies were drawing cautiously back into their family defences doubting the Queen's innocence and the King's wisdom in exposing so great a prince as de Rohan. But she sat silent, with slender hands folded in her lap and eyes fixed on the trees where a few birds still faintly chirped and twittered. The singing was over. Love-time was done for thrush and nightingale, and only the dove remembered and from some deep shadow uttered her eternal moan of dreams. It dropped, a round pearl of sound, from the very hand of silence.

The faithful Madame Campan would have given much to speak her mind, for drifts of event and opinion which it was vital should reach the Queen broke against her daily. Her lesser rank gave her freedom with people who would never have spoken their minds to any of the great Court ladies and knowing these things she feared a certain stubbornness in the Queen, partly the result of anger, partly temperament, which might hurry her into dangerous decisions in a most dangerous crisis. But when royalty is silent it enforces silence on those about it and she could only wait in deadly anxiety. The King was almost invisible, holding long councils with his ministers. All now realized that Boehmer and his affairs had precipitated a crisis which would shake the throne. The air was charged with thunder-glooms and none knew the direction the storm would take.

Presently the Queen looked up: "How did they capture the woman?"

"Driving madly from Bar-sur-Aube, making for the frontier as hard as she could go. She had miscalculated by a day. She is in the Bastille now."

Marie Antoinette drew a long deep breath like one relieved from a terror.

"Thank God! I feared I might die before they captured her. Now the truth will be known."

Madame Campan was silent. The truth could never be known. De Rohan's fatal order to his secretary had saved his own head and destroyed every scrap of evidence. It was now only a question of the Queen's word and there were few indeed in France who would be so poor as to value that at more than the dead leaves drifting about her.

She said no more, but perhaps there was a faint tinge of colour in her face. How she had longed and prayed for that news none but herself could know. She might begin to hope.

A step sounded far off on the shady path and presently nearer. It meant nothing to Madame Campan. Probably one of the gardeners, mattering as little as the grasshoppers chirping about them in the perishing grass. But a faint painful colour stole into the Queen's cheeks, though she still gazed steadily at the fair hands folded in her lap. It drew nearer and nearer, and presently a man, parting the branches, came out into the glade where they sat and looked about him.

It was the Count Axel de Fersen, and evidently he was not strolling aimlessly, but had a purpose. He halted and bowed, sweeping the grass with his hat, then stood bareheaded, a sunbeam falling on his fair northern hair and clear blue eyes — clear and blue as icebergs swinging down from the North Cape — a very gallant gentleman. He said not a word, but stood waiting until the Queen said uncertainly: "Monsieur?" with a trembling question.

Again he bowed low.

"Madame. May I have the honour to speak a few words to your Majesty? I felt this was an opportunity not to be lost."

"You have something of consequence to say? I am very weary today." She looked it. Her twenty-eight sad years weighed on her like lead. It was an effort to raise her eyes to his face.

"Madame, I believe it to be necessary. But you will be the judge."

She raised her hand in a gesture that bid him speak, Madame Campan watching him with profound interest, touched with hope. This young man inspired confidence in all honourable men and women who knew him, and detestation in the baser sort who dreaded the cool contempt hidden by northern reserve and self-control. He had therefore his warm friends and malignant enemies. To Madame Campan, who was his friend, it seemed at the moment that his presence was like a stream of clean air in a close and sunless room.

The *roucoule* of the dove fell into the silence as he collected himself to speak.

"Madame, since the arrest of the Cardinal, the Court — Versailles at large — has seethed with rumours and tales true and false. I have listened to all in silence, for it may be needful the stark truth should reach you, and. I dread lest it may not. It was therefore my part to. make myself acquainted with all."

"You mean, monsieur, that you will spare neither my feelings nor my royalty if you believe there are things. I should know?"

"I mean that. And I shall wound both — which I would give my life to guard."

He spoke so plainly and simply that the words conveyed no bravado, nor any touch of lover's passion. But still the Queen did not look up.

"You offer me true service," she said. "Speak fearlessly. I will listen with courage."

"Then, Madame, you should know that all the world with but few exceptions believes that you were concerned in the intrigue and that the Cardinal acted as your agent. They believe that Lamotte and he are to be made your scapegoats, and that the necklace is in your possession."

"My God!" she said very low. Then, looking at him with a curdling terror, she said swiftly: "That bears out what I foresaw. I will tell you and my good Campan what haunts me — what I dream of awake, for sleep I cannot. I think it is a plot, a much greater plot than we have thought. Perhaps some of the great nobles behind it. They want to ruin me in the eyes of the King and the French people. And I believe that they have hidden the necklace somewhere in my rooms, and they will pretend to find it there and that will be the end. You will see! And then I shall be taken from my children — and — and —"

The words broke on her lips. Madame Campan interposed eagerly. De Fersen struck his hand on his sword hilt with a laugh gay as sunshine.

"Dreams, Madame, dreams! It is a case of the commonest swindling," he said, "and the only plot in it was to steal the diamonds and enrich such sharpers as the Lamottes and another rascal named Villette. Am I not right, madame?" — to the eager-eyed Campan.

"A thousand times right, monsieur. There is no question at all of such a horror. But I rejoice you will speak frankly with her Majesty. The words have burnt on my own lips, and you know more than I. Madame, this is a godsend. I entreat your Majesty to hear with patience."

A little electric shock of vitality seemed to communicate itself to her from the eagerness of the other two. She said simply: "I thank you both very sincerely. Yes, that could scarcely be, but when one has suffered so much all terrors become possible and natural. Well, monsieur? Have I no friends?"

"Madame, there are very few who believe the truth, but not many, and this story added to the vile libels which have been circulating in Paris will make the position extremely difficult. It is said that the woman Lamotte now in the Bastille swears she will carry it through to the bitter end and will drag — no, how should I speak such filth?"

"Repeat it, monsieur. I must know."

"Will drag your Majesty from the throne with her if she must suffer."

"And the Cardinal?"

"He repeats that he had your Majesty's assurance and letters all through. That he believed and believes them to be yours, and that moreover he had a meeting with you in these gardens where you assured him the past was forgiven and permitted him to hope for the future. On that assurance he bought the necklace."

"And hearing all this you still believe in me?"

His smile was sufficient. He went on quietly with his statement: "Madame, I wish to point out also that the Cardinal's high birth gives him great allies. I have been able to ascertain that the Condes, the de Noailles and many more are banding themselves together in a league which will spare neither money nor effort to carry him through scatheless. There is not one but feels that the disgrace of a man of the same blood — a de Rohan — would stain every one of his kith and kin and even the whole order of nobility. It is war to the knife between the nobles and the Throne if the Throne prosecutes. We have got the woman now and the villains may suffer for all they care but not the Cardinal. It may be necessary —"

In a flash she was on her feet, beautiful as a flame of fire.

"I see your drift, monsieur. I see it well. It is the old counsel of cowardice for me. You have not faith in my cause. Then I tell you this — I, Marie Antoinette, Queen of France, Archduchess of Austria — that if for fear's sake I forgave that man and permitted him to escape the punishment of his crime I should deserve to fall from my throne and lie in the gutter beside the Lamotte. Thank God, we have got them both!"

Madame Campan threw herself on her knees before her.

"Madame, the Count is right. It is a frightful danger. I knew the Cardinal should never have been arrested. He should be conciliated —"

The Queen burst through her words: "Conciliated? A vile wretch who believed that his sovereign was an intriguer and dared to believe he could make love to her — to a woman he believed would sell her soul and her royalty for a handful of diamonds? You are mad, you and the Comte de Fersen. People might well believe me guilty if they saw any mercy accorded to a villain like de Rohan — the worse villain because of his great blood and his profession."

"His profession," de Fersen repeated eagerly. "That is true. But there again, Madame, let your Majesty remember that in attacking the Cardinal you attack not only the French nobility but the whole mighty power of Rome. It is arrayed behind him now. Can your Majesty believe that the Vatican will permit a cardinal to be disgraced — a man who, whatever his life, knows the inmost secrets of the Church? Never! — I beseech you to use your influence with the King to undo at once his fatal arrest. His rank entitles him to be judged by his Majesty and no one lower.

Then, Madame, when he has given up his secrets let him have a year's exile and thus satisfy the nobles. Your Majesty will need them."

"If I needed them a hundred times I would not buy them at the price of shame and a craven heart. And let me tell you, you are both mistaken. Who would not believe I had something to hide if I skulked in the dark and feared to let common justice handle my accusers. No — I know your fidelity, one and the other, but you are grossly misled. The French people have hated me but they will respect the sight of their Queen who dares to meet her accusers like an honest woman."

The man and woman looked at her in despair. They could not make her understand that for her there would be no justice.

"And I glory in it that I — *I* persuaded the King to arrest him. He hesitated but I would not have it. I forced him to see the cruelty of my position and at last he saw and agreed."

She had never looked more beautiful, with her eager face and panting bosom, and the words leaping like sparks of fire from her lips. But de Fersen caught no contagious flame. His manner was indescribably anxious and sad.

"Madame, your view is noble and like yourself. Yet in the world we live in nobility itself must walk sworded and shielded, and I take humble leave to tell your Majesty you are not wise. It is yourself whom you put on trial with the lowest of earth's creatures. I who venerate the ground you walk on would a thousand times rather see the door of the Bastille open and give free way to all those scoundrels than behold the Queen reduced to defend herself against them in a dreadful equality. But since that cannot be I beseech you on my knees to free the Cardinal and let him assist the prosecution."

Madame Campan, still on her knees, ventured to touch the Queen's robe. No more, for in moments of anger the training of race and command set her apart from ordinary mortals.

"Madame, Madame, I beseech you to hear us. Every word the Comte says is true. It is ruin to proceed further."

She blazed upon them.

"Ruin for the Queen of France to have her calumniators brought to trial and punished as they deserve? The Queen to be the only person in the realm who can claim no protection from justice? I thought you both my friends. I see that in your hearts you believe me guilty and so counsel me to seek a disgraceful safety. And where do you believe I have hidden the necklace, monsieur?"

Her proud eyes lanced his heart; her disdain scathed him, but for her sake he did not flinch.

"Madame, pardon me. Do I not see that such a suggestion is horror to your noble pride. But there is deadly danger. It is known that the Cardinal's papers were all destroyed owing to the fatal lapse made by the officer who arrested him. It will be but your word against —"

"*But* my word!" she interrupted, no longer able to contain herself. "I have fallen low indeed when such a man as yourself can address such a word to me. Well, monsieur, it is time you left my presence, but before you go, know this: that with *but* my word and my pure conscience I shall drive these wretches before me to their rightful ruin. I thank you for your counsel."

The words were of course dismissal. His hat had dropped upon the grass beside him. He stooped and picked it up, then bowed deeply.

"Madame, it is possible your Majesty may be right, but I fear not. I thank you for hearing me. If the evil deed sown by evil ripens I am at your service until death, whenever you honour me with a command — or a wish. I repeat that my life is at your disposal."

Her face did not soften. He backed toward the trees, still bowing, and, parting the branches, vanished as he had come. Madame Campan was sobbing.

"Madame, your Majesty has banished a true friend. That man would die for you indeed and his is a noble heart. Do not forget him if ever you need a service more than common."

But the Queen said nothing. Her face was pale and fixed as she turned toward the Palace and the miseries waiting there for her, and she herself at bay and as little fit to reason her way through them as the stag with the hounds yelling at his throat.

She would hear nothing. The King had just issued Letters Patent to the Parliament declaring that he was "filled with the most just indignation on seeing the means which by the confession of his Eminence the Cardinal had been employed to inculpate his most dear spouse and companion."

"Inculpate." Fatal word to be used in connection with a queen! What queen of France had ever before been virtually put on her trial with the myriad hyena-eyes of a people who detested "the Austrian" waiting to see her ruin?

The day drifted slowly by and night was darkening down over distant Paris and a faintly lurid glow streamed upward from the city into the darkness. What hatred, intrigues and vilenesses breathed their vile lives beneath. it! In the Bastille, Jeanne de Lamotte recklessly contriving her web of lies to cover the Queen with shame; Cagliostro, cynic and cheat, plotting his frauds not far off, and the duped Cardinal driven in self-defence to herd with them; Lamotte and Villette at large in England and Antwerp, still further to poison public opinion against the unhappy Queen. And her own pride and purity playing their game for them and coupling her high name with theirs in every low fellow's mouth.

And with his forehead in his hands de Fersen sat thinking, foreseeing, as far as blinded humanity can foresee, a dreadful future. The very virtues of the Queen flung her into the hands of her enemies, and her faults — for his love was no boy's passion that the sun dazzles until its spots are invisible — he knew would rise against her in the fiery trial coming on in deadly array. She had had a woman's dignity but not a queen's. She had known but too well how to make men love her but not how to make them dread her. Yet again — how he knew her! Sitting there and looking into the future he believed that sorrow and misery would develop that one thing lacking and make her a queen of men indeed. It had come too late for her happiness, but it would come. She would know how to confront her enemies though she had not known how to confront her lovers. His heart yearned over her with unspeakable tenderness. She would know. He should see her high above them all even if they broke her, eternally in the heavens while they yelled like wolves on earth. And he would stay to see it and more. "Thy people shall be my people," he murmured in the words that have come down the ages, and never heart meant them more truly or fulfilled them more nobly.

Who can define love, the only passion we share with Divinity? In Fersen it had wrought like fire, burning out all the dross and ashes of a life lived for pleasure and aims as light as thistledown. He believed himself a man like others and, behold, at the touchstone of Fate, there was revealed a great genius in him — the genius for love and as rare as any other of the manifestations of genius. To himself it was an astounding revelation. It was a new birth, as it is called in religion, reshaping his every thought, revaluing the whole of life. Well, he must possess his soul in patience until the perfect work was finished in him, and then, he knew as though it were written in light before him, the day would come in which he should act as it beseemed him — and her. Thought of possession he had none. That is not the plane on which genius works in any of its manifestations. It is to aspire endlessly, endlessly to achieve, some deep need of the longing in the soul and to see the heights eternally receding into highest heaven.

And in a baptism of fire this is accepted as the profoundest good. So his soul saw it.

Chapter XX

IF the Queen thought she had sounded the depths of bitterness when the trial began and believed that truth must make itself manifest in the forms of law she had much to learn. It had scarcely begun when with a bleeding heart she acknowledged she had been bitterly mistaken and that there was no justice for her, for the French people were waiting like a hungry wild beast to see her fair fame flung to their greedy jaws. Little had they ever hoped that the Austrian would be delivered up to them thus by her own folly! They trembled lest the King should allow the right of de Rohan to be judged by his Majesty only and Paris thrilled with joy when the news was confirmed that the Queen — the *Queen!* — had insisted that he should plead before the Grand Chamber like a criminal. They had got her at last!

Too late she understood the madness of her mistake.

Now the case had passed into the hands of members of the Grand Chamber, and amazing sights were seen. The princes and princesses of the princely families allied to the House of Rohan (which in themselves represented half the peerage) spent their time in canvassing on behalf of the Cardinal among the members and seconding their appeals with huge sums of money distributed among them and the clergy. It was known that at least a million livres went in that way. They all collected — princes and princesses — on days when the case was proceeding and, dressed in mourning to express their shame and affliction, ranged themselves along the way by which the members of the Grand Chamber must pass to their duties, to salute them with the lowest, most respectful, bows and expressions of deepest depression. What member's hard heart could resist such tributes of honour from men and women bearing the most distinguished names of France?

As for the nobility, loyalty to the Throne appeared to have vanished and in their blind anger they did not realize that nobility stands or falls politically with the Throne, and that they were destroying their own foundation. They had precipitated the French Revolution with their foolish chatter and self-interest.

But it was not only the nobles. The clergy, in defence of their order as represented in the Cardinal, rose like one man. The Pope, claiming sole jurisdiction over the Cardinal, demanded that he should be judged in Rome. And the King's aunts, bigoted old women as they were, adopted the Papal view and were shrill in their demands that the Cardinal should be deported to Rome for judgment where it was known the matter would be gently and discreetly hushed up. Even that might have been better for the Queen's cause, since it became more evident every day that the scandal would shake the Throne to its foundations and that at all risks and hazards the trial should be cut short even at the cost of escape for the offenders. But if that course had been too hard for the Queen at the beginning it was impossible now. Too late the King saw the danger, and now had not the courage to break the matter off short, especially as the trial had become the choice amusement of the Parisian and other people who crowded there every day as to the theatre to listen hungrily while their Queen's name was dragged through the dirt. It would have taken braver and wiser men than the King and his ministers to deprive them of their amusement and face the howls of execration that would have arisen in defence of defrauded justice if they had dared such a thing.

The Queen had nailed herself on her own cross and must endure her crucifixion. There was no way in which her heart was not pierced every day. Frightful assertions were made by Jeanne de Lamotte and though her lies were disproved again and again enough survived to ruin the Queen in the eyes of those whose earnest hope it was to find her guilty.

Madame Etiquette, formerly the worshipper of monarchy, was one of her strongest enemies. She joined the party of the Cardinal and acted as an electioneering agent on his behalf, collecting and paying for votes in his favour and with the rest of the nobility did her utmost to incriminate the Queen that the Cardinal might get off scot-free. And after all who could blame him for accepting the Queen's advances — the base Queen who meant to ruin him now she was found out!

They succeeded only too well. The whole country was flooded with atrocious libels and nothing was too vile to be believed. Had the King consulted his own safety he would have sent the Queen out of the kingdom and thus retrieved his popularity. But he was not only a man of honour but a lover. He made her cause his own and those who attacked her knew they attacked him, and still persisted.

De Fersen (who was seldom at Court now) watched the tragedy with feelings he himself dared not sound in their deepest depths. He never approached her except with the courtesy which avoids all comment.

So the sad year went by on heavy feet and for three hundred days the trial lasted and the Queen was tortured before the people. The very atmosphere was changed about her. Where her smile had been grace and honour it was now avoided. She surprised looks passing from one to the other which burnt her with angry shame, and it was all but unendurable, knowing how all had been feasting on the garbage provided by Jeanne de Lamotte each day, to receive them with royal tranquillity and unconsciousness of the stories which ought to damn any woman if credible.

Guilty, it must have killed her, but innocence has a mysterious strength fed from clear springs in the high mountains of the spirit and on that and that only she lived. Part of her support was a noble scorn of her enemies in and out of the Bastille. If they chose to make their heroine of that vile woman uttering her daily dole of filth in the court — unchaste, abandoned, a proved thief and cheat — need she herself so greatly miss their flattery? What, after all, had it ever been worth, that life should be unendurable without it now? And the hero, de Rohan, florid with dissipation and high living, craven with terror yet with furtive gleams of hope as the tide of bribery and canvassing rose steadily and promised to float his stranded barque into harbour; Cagliostro, with his portentous face of scoundrelism, flat-nosed, greasy, full of greediness and sensuality, casting his brazen impudence about him in jests highly to be relished by his kind! These be thy gods, O Israel! thought the sad Queen, deriving a bitter consolation from the vileness of her foes and their followers.

One day as the end drew near, Thérèse de Lamballe was pacing on the terrace at Versailles, so deep in thought that she did not hear the light steps of de Fersen swinging up the steps, until, looking up startled, she greeted him with her own smile. In latter days of horror he was often to remember its selfless sweetness and the unconscious dignity that seemed to set her apart from ordinary mortals. Not even his love for the Queen could blind his eyes to the starry beauty which claimed his worship also, though of another kind.

"Walk with me awhile," she said. "I am very anxious to have a few words with you." And in silence he fell into step beside her.

"The verdict will probably be given tomorrow," she said, as they turned at the end of the terrace. "You hear more than I. What will it be?"

"I hear much," he said. "The whole thing has been a carnival of disgrace from beginning to end. That the woman Lamotte should have been allowed day after day to pour out filth against the Queen in ways wholly unconnected with the diamonds proves what powerful influences are at work against her. And have you observed how lightly it is passed over when Lamotte is proved a liar. Yesterday she was asked to declare the name of the man who received the necklace on the Queen's behalf. She pointed out Leclaux, the valet of the Queen's bedchamber. Brought into court he proved beyond doubt that he had never seen Lamotte but once, at the home of the wife of a surgeon at Versailles, and that he knew nothing of the necklace. But *that* did not fly through Paris. Truth was displeasing to the Queen's enemies."

They turned and returned in silence.

"And Boehmer?" asked the Princess at last.

"Oh, he is well enough off. The Cardinal's friends have paid him. His necklace is only a small part of the money they have spent. And of course now his evidence is whatever that party wishes. I declare to you, Princess, on my honour as a gentleman, that I so loathe the spirit of the nobility and the people of Paris in this matter that I would leave the country tomorrow for ever but for one reason."

"I know the reason," said the Princess in her quiet tones. "You feel the day is not far distant when the Queen may need a defender, and Sweden is far! That is my feeling also. If this verdict does not publicly vindicate her — and even then —"

"Even then!" Fersen said gravely. "In my opinion, however the verdict turns, the Queen can never hold up her head again. The verdict may make her position worse but never better. How are the people to respect as their Queen a woman dragged through the mud like that. O that this madness should ever have been allowed."

The desperation of grief in his words and face silenced the Princess for a moment.

"There is no help?" she said at last.

"There is no help," he repeated, "for all these things are so. And the day of the People is coming in France. The People! Good God, what a rule of cruelty and corruption do we face!"

"The only resource left is to educate our masters!" said the Princess. "They need it!"

"They do not need it and could not use it if they had it," de Fersen answered seriously. "What they need is a regenerated monarchy and a strong hand over them. If all men were in the same rank of intellectual culture and heritage or if it were ever possible they should be (which it is not) one might talk then of the Rule of the People. As to education, it is a two-edged weapon, and the best security for the masses doing their duty is that they should know nothing else to do."

"You speak with scorn, monsieur."

"With truth, madame. And truth bears sometimes the mask of scorn. As to the verdict, I think the issue certain."

She halted and leaned her shoulder against a stone vase filled with flowers, for a trembling took her.

"Tell me."

"The Cardinal and Cagliostro will be acquitted. Lamotte, having no interest to protect her, will be found guilty. They must do that to save their faces in acquitting the Cardinal. It has been impossible for him to prove he was a dupe all through, though one may or may not believe it. One aspect of the case is that he may have wished through any means to dominate the Queen."

"We are walking in dark places," she said in a low voice.

"True, and I believe the day is at hand when the utmost courage will be needed, combined with wisdom of which I see no sign. For my part, I cast in my part with France until the sky clears. The storm will be f rightful. But you, Princess; I entreat you to consider your safety when the time draws nearer. Others are spreading their wings for sunnier shores. The Polignacs, the King's aunts, all, all are going. Why not you?"

She looked him in the eyes with the peculiar beauty of her smile.

"Because, monsieur, like yourself I love the Queen and doubly so for this calamity and the fortitude with which she meets it. It is heartbreaking to see her face the treacherous world with that royal calm, knowing the agony she suffers. What — what is to be the end?"

"Ruin. Yes, madame, I love the Queen, and hope some day to prove it. Lay my homage at her feet when you see her. Ask her forgiveness if my earnestness to serve her has not always been courtier-like. Tell her —" His voice strangled in his throat. He could not finish the sentence.

"Monsieur, I will tell her," said the Princess.

She passed slowly along the terrace, tall and majestic in her white draperies. He watched her receding in the distance, and it seemed to him in a strange flash of psychic vision that much else was receding with her, the old order, the knightly manners, the beauty, splendour, gracious ways of men and women, all melting into the past with a vanishing sadness of delay.

Did he forget what lay beneath that fair surface — self-interest, cruelty, cunning and the rest of the ugly brood that nest in palaces as in cottages? No. But like all noble hearts he saw the ideal high in blue air and could not count the airy leagues that divided it from the actual.

Next day as the dusk fell quietly the Queen sat alone with the Princess and Madame Campan. It had been so contrived that no others should be with her, for they dreaded the reaction of joy or grief, and in spite of de Fersen's prediction none certainly knew how the matter would end. End? But there was to be no ending. It would only be the beginning in any case — the beginning of new and dreadful days.

She sat in her boudoir waiting, waiting until the news should come by courier, and time grew intolerable with the ticking of the clocks and the anxious silence of the other two women, and still, hands clenched in each other, she endured. The gesture reminded her of her son's birth — the Dauphin, the hope of France — thus she had endured then, and remembered the agony of relief at the end and the joy — the joy! Would it be the same in this more cruel pain? Would these men who had meant nothing to her before, and now had her fate in their hands be merciful, or rather just — simply just — and crush these vipers who had lain in a Queen's path?

They could not tell what her thoughts were — her face was so calm — but all their fidelity and love waited upon her through anxious eyes.

The dusk fell deeper. One could no longer see the distant walks and groups of statuary. She refused lights, though they glimmered here and there in many windows. The quiet in the room was extraordinary and thus for a while it continued.

Suddenly there was a distant cry — or so it seemed — the shouting of many voices — louder now, like the roar of many waters released. Louder, coming nearer, as if Paris were pouring its thousands upon Versailles. Shouting, rejoicing, cries! It had come!

The Princess flew to the window, holding her hand to her throbbing heart. Madame Campan fell on her knees and prayed, face hidden. The Queen sat motionless.

How long it lasted none of the three ever knew, but the room filled with shadows, darkened while the noise in the distance grew. Suddenly the door burst open, the King came in alone, stumbled against a table, recovered himself. They could see him only as a deeper gloom in the gloom, his face invisible.

"Paris is rejoicing!" he said, his voice thick with rage. "The Cardinal is acquitted and Cagliostro. The woman is found guilty."

"The Queen also," she answered.

There was silence.

Chapter XXI

WHEN the Great Trial in which a queen was the real prisoner ended there were men in Paris who exulted, seeing the red dawn of a bloody day. They read the signs and knew. The nobility exulted also, cackled, chattered, rejoiced, not knowing they had signed their own doom. Not long afterwards most of them were fleeing to England and Italy, perishing leaves blown upon a blast of ruin, and those unable to flee were marching with what dignity they could to the guillotine — the People in the saddle at last booted and spurred galloping to their own doom in the bloody Nemesis of the Napoleonic wars which left France drained of manhood.

The Cardinal, acquitted and condemned to a mild exile, by a belated exercise of the King's power; Cagliostro acquitted and betaking himself brazen-mouthed to England to cry his wrongs there and prosecute his charlatanries until London grew too hot to hold him; Lamotte, whipped and branded with the V for *voleuse*, "thief," on her shoulder, spitting like a wild cat, shrieking, cursing, hurling infamies at the Queen and all about her — these things horrible enough once were settling into the dark background of the Queen's life and taking their place as factors profoundly influencing the future to be accepted — never to be escaped.

There was not one single moment in which Marie Antoinette believed that the harm done could ever be undone. She had learned her lesson. The young Queen of France was dead and shaping out of that lost exquisiteness like a soul reincarnating in another life was a woman in whom the old impulses of truth, generosity and love were to fight transfigured in a new and terrible arena.

A few days after her ordeal ended she summoned Thérèse de Lamballe to her private cabinet. Until then she had hidden herself and none but her waiting-women had seen her and they as little as possible. "Her Majesty is indisposed," and the statement had roused the jeers and triumph of her myriad enemies. "Ashamed to show her face and no wonder!" delighted Paris and the nobility cried in all their streets and salons. She knew their glee; a little while ago it would have spurred her to some flash of brilliant courage in facing Court and people. It did not now nor did it even influence her. It was necessary that she should be alone, viewing the future with open eyes, facing her own ruin, considering only what could be wrested from that gulf for France, the monarchy and her son, and determining the part she herself must play to that end.

When at last she believed she knew her next step she sent for the Princess.

Very great astonishment awaited her when she found the Queen sitting by the fire pale indeed, but calm and even smiling. It was as though she had risen from a long illness and the mysterious restorative processes of healing were begun, bringing the dawn of new life and strength. The Princess's first feeling was thankfulness that she apparently realized so little the terrors of her position. Her next was awe. No, it was not ignorance. She knew and feared no more for herself because so little was left to lose.

"Madame —" she began with trembling lips, and halted as the Queen waved a delicate hand. There was to be no emotion. The time for that was passed.

"Don't move me, my dear!" she said with a little smile. "I must not be seen to have wept. But there are things to be said. Draw a chair beside me and listen. Your hand is freezing; it must have been death-cold coming through those long corridors and galleries."

It was May, but a bitter day, a driving, sleeting rain against the windows, and the empty chill of the great palace could be felt even through the firelight and flickering candles of the cabinet. Thérèse almost shuddered as she knelt and stretched out her hands to the blaze, looking up with expectation as the quiet voice went on: "You see me quite composed now, and there are many things to settle. But before these are spoken of I wish to say that you and the Comte de Fersen were entirely right as regards the Cardinal. There should have been no trial. I have ruined myself by my folly and rightly. My only care now will be to save what can be saved for my husband and children, and what they represent."

She spoke so simply and with such grace of humility that Thérèse ventured to lay her hand on her Mistress's. For a moment they clasped each other, then the Queen drew hers away and went on: "Do you remember that during the trial the woman Lamotte among a number of threats declared that she was writing a memoir of the necklace affair which would be published in France and England. No doubt she had done this in the Salpêtrière prison and it will be perfectly easy to smuggle it to England with the connivance of my enemies."

Thérèse looked up quickly. A frightful danger that a book filled with such infamies should travel over the world where all would read them and feast on the martyrdom or shame of the Queen of France!

"It cannot be possible, Madame. The King's orders —"

"You forget, Thérèse. The King's orders run in Paris no longer and we cannot bribe high enough to outbid our enemies. Those memoirs will be worth much money. But listen. You know England. Do you know any highly placed man there who could stop the publication? Think — think with all your strength."

"I will try, Madame, and rejoice to be employed."

"Then let us set to work. I have great confidence in the English. I think they have an instinct for justice, which is lacking here. Is there one with enough kindness for France to wish to spare her another orgy of shame and slander?"

The Princess reflected steadily for a moment. She had had many friends in England, but that was in the days of frivolity, gaiety and pleasure. On whom could she count now that winter was come and the swallows all fled to sunnier lands? At last: "Madame, you have heard of Richard Brinsley Sheridan — a minister but I forget of what. It is so hard to understand English ways. A strange man, very brilliant and impulsive, and writes witty plays something in the manner of Beaumarchais but yet not cruel. Chivalrous, something in our own way. Irish."

The Queen looked up with a gleam of hope.

"That country has always been friendly to France. I thought of Charles Fox, son to Lord Holland, but —"

"No, no, Madame. He is a dissolute indolent man and a friend to what he calls freedom — such freedom as we see here! Sheridan is of the romantic type, with himself for a hero. May I write? He is a great intimate of the beautiful Duchess of Devonshire and she too has much influence. I know her and like her."

"If you wrote as if from yourself to the Duchess and enclosed a letter for Sheridan it might be safe," the Queen said thoughtfully. "We know that all letters to important people are opened and read now, but a letter from one woman to another may pass. Yes, do it, and without loss of time. Lamotte will not let the grass grow under her feet."

There was a pause. The Princess rose as if expecting permission to go, but the Queen did not speak for a long time, and the rain pattered against the window.

"Later on," she said slowly at last, "I shall hope that you will go to England, my dear. You could serve us well there and — I do not want you in France."

Kneeling again beside her the Princess said simply: "Madame, I am wholly at your Majesty's disposal. But would you send me there because there is danger here? For if so —"

Marie Antoinette stooped and kissed her: "Dear, you and I both belong to people who have not let danger stand in the way of deeds. I believe honestly that you can do most valuable work there in this and other ways and —"

"You will not be lonely, Madame, now that all your friends are fleeing?"

"I shall be lonely but not friendless. Thérèse, I have understood in these last days how much I have neglected my sister-in-law. Madame Elizabeth has a noble soul and I mistook her silence and reserve for foolish disapproval of harmless fun and laughter. She was wiser than I. I have sent for her and told her this and we are friends."

Another pause and Thérèse said softly: "Madame, that was well. But for me, there is a story in the Bible which sums up all my hopes. It is that of Ruth, 'Where thou goest I will go … The Lord do so to me, and more also, if ought but death part thee and me.'"

They looked into each other's eyes in silence and with complete and perfect understanding. No more words were needed, for in that moment a compact had been made and sealed. The Princess rose in readiness to go, then said quietly: "Madame, has your Majesty realized how true a servant is the Comte de Fersen? I venture to hope that you will see him. He was perhaps hasty in his remonstrances — he feels that himself — but I know no truer or more gallant heart. Send him to England. Let him see Sheridan!"

The Queen's heart beat quicker. She dreaded seeing him for many reasons — how face him after the terrible fulfilment of his warnings and with the memory of her cruelty and foolish arrogance? And he had said he loved her. Those words should never have been uttered, yet having been uttered it would be a bitter humiliation to meet his face changed and altered, to find only compelled courtesy where once his soul had spoken. Her unfailing courage failed her there. She could not see him yet, but also she could not send him from the country and miss his steadfast presence.

"Not yet, Thérèse. I know — I agree with all you say, but I will not ask for help yet. Write first and see what happens. I am not fit to see him now —"

"Madame," the Princess ventured, "time is precious and he could go today. Then not a minute would be wasted. Oh, Madame — I could instruct him."

She could not explain the complexities of her own heart to herself, much less to the Princess. She could not see him, she dared not let him go.

"Write first!" she said, and Thérèse went noiselessly away.

She wrote to the Duchess of Devonshire as fully as she dared and to Sheridan with perfect candour. He would see and realize the anxious position of the Queen and the Government of France. The Queen desired to ask his assistance in a matter of much moment and so forth, all written with the gracious courtesy which would recall not only her beautiful face to his mind but happy days in all the merriment of London headed by the gay young Prince of Wales who adored Sheridan and took his word as law in everything but his pleasures. That connection was not to be despised either, as Thérèse knew. The future King of England would not stand by and see another king and queen so mocked and slandered and insulted. These things fly like thistle-seeds in the wind and the Channel is a narrow parting.

Days went by, weeks followed, and still no answer. And what should have been impossible had happened. The Lamotte escaped to England to live triumphantly on such a share of Boehmer's necklace as she could screw out of her husband and Villette. It was by no means as large as she had hoped, for she was not of much consequence to them both now that all the world was welcome to slander and vilify the Queen of France. But with all her venom alive she could sting, and her base bright wits were flung into that devil's joy. In England also the Queen's name was tossed to and fro and gibbeted, as Jeanne whispered and lied and hinted.

Even if Sheridan had written they could not be sure of an answer, for daily the Revolutionary net closed in about Versailles. Fersen never saw her. The entertainments and pleasures were all ended. Very few people crept about in the vast palace now and the Queen shut in her rooms saw no one but her women and those political enemies or would-be friends whom the King's affairs obliged her to meet.

Suddenly one day like a thunderbolt from blue skies the Princess received her answer, but not from Sheridan: from Jeanne de Lamotte.

MADAME,

As the friend of the woman I scorn to call her Majesty I desire to let you know that there is now prepared in London a very fine full edition of her life and doings which no doubt the world will enjoy, for never was adventuress more audacious in her pleasures and her greed. There are five thousand copies for sale and the production has been costly beyond what you could imagine. Shamefully as I have been treated and the blood of the Valois (much higher than the Queen's own) degraded in me, though nothing can degrade a generous soul, I am generously prepared to make her the first offer of purchase. I will sell the whole number to her for sixty thousand pounds English money and will promise no other edition shall appear. But she must be prompt if she wants it, for the world naturally desires to know how far a queen, wife and mother can step down from her high station. I therefore offer her the opportunity and should not be surprised if the Cardinal de Rohan, who has treated me with the same shameful ingratitude as his Mistress, would be ready to help in the purchase. I am to be heard of at the house of Monsieur Williamson, Bloomsbury Street, London.

Thérèse was at the moment at Versailles and she had scarcely read it when she summoned Fersen to her *salon* and thrust it into his hand. Instinctively she relied on him and none other, knowing that he had no axe to grind; nothing but selfless devotion for the Queen and the sinking monarchy. She watched his calm face as he read, herself in a transport of fear and disgust.

"Does one deal with such people?" she asked breathlessly.

"One does if one must!" he said between his teeth. "I will cross tonight. That woman should have been executed. It would have saved much blood. Say nothing to the Queen. Why let her suffer a pang she can be spared until it is absolutely necessary?"

"But the money?"

"That can be raised. I have friends. It is not a thing to delay me now. Madame, adieu; I thank you for a privilege."

He was gone. Even in a later and more momentous journey he recalled the slow torture of that gallop to the sea. For he rode, knowing it would save time, taking relays where he could, sparing his horses as mercifully as was possible, yet riding like a man who races with Despair to save the Queen's honour. The thought that drove him was that she could bear no more; it would kill her if this infamy prospered and he knew that not only would the world's light go out with her but also the last hope of the monarchy of France. None knew better than Fersen the dreadful ebb of the royal fortunes and only the King to stem it if she were gone. The King! — a good man, but with no dash, no decision or initiative and the fatal gift of cooling his friends and heating his enemies in every encounter. It said much for Fersen's knowledge of him that it had never crossed his mind to see the King and take his commands before he started. He never had any commands to give, no royalty with which to inspire those about him. Endurance, yes — but no swift outleap of magnificent inspiration such as the Queen shot in one glance of her blue eyes. "What a Queen — what a lady!" even the dullest man must say when he saw her. And the King — negligible, slow, hopeless!

"If I were King of France," Fersen thought as the long rows of poplars ran swiftly back to Paris before his galloping horse — "If I were! If she —" And then he would dash the thought from him as disloyalty and fix his mind only on his errand.

Of course the wind was contrary when he sighted Calais — a grey wind blowing from the north. That too was delay unbearable. When he reached London it seemed a month since he had seen the roofs of Paris. He betook himself to an Englishman, a lawyer named Gray, plain and trustworthy, with whom he had had dealings in the past, laid the case before him and was received with a pitying smile.

"My good sir, I am sorry to damp expectation but you can trust a woman like that exactly as far as you can see her, if so far. What is to prevent her keeping a copy or two and reprinting the moment she has the money? It is probable that a new edition is ready now."

Fersen pleaded the dreadful urgency of the case in vain.

"In my opinion, sir," said Mr. Gray deliberately, "this business can never be carried through. The woman is a rogue and there is no security for a thing she promises. I should drop the matter and retire to France were I you. I will do what I can on the spot, but it will be — nothing! Such people are better defied or ignored."

Fersen shook his head sadly. No chance must be left untried. Some way might suggest itself.

"I understand your feeling though I cannot share it. Then by all means let us interview her."

He sent a messenger and Fersen was compelled to wait in the dull room in the dull London street, a heavy clock tall as a man ticking inexorable minutes and Mr. Gray's pen scratching beside him as if no such trifle as a queen's despair could interrupt its course. The ceaseless rain of England fell in a muddy smudge outside, and inside were chill discomfort and a man to whom this terrible thing was a matter of business routine and no more. At last, the messenger returned. The Countess would see them immediately.

Of his strange life that moment seemed the strangest to Fersen when the door of the dingy Bloomsbury drawing-room opened and the Lamotte swam in, ostensibly alone though his quick ear detected the sound of a man's boot outside. He had seen her during the trial, having attended often enough that he might makes notes of important points of attack and defence. She had been a vixen there, hard red spots on either cheek that showed through the rouge, fiercely glittering eyes, bitter, biting, scratching, fighting with tooth and claw in defence of her worthless life but with terror for a background. Now, vixenish still, with a hard set smile she was mistress of perfect assurance. On the sacred soil of freedom she was safe and moreover could she have been set down in France that moment the King had no power to detain her or the Queen to silence her. She came in, handsomely dressed in a rich lilac brocaded-silk covering the shoulder shamefully scarred with the brand of a thief, her face made up and rouged to perfection but much more openly hard and shifty than before. That mark the trial had left upon. her. She swept a slight curtsey which neither of the visitors noticed, then fell into a chair and stared at Fersen; she spoke in French.

"I have the pleasure to recognize Monsieur de Fersen, the confidential servant of the Queen. Well, monsieur, I am happy to hear your wishes. It is something to see the shameless Austrian begging at my feet. There are women treated as I have been who would prefer revenge to any consideration of money profit — which indeed I despise — if my poor maligned maltreated husband did not insist upon it. Money, thank God, does not control the actions of a Valois. Have you brought it?"

Fersen's habitual self-control stood him in good stead and his shrewdness also. It would have been madness deserving doom to enter a house with money about him and the Lamotte in control. Though he caught the warning in Robert Gray's eye he was already prepared and answered with cool precision and no title of courtesy.

"It is in London but not here. What do you undertake in return?"

She flamed like a fury at his contempt.

"If you want the books, mind your manners! You want them, I don't. You had better not drive me too far. I know things of her that decency has kept hidden up to now, but I won't answer for the future. And let me tell you I have had help — splendid help — in carrying this through. What do you say to a minister of France helping me with knowledge of things that even I couldn't have reached? Her day is done. I may live to see her branded and whipped as she branded me!"

Her eyes shot hell's sparks of hate. Had she been a man — but again Fersen was steady as a rock and Gray, used to criminals, watched her with contemptuous curiosity but very much on the alert for his client.

"The books?" repeated Fersen.

"They are in the cellars of this house and there is not the slightest difficulty in having them removed the instant the money is paid."

"A bank draft?" Gray suggested.

"Yes, when we have cashed it. Well, have you decided?"

Fersen looked her in the face.

"What guarantee that you keep no copies nor the documents from which they were made?"

She tossed her head in the air.

"The word of a Valois!"

"I asked for a guarantee."

She all but spat at him, teeth and claws flashing in a tigerish rage, but sixty thousand pounds and the manner in which Gray reached for his hat impassively calmed her.

"The bookseller's account for the number he has printed and the documents and manuscript to be gone over in your presence. You can do that now."

Fersen heard a breath at the door and looked up swiftly. He caught a vanishing gleam outside. A den of thieves and a queen's fame hanging on their honour. He turned and spoke in Latin to Gray — continental Latin in its inflexions but the other — an Oxford man — understood.

"If even they kept no copies they would spread the news that we had bought it and the deduction is clear. I will not buy."

Gray made a reserved gesture of approval.

"You do very right. Your client must face the consequences. It is less dangerous, believe me. I will do what I can with our authorities. Is that all?"

It was decided as simply as if an afternoon call were ending. One almost expected the gracious adieux of hostess and guest except for her victorious smile as she watched them. No doubt they were considering payment. My God, how she had whipped them all from highest to lowest! She had piped and the world danced to her tune. It should dance to a wilder measure yet.

Fersen had not laid his hat aside. He put it on his head and stood there very tall and with his caged riding coat hanging about him.

"I shall not buy. The Queen's name is above you as heaven from hell. You cannot touch it and truth's triumph is sure. Crawl to your den, but if you cross her path in France I will kill you as I would kill a viper. Remember. It is the truth."

He turned, followed by Gray, as white with rage but courageous she mocked them to the last.

"The Queen's lover — and how many of them! *Ohe*, the Cardinal, the English Duke, the —"

The door closed between them and a man shot out of another room on the landing, pistol at the ready.

"You will not buy, messieurs, but you had better. I pardon no insults to my wife."

Gray put a whistle to his lips and blew a shrill blast, and the hall door burst open as four constables leaped in and up the stair.

"In the King's name arrest the man for blackmail and attempted murder. The woman also! But no hurry for her. There's no other door."

211

They handcuffed him, yelling vile curses and when they could stifle him no other way gagged him and left him lying while they dashed into the drawing room to secure the woman.

No other door! But where was she! The large room was empty. Nothing under the bare table, behind the curtains. The balcony! Fersen and Gray flung up the closed window. Yes, there, there! Behind a small tree in a cement vase, hiding, flattening herself against the rails, green with pallor, staring-eyed, but a cat still with clawed paws ready.

"Come near me and I will leap into the street! Murder! Murder!" she screamed in English.

Believing she might do it, she had them at a disadvantage for a moment and the two consulted hurriedly. Could they lasso her? A ladder. Yes, a ladder! A secret word to the constables and one ran downstairs. A crowd was assembling below, pointing. They would help in the law's name.

Then, standing on the veranda the two watched her calmly as she hurled insults at them. Leaning against the balcony she yelled and gesticulated, a mere fury, unseeing, unhearing the stir beneath, and worse, worse the slow yielding of the balcony at her back. Old, rusted with disuse it was giving! Fersen saw and with the human impulse to save leaped forward. She mistook him, yelled, thrust herself back against it instinctively; and it and she were gone!

A wild shriek, an answering horror of confused noise from below and Fersen and Gray rushed down the stair like madmen, leaping the steps down — down.

But she had been swifter — she had outmatched them. When they reached the area there was no more Jeanne de Lamotte-Valois, but a mass of bloody pulp. Dead — dead.

Chapter XXII

WHEN Fersen took boat he was an older man than when he had seen London. He had learnt that love and power and rank and wealth — and even death and life — are helpless against the cruelties of man. Her evil had not died with her. Her husband arrested could give no account of the books. He had been her tool, he said, and he knew nothing of where they were. London was searched, but in vain. Sheridan sent for Fersen — Sheridan still the most brilliant of human beings, bold, witty, the gay loose air of the libertine about him, but a little touched at the French Queen's plight and the grief of the charming Princess whom he remembered, "so sweet, so *spirituelle*," as he said in the imperfect French of which he was so proud.

"But present my homages, Monsieur le Comte, at the feet of her Majesty and her Highness and assure both that the utmost influence of his Britannic Majesty's Government shall not be wanting to stifle a hateful scandal. You are very well aware that it is as easy to stop thistledown from floating on a breeze as a woman's tongue, but our utmost shall be done. If she used a continental press — why then, I fear we have no possible way of dealing with it!"

He shrugged his shoulders in a French gesture not badly done. He was always playing his part on a recognized stage and this time it had a tincture of the grace of Versailles because it concerned the French Queen. His adieux were nearly in the best manner of the Court. But Fersen left his presence dumbed and broken. He had failed. There was more agony for her to face — more! — and when would it cease and how? Nothing could be proved against the man but that he had resisted the police with threats and he was released before long to his subterranean life and work, with, for all Fersen knew, the threads of the plot intact in his hands. Why should they care in England? And there they had no Bastille where suspected offenders could rot till death. Yes, he had failed — and in her service!

He rode back to Paris swiftly, but no longer upborne or unconscious of the long leagues of straight road, the stiff poplars, the passing of villages haggard with want and woe. Dimly and terribly he realized the passing of a whole social order, the uprising of a new with Jeanne de Lamotte for its priestess — the reign of the people spurning their masters from the throne they had held so long but themselves driven by a power more despotic by far which would hound them into war and death.

How would it end? What new and frightful portent lay under the glee of Paris at the Queen's ruin? For what monstrous birth were the times pregnant?

Did the publication of the libels greatly matter? The accursed thing, like the Jinn rising from the vase in smoke, had so darkened the air that all sense of beginnings was lost. In Jeanne de Lamotte Fate having used its instrument had crushed her like a writhing snake and passed on careless, but she had done her work well. It would not die and other figures would fill the terrible stage and carry on her drama and posture to the light of flames and the music of lamentations until for them also the black curtain fell. A cosmic drama — with what wild hidden faces for audience and awful applause and rejection? He shuddered in the thought.

He went straight to the rooms of the Princess to give her an account of his stewardship — say, rather, of his failure. That was bitter in his mouth as he met the hope in her eyes and with his first word dashed it.

"I have failed. The wretch is dead, but I have no hope that the memoirs will be stopped —"

She pushed a chair silently to him seeing he was worn almost to exhaustion by the strain of the effort and listened silently while he told his story, every muscle of her face tense. When it was finished she said slowly: "You could not achieve the impossible? What else was there to do?"

"I should have got her somehow as a hostage. Shut her up, held her life as a pledge. No, I failed. Mercifully the Queen does not know. She has been spared this forlorn hope."

The Princess sighed: "She has known all through. One can hide nothing from her."

There was a long silence. Then he said: "That is the last bitterness. You must choose another messenger, Princess, when you want deeds greatly done. Have the goodness to lay before her Majesty my useless regrets."

She leaned forward.

"Monsieur, her Majesty wishes to see and thank you herself. You are to see her when you leave me. There is one thing I wish to say for your guidance. She changes and strengthens every day. It is she who takes the lead in all things now. The King is nothing. She has placed herself in the forefront of the battle."

Incredible — that that delicate worshipped beauty should be transformed into the statesman, the ruler — Could he believe it? And yet had he not always believed that there was fire sheathed in her to leap aflame and responsive to any noble call? That was what he had known, loved, and adored even before he recognized it. The wizardry of love, omniscient as God. Even the flicker of a smile crossed his face as he rose.

"Don't spare her!" Thérèse said anxiously. "Her words to me were, 'I could have been a comrade always. I could have helped if I had understood. Now I understand.'"

"I also!" said Fersen. "No, madame, I shall not spare her Majesty now or ever. She has risen above that child's talk. I thank you very sincerely. You are always my guide."

So he went to the meeting, his heart swelling with pride and a kind of austere joy. It compensated him for much agony. And again he smiled, remembering a proverb of his own land, a homely one but true: "Those who carry umbrellas do not see the rainbow." No, this might have been choked in her all her days — smothered in foolish splendour and flatteries. Now she was Queen by Right Divine and he kneeling at her feet.

As he waited for her in the small room of reception at Versailles he could prepare no words. All must be as it would. Outside in the great gardens the glittering fountains were playing and the air was kind with spring and women walked up and down the ways with men in attendance laughing and talking as if nothing had happened to disturb routine or ever could. Were they a little bolder in passing through forbidden places and looking harder at the palace windows in case a royal shrinking figure might be seen there? Were the laughs shriller, the disputes louder, as one took the Court side, one the Cardinal's?

He forgot all else. She was coming. A woman opened the door, assured herself that he waited and went out. Changed — changed from the old days of the pomp of the Queen's entry!

A handle turned and she came in alone, bowing slightly with the grace that none had ever matched or would, pale but perfectly composed, and smiling her thanks for his wild ride.

He knelt and kissed her hand, and she sat, motioning him to a chair, but he preferred to stand as he told his story briefly, with no redundant works and as a soldier reports to his general. He feared a touch of emotion lest it should break him down into some uncontrollable passion that might set them apart for ever.

Her uncomplaining composed suffering half broke his heart. Words bubbled against his lips. Words? What use? What use!

He ended: "And therefore, Madame, I report myself a failure. It is Mr. Sheridan's opinion and mine that the libels will be published. I cannot tell which is greater — my grief or shame."

"There should be neither," she said calmly. "You have done your utmost, and the thing has spread so far now that I think more makes little difference."

His own thought, but a most terrible realization for the Queen of France! She looked at him, catching his disturbance, then continued, with stiffly controlled composure!

"All is changed. What use to deceive our certain knowledge? The greatest of the nobles allied themselves with our enemies. They will live to regret it, true! But the Crown cannot stand alone, and new men from the middle classes, greedy men with careers to make, are stirring and busy. The ox must die that the worms may fatten. Monsieur, you should not have had the trouble of your journey. I should have known it was in vain."

"You are too gracious, Madame," he said, breathing quickly as if the hurry of his ride were on him still. "But what do you foresee?"

"What the world has seen before. A new order arising. A losing fight. Monsieur, I have a favour to ask you. This country is not yours. I beg you to retire to your own where your truest allegiance is due and leave us to our fate and —"

He would have interrupted, but she waved a white hand and went on: "I beg you also to persuade Madame de Lamballe, who values your opinion, to retire to England, where she has good friends. Many of the nobles have fled, many are flying, and the way is closing. Soon it will not be possible. She should go. I ask you to influence the Princess to flight."

"And leave you, Madame, leave you to the griefs you have borne, to those you foresee? Never — never, while life is left me. On my knees, on your hand I swear it!"

He flung himself on his knees and caught her hand and kissed it, looking up transfigured as a man who sees Death in a dream of glory and adores him with the passion life cannot win. She looked down upon him, the nerves of her face quivering. So the vibration of spring comes in trembling air and winnowing leaves after long winter and the silences of frost.

"Then you did not believe me guilty? You did not suspect me? You have acquitted me?" she said slowly.

He knelt with joined hands to the woman — not the queen.

"Acquit you? Do I acquit the passion of Christ, of all the martyrs, all the saints? You torture me in the question, for if you could think such horror of me — O my God, what manner of man am I?"

Her eyes blessed him. She took his two hands in hers and so held them clasped, unconscious even as he of any danger in the moment and with a high and simple sweetness that summoned what was noble in him to instant response. A very different passion from that of the lover swept both upward in that moment, and one with a more sacred fire. Presently, loosing his hands, she looked into his eyes: "My friend, I think I knew. Certainly I know, but my soul thirsted for those words. Now I will tell you. I have seen Barnave — the man who will be spokesman of the people. Great dangers are coming. My life is dedicated to my husband and children and to undoing the injury I have done them all unknowing. Since you will not go I ask you for great gifts. Your sword, your service, possibly your life. And I offer you for reward —" She hesitated on a breath.

He rose and stood before her.

"Your words, Madame. That is my reward. Paradise can give me no more. I am overpaid. I bless you. I bless God that I have lived."

She rose also, her pale face glimmering in the dusk, her pale hands like lilies in dark water. She stretched them to him.

"In the name of my husband and children I thank you. I love you."

The hands did not touch him. He drew no nearer. Between them flowed a deep river unbridged by any human possibility. Both understood and accepted their division.

Steps at the door. The handle turned. The King entered heavily.

"Madame, they told me the Comte de Fersen had returned from England. How dark you sit! Is he here? Lights, lights!" He called, and lacqueys entered bearing the great wax candles in silver stands. Fersen stood to attention by the door, and the Queen taking his hand herself led him to the King.

"I present to your Majesty a friend and servant so loyal that in all the world can be no loyaler. He who is not by birth your Majesty's subject has dedicated his sword and service to us and to our children in the dark days that are upon us. I recommend him to you not for honours and rewards but for dangers and death and I entreat your Majesty to love him for his loyalty as I do."

Her voice did not falter.

The King said dully: "Monsieur, I accept her Majesty's recommendation and your good service. What more can I say?"

Fersen knelt and kissed his hand.

The world knows the history of the Revolution.

Fersen seldom left Paris, remaining steadfastly on duty. Could he in waking or sleeping dreams behold a day when the one hope of the royalty of France would be in his strong soul and strong hands, when, with his life in his hand as though it were nothing, he should conduct them on that blind flight of hope and terror to Varennes? Who can tell? It may be, for the eyes of love are clear and his soul was clear and strong as fine steel.

He waited. And had his counsel been obeyed in that flight history might have been a different tale to tell than that of a king's and a queen's murder and a child's ruin and despair.

The Princesse de Lamballe also waited.

Compelled to visit England she returned at the call of the Queen's need. Could she foresee the reward of that fidelity, her head with its pitiful long tresses tossing on a pike in the midst of a yelling crowd of murderers in Paris, her body mutilated and lost among the victims of the same massacre? Yet had she known it none the less she would have come. For the faithful there is only the way of fidelity, none other in all the world.

And the Queen — in what dream could she imagine the future — she the royal daughter of the Caesars! Was it possible that she could foresee the cart of the executioner driven slowly through the streets of Paris, yelling crowds about the woman sitting in it wrapped in a coarse shawl, discrowned, widowed, her sight nearly destroyed by weeping and the darkness of her prison, her little son torn from her to be ruined mind and body, the white hair blown about her thin face — lost beyond all human help? Could she have imagined that ghastly sight even then, with the growing wisdom of utter loss, she would have known that in the darkest Blooms of midnight sunrise is hidden, and to the noble there remains always their own nobility and the Divine from which it springs. She was never so much a queen as when she went to the scaffold.

But of all the jewels in the world's history, stained with blood and shame the most terrible is the diamond necklace that wrought a queen's ruin and the end of an era. Through its glitter there ran indeed the fires of hell.

13595140R00123

Printed in Great Britain
by Amazon.co.uk, Ltd.,
Marston Gate.